The Franklin Affair

An Henri Gruel Adventure

By

Ty Drago

Regency Press
Cleveland Heights, Ohio

This is a work of fiction. Other than clearly historical personages, all the characters and events portrayed in this work are fictitious, and any resemblance to real people or events is purely coincidental.

THE FRANKLIN AFFAIR

Copyright © October, 2000 by Ty Drago

All rights reserved, including the right to reproduce this book, or portions thereof, in any form.

REGENCY PRESS is a division of Crack of Noon Enterprises, Incorporated. The name Regency Press and the Crowned R are registered trademarks of Crack of Noon Enterprises, Incorporated.

ISBN: 1-929085-75-3

First hard-cover edition: June, 2001

Printed in the United States of America

0 9 8 7 6 5 4 3 2 1

Regency Press
Cleveland Heights, Ohio

To my beloved wife, Helene, who believed -

Chapter One

"Most fools think they are only ignorant" - *Benjamin Franklin*

"Please understand, Master Henri, that we wish no harm to this honorable gentleman."

"Of course, sir," I said, although I understood no such thing. Since these two men, distinguished and far older than I, had first entered the drawing room of La Barbarie, my family's country house in Nantes, near the French coast, I had understood precious little. Indeed, one might justly say that I floated upon a sea of turbulent confusion. It was a station with which I would become most accustomed in the weeks ahead.

It was December the 5th, in the year 1776. The night was cold, and a foot of snow blanketed the frozen ground. In the hearth, a fire burned mightily, its flickering light casting everything into a strange, iridescent dance. We each had wine beside us, served in pewter goblets by Madame Jogues, the caretaker's wife—though none of us had thus far felt inclined to partake.

"It is only that we fear the message that he may take to our good king, and to the people of France as a whole." The speaker was Jacques-Donatein Leray de Chaumont, a man of considerable national reputation. He was a great bear of a fellow, with large, fiery brown eyes showing from below his powdered wig. Though born into the merchant class and wed to a woman who had once served in my father's household, Chaumont had elevated his station through the clever and often ruthless acquisition of wealth. Successful business ventures had made him a man to be reckoned with, even feared, and had earned him full membership in France's highest social circles. In truth, his personal economy was even more advantageous than that of my father, whose own holdings were not inconsiderable. Chaumont was one of the superintendents of the Hôtel des Invalides in Paris, as well as Quartermaster for the French Army, and was rumored to enjoy considerable royal access.

I had grown up knowing this man and his wife, Thérèse. I had always found him to be imposing, loud of voice and manner and—in a word—intimidating. Tonight was no exception.

Beside him, taciturn and expressionless, sat the man whom Chaumont had introduced to me as Father Hilliard of Paris. This clergyman was younger than his companion, lean but broad at the shoulders and possessed of a fierce, almost predatory look. Hilliard's eyes were as dark as coals and his hair was almond brown. As a clergyman, he wore no wig, but kept his hair drawn carefully back in the style of the day.

"I must admit, Master Henri, that was I surprised to learn from my wife that your father had seen fit to place you here as host to our honored doctor," Chaumont said.

"Most surprised," Father Hilliard added, one of the few times he had spoken since the two of them had appeared at the threshold of La Barbarie half-an-hour before. Chaumont was smiling condescendingly, while his clerical companion glowered darkly. I wasn't sure which expression disturbed me more.

"After all, my boy," Chaumont continued, "What are you? Fourteen? Fifteen years of age?"

"I am sixteen, sir," I said quietly. "I shall be seventeen this coming spring."

"Still, I must confess that sixteen seems a tender age for such a responsibility." Then he read my frown and amended, still smiling: "I do not mean to offend you, Master Henri."

How strange it is to look back upon that night with an old man's eyes, and with seventy years of experience to color those events. Now, as I take pen in hand to set down, at long last, the business of my life, I find this descent into my memories both exhilarating and frightening—much like riding a child's sled down a steep hill in winter. How well I remember the boy who sat in that armchair, the very chair my father had occupied on so many summer's nights, as he told us, his five daughters and two surviving sons, of his adventures abroad. How clearly I recall my uncertainty regarding my two guests and their strange request, made in the name of patriotism.

"My father sent me here to serve as host in part because of my skills with language," I told them, striving to sound self-possessed. "I speak English fluently, sirs...and Spanish and Dutch. While I have not been to the American Colonies, I have visited my father's holdings in Santo Domingo in the West Indies, and as such have had at least some modest experience with worldly matters."

The two men glanced at each other, sharing a look that I was too young to decipher.

"Well then," Chaumont said. "If your sire, the noble Bathelemy-Jacques Gruel, has marked you for this duty, I shall not gainsay his wisdom."

"I thank you, Monsieur," I said, relieved, believing that I had passed some test.

"So then, I must say to you again, Master Henri, that what we ask of you, while important, is in no way meant to bring harm upon the good doctor."

"I'm glad of that, sir," I said. "My father made it plain that I should see to the American's comfort during his stay in Nantes, not conspire against him." The word "conspire" came out without my thinking and I immediately regretted it. But if either man took offense, he gave no sign of it.

"Conspiracies," Father Hilliard rumbled. "Fear of them is what brought us here, boy."

"The fact is, young Monsieur," Chaumont said patiently, "that the American has come to our shores with conspiracies of his own to realize. He means to meet with our king and to negotiate a purchase of arms, perhaps even a military treaty."

"I see," I said, though again I "saw" little indeed. Surely the reason for the doctor's visit was no secret. My father had explained this to me plainly enough before I had set out for Nantes from our home outside of Paris. Uncertain of what to say, I said nothing at all. It is, perhaps, the only time during that night that I acted with a man's prudence.

"The American Colonies are in revolt," Chaumont said.

"An *illegal* revolt," Father Hilliard added.

"They have declared their independence from the British Crown," Chaumont continued. "They did so, quite publicly, back in July of this year. Since then, they have been romancing the various crowned heads of Europe, with an eye toward garnering support for their cause. Diplomatic commissioners, armed with copies of their 'declaration', have been dispatched to Spain, Austria and perhaps even as far as Russia. Now, they come here, to France, to beg our aid."

"Should we not aid them, then?" I asked. "I lost four older brothers in the Seven Years War, Monsieur. Though I was barely three years of age at the time and, as such, have little memory of them, it was a blow from which my father has never fully recovered. I grew up watching what the grief did to him. I would like nothing better than to see the Colonies beat the British soundly and chase them back to their little island, for good and all."

Father Hilliard made a low sound in his throat, not a word so much as a growl.

"I understand your feelings, Henri," Chaumont said gently. "And I share them. What good Frenchman would *not* share the wish to see Britain put down, if only to ease the sting of our own defeat at their hands? But there are greater considerations that cannot be ignored. Paramount among these is the matter of the Colonies themselves and the message that their action sends to Europe."

"And what message is that?" I asked.

"Insurrection, boy!" Father Hilliard exclaimed. His face had gone very red. "Rebellion! *Treason!*"

Chaumont steadied his companion with a gentle hand upon his arm. To me, he said: "Consider this, Henri. Already talk of what the Colonies are doing has spread throughout France. The so-called 'philosophers' amongst us see this as not merely a dispute over taxes between a colony and its parent country. They see it as the unveiling of a new world order. What the Americans intend, Henri, is to do away with the monarchy. They would replace it with a republic, as dangerous and unwise a form of government as has ever been devised. The Romans attempted it in the time before the coming of our Lord, and abandoned it in favor of a dictatorship that kept them strong for a thousand years. The American Colonies have not learned from this example. They have forsaken the historically proven path of anointed monarchy in favor of this naïve and self-destructive one. It will be the ruin of them, Henri. Worse still, it may be the ruin of *us* as well."

I made as if to speak but Chaumont silenced me with a gesture.

"Ideas cross the Atlantic as surely as ships do, Henri. The cancer spawned by these misguided Americans is already here, festering in the streets of Paris and elsewhere. There are those who speak of petitioning the king for greater governmental representation, threatening the holy authority of the Bourbons!" He said this as if it were the direst of circumstances—though, sitting in my father's chair, I could see little danger in the spread of a few ideas.

"This man who will be your father's guest in this

house," Chaumont said, "is a renowned personage. His presence in France will lend...validity...to the dangerous notions that already fill our streets."

"If that's so, sir," I said. "Why does the king not ban him from our shores?"

Father Hilliard nodded, as if he thought this was a fine idea.

"If only it were so simple as that, Henri," Chaumont replied, smiling thinly. "But France has interests in the New World...interests which could be threatened were we to so openly reject the American commissioner's advances. No, we must accept the doctor and make him welcome. But we must watch him closely...know his movements and liaisons. This, my dear Henri, is why we have come to you."

"What is it you wish of me, Monsieur?" I asked. My heart was pounding. Never in my life had I been made privy to such intrigue. It was more than exciting. It filled me, like fire.

"It is not what *I* wish, Henri," Chaumont said. "Nor what Father Hilliard wishes. Were we to come to you in this way, acting on our own authority, I should expect you to report us to the local constable at once. No, young sir, we are here by the authority of the Comte de Vergennes, His Majesty's foreign minister and, through him, by the holy authority of King Louis XVI, himself."

This speech, delivered with absolute conviction, fell upon me like a cresting wave. I was dumbstruck! The very notion of the king requiring my assistance for *anything* left me stupefied and as tremulous as a reed before a whirlwind. In my youthful mind's eye, I conjured the fanciful image of good King Louis, seated at a gilded writing desk somewhere in his palace at Versailles, penning his commands to me on fine, rolled parchment and sealing it with the signet on his ring. "Take this to Henri Gruel," the king commanded in my imagination "*He'll see to it for me!*"

Of course, I had been shown no such sealed parchment, nor indeed any written confirmation of any kind regarding Chaumont's claim. A grown man would have made a point of this absence. I did not.

"I am at the King's service," I said with a child's pride. Chaumont nodded gravely. Father Hilliard actually smiled, but it was a hard, bitter thing that really bore little resemblance to smiling.

"Then listen to what I tell you, Monsieur Gruel," Chaumont said resolutely. "Here is what France requires of you. The American doctor will reach Nantes within two days. He is, as you well know, a gentleman of far-flung reputation. His words in print have preceded him, as have his inventions, which include the stove and the miraculous lightning rod. In deference to these accomplishments, the local merchant firm of Pliarne & Penet, associates of your father, intends to busy the visiting commissioner with banquets and other celebrations in his honor while he is in Nantes. During his stay at La Barbarie, he will no doubt receive many guests. He may come and go at odd hours. You, sir, are to mark his comings and goings carefully. You are to learn all you can about whom he visits and what his business with them may be. Then you are to report this information to me."

"To *us*," Father Hilliard corrected. He and Chaumont exchanged another indecipherable look.

"Quite so," said Chaumont. "My wife, Thérèse, will be here to help you, but the task, itself, is yours, Master Henri. For the sake of France, watch this man closely. Will you do this, sir?"

"Yes, sir," I replied at once, nearly rising to my feet and snapping to a soldier's attention. "I will."

They left me shortly thereafter, making their goodbyes at the door, with Chaumont's wife, the former Thérèse Jogues, looking on. She was a tall, dark-haired woman of middle years, with strong features and luminous, dark brown eyes. She was the daughter of Monsieur and Madame Jogues, an elderly couple long in my father's employ. Some years ago, Thérèse had caught the eye of the wealthy Chaumont, who had married her and thus taken her from our service. But now she had returned, offering her skills as a maid and cook at her husband's behest, ostensibly to assist her aging parents in the care and comfort of the American doctor during his stay at La Barbarie.

As Monsieur Chaumont and Father Hilliard departed into the night, leaving me alone with in the vestibule, Thérèse approached me and, seeing my troubled face, placed a kindly hand upon my shoulder. She was taller than I, as I was not yet of a man's height and would never achieve what anyone could justly call physical stature. "Would that such matters as this need not trouble you, Master Henri," she said in her soft voice. "A boy your age should be courting ladies, not politics."

May I fare better at this courtship than I have at the others, I thought bitterly.

"I'll gladly offer what help I may," she said. "But my husband knows his business. I've no doubt but that, between the pair of you, you will discover what intrigue this American may bring with him. Have no fear, Master Henri."

Yet I did have fear. I had been placed in the role of both host and spy to a man some fifty years my senior. Events were taking shape around me that I could not fathom, and they left me feeling dizzy, as though I were standing on a high place, looking down into the darkness of a fearful abyss.

But His Majesty needed me. France needed me, as it had my brothers. I had been little more than an infant when the four of them had ridden off together to defend French interests. The conflict, fought largely over colonial territories in the New World, had gone badly, finally costing France its holdings throughout most of the Americas—not to mention the lives of many thousands of her sons.

Despite my tender years, I could well recall the sight of a wagon riding slowly up the hill toward our family's estate in Nogent-le-Rotrou. In its bed had been four wooden caskets, and in its driver's hand a letter addressed to my father, expressing the King's regret at his loss. My father had insisted that he was proud of their sacrifices, even if those sacrifices had accomplished nothing for France. He hadn't known that I could hear his footsteps as he wandered about our home at night, wrapped in his grief. But I had heard them and, even after thirteen years, I still did.

I still did.

Now I had been given a chance to seize the honor that had eluded my brothers. Fearful and uncertain though I might be, I vowed not to turn away from my mission. What intrigues this American visitor brought with him upon the morrow, I would be there to watch and to listen—for France.

Chapter Two

"He's a fool who cannot conceal his wisdom" - Benjamin Franklin

La Barbarie occupied fourteen acres southeast of Nantes, two hundred and fifty miles from Paris. The house stood atop a low hill, with trees all around it—a square, three-story structure of gray stone with chimneys at every corner. The house was approachable only from the north, by way of a winding carriage trail that navigated up through a gently sloping winter's tapestry of snow-covered ground and ice-sheathed trees. On a crisp, winter's night, such as this one, the clatter of an advancing coach carried from some distance off.

Thanks to this, the Jogues', Madame Chaumont and myself received ample warning of the American's approach.

He arrived on the 7th of December, just two days after Chaumont and Father Hilliard had recruited me as their agent against him. At the first sound of his approach, I bade Monsieur Jogues to be sure that the guest bedchamber's fire was lit and that the room had been made warm. Then I asked his wife to go into the kitchen and ready hot food and drink. As my father's servants went forth to conduct these errands, Thérèse moved to stand beside me in the doorway, which we had cast open—despite the chill—so that the weary traveler in the carriage would see that his welcome awaited him.

The Franklin Affair

The large coach was drawn by two horses, its driver wrapped in blankets and hunched over against the cold. The carriage windows, understandably enough, were shuttered. As the horses clattered to a stop before us, I noticed that the carriage bore upon it the crest of Pliarne & Penet, the merchant firm with whom my father was closely associated and which had appointed itself unofficial caretakers of our guest during his stay in Nantes.

Several moments passed as the carriage settled. Then, before the half-frozen coachman could climb stiffly down from his seat, the facing door opened. The man who emerged was of medium height, quite stout and wrapped in an unembroidered brown coat, its fur collar pulled up close around his ears. His face was oval and aged, heavily jowled, but with large, expressive eyes hidden behind modest spectacles. A hat, fashioned of what appeared to be rabbit or beaver pelts, warmed the top of the gentleman's head. In his right hand, he carried a Crabtree walking stick, with which he carefully tested the frozen mud that layered the ground. The coachman moved to help him, only to be waved gently but firmly away.

As the driver collected two pieces of heavy hand baggage from the rear of the carriage, the old man reached our threshold and stopped there, looking first at me and then at Thérèse, to whom he offered a broad and surprisingly youthful smile. Then he addressed me in English: "Monsieur Gruel, I presume?"

"Indeed...sir," I replied, struggling to find my voice. "Welcome to La Barbarie, Dr. Franklin. You honor us with your presence."

Then, for an awkward half minute, the three of us stood there at the threshold, Thérèse and I in the lighted vestibule and Dr. Benjamin Franklin on the cold, dark stoop without.

Finally, Dr. Franklin smiled again as a chill breeze caused wisps of his white hair, which peaked out from under the brim of his fur hat, to dance upon his wrinkled brow. His blue eyes sparkled in the faint light from

Thérèse's candle. "Sir," he said, with mischief in his voice. "Would you not be just as honored in the warmth of a drawing room?"

"Yes...of course, doctor," I stammered, feeling my face flush. "My humblest apologies. Please do come in."

"In a moment," Franklin replied, smiling. To the coachman he said: "Much thanks to you, Tomas. And to your good wife as well for sparing you on such a night."

Despite his obvious chill, the coachman grinned. His teeth, what few there were, had been stained a poor yellow. "The honor was mine, Ben. I wish you a pleasant stay with us!"

His coach clattered away across the frozen mud as Dr. Franklin stepped thankfully into the warmth of the vestibule. Thérèse shut the door and immediately advanced to accept his coat and hat. Then the doctor ran a hand through the thin curtain of long white hair that crowned his balding head and fixed me with an expectant eye.

"Dr. Franklin," I said. "I am Henri Gruel, son of Bathelemy-Jacques Gruel, the master of this house. My father regrets that he could not be here to greet you in person, but business obligations prohibit it. I am to serve you in his stead in all matters, and am your humble servant, sir."

"Well spoken, and most generous of you, Monsieur," Franklin said. "In that spirit...if you would be so kind...as my first request I should very much like to know the name of this lovely lady who shares your welcome."

I regarded him quizzically, and then cleared my throat and said: "Dr. Franklin, may I present Madame Chaumont, wife of Monsieur Jacques-Donatein Leray de Chaumont."

Thérèse, who did not speak English, smiled with delight as Franklin took her hand and kissed it most tenderly. "A pleasure, madame," he said, his eyes playing over her face. "Your beauty warms an old man's wintered bones."

She looked to me for a translation. Feeling somewhat unsettled, I obliged her. She flushed and muttered an abashed "Thank you". Franklin beamed at her.

"Um...I'm surprised to find you alone, doctor," I said hesitantly. "My father informed me that you were traveling with two others."

With obvious, almost schoolboy reluctance, Franklin forced his gaze away from Thérèse. "Yes, my grandsons Temple and Benji were supposed to accompany me. Sadly, Temple took ill at the last minute and Benji, being only seven years of age, was loath to make the trip without his older cousin."

"I shall be sorry not to have met them," I said politely.

Franklin sighed. "Their absence made my journey long. Fortunately, I had my gout to keep me company." He stretched one leg and made a sour face. "I never go anywhere without it."

"Oh, I'm so sorry to hear it," I said. "It must be terrible to suffer a winter's voyage with such a condition."

"It does take one's mind off the *mal de mer*," he replied sardonically. "Still, the voyage was not without its bright spots. My ship, the *Reprisal,* happened upon two British merchant brigantines and took capture of them. Together with their cargo, they should fatten the purses for the American cause in France."

"These ships were seized in battle?" I asked, fascinated.

"One might say so," Franklin replied. Then, with a sly smile: "Lest I be called fanciful, I should stipulate that the battle was a brief one. The two British ships offered little resistance. Most amusing of all: of the brigantines, one was called *Helene*, but the other...oh, the *other*...was named *George*...though whether this was in honor of the tyrant in London I cannot say."

"That's indeed a tale!" I remarked sincerely. Despite my secret concerns against this man and his cause, I found the notion of the British merchant fleet being dealt such a loss quite appealing. "Well then, Dr. Franklin, perhaps we should make your welcome a celebration of sorts. I have asked that hot food and drink be brought into the drawing room. If I may, I shall have Monsieur Jogues, the caretaker, move your personal effects up to your bedchamber."

"I thank you, Monsieur," Franklin replied. "And, I must say, your English is excellent."

"You flatter me, doctor."

The old man chuckled. "I save flattery for ladies and royalty, young man. So, unless you wear either a petticoat or a crown, you may rest assured that any compliments I pay to you are quite sincere. Do you speak other languages as well?"

"Spanish and Dutch," I replied. "My father had all of his sons tutored in the various European merchant tongues, but I had the good fortune to possess the keenest ear for it."

"Fortune, indeed. My own French is rather poor, I'm afraid."

"You seemed to manage quite well with the coachman, sir," I said generously.

"Tomas was patient with me," Franklin replied.

"And also somewhat forward...to have called you by your Christian name."

Franklin paused as we were about to enter the drawing room. "I asked that *favor* of him, Monsieur," he said. "In my country, station is of less import than here in Europe. I have, amongst my belongings, a slip of a paper which declares that all men are created equal."

All men equal. It was a notion that I found quite absurd. By that reckoning, I would stand as peer beside the king, himself. For the first time, I began to understand what Chaumont had meant when he had said that this man's ideas were dangerous. "Forgive me, Dr. Franklin," I remarked after a moment. "But I must admit that you are not at all what I expected."

The old man laughed, a soft, almost musical sound, full of mirth and so infectious that I nearly joined him. "Well, my dear Monsieur Gruel," he said. "I hear that rather a lot. Rather a lot, indeed!"

Chapter Three

"They that can give up essential liberty to obtain a little temporary safety deserve neither liberty nor safety." - Benjamin Franklin

The drawing room proved invitingly warm.

As Thérèse departed, leaving Dr. Franklin and myself alone in the darkened, fire-lit chamber, she treated me to a brief, supportive smile, full of meaning, which I understood and appreciated with a boy's passion for intrigue. If the American noticed what passed between us, he volunteered no sign. Instead he moved spryly across the floor, his Crabtree stick tapping rhythmically upon the boards, before settling down in my father's cushioned settee, as comfortable and at ease as if *he* were the host and *I* the guest.

"Come and join me," Franklin said cheerily, reaching for the carafe of warm rum that Madame Jogues had left for us. Two covered bowls of hot meat broth stood nearby. Slowly, feeling oddly disoriented by Dr. Franklin's curiously familiar manner, I sat on the sofa across from him watched as he poured warm rum into a pewter cup and handed it to me. I thanked him and sipped at the rich spirits, letting them fill my belly.

"Excuse me, Monsieur," Franklin said. "Can you tell me which way is west?"

"West?" I asked.

"West." he said. "In which direction does it lie?"

I pointed toward a corner of the drawing room. "That way, I believe."

"I thank you, sir," Franklin said. Then he placed his walking stick upon the floor, turning it so that it pointed in the direction that I had indicated. "This is an eccentricity of mine, I'm afraid. I like to have my walking stick always pointing homeward."

"I see," I said, not truly seeing at all. To my youthful perspective, what possible comfort could the positioning of a wooden stick offer to a heart lonely for home? In later years, I have come to appreciate this practice, and even to emulate it on more than one occasion. I have learned that, when feeling desolate, there is some respite to be found in always knowing the direction to one's own hearth.

"You must forgive an impertinent question, Monsieur Gruel," Franklin said, watching me imbibe. "But you seem a bit young to be acquainted with such strong drink. Of course, the French have different ways."

"My father imports this rum from his holdings in the West Indies," I said. "I was raised on it."

"Of course. I should have realized that. My apologies. Ah…soup!"

Franklin consumed food and drink with a passion that I had never before witnessed. Every sip of hot broth, every draught of warm rum was to him an individual and unique event, to be experienced and savored and then remembered fondly before taking the next. He seemed to pause between spoonfuls—with a mouthful of Madame's hearty soup cradled in his rosy cheeks—and close his eyes, as if he were inventorying the flavors contained therein, one at a time.

"Monsieur," he said at one point. "My compliments to your cook. You have a fine household here. And a fine house in which to contain them."

"The household is my father's," I said. "I am merely here to act as your host in his stead. This is our country home, and is usually occupied only during the summer months. The rest of the year we pass at our estate near

Paris."

"Ah, *Paris*," Franklin purred. "I look forward to seeing it again. It has been so long."

"I'm afraid I don't know Paris very well," I said. "Our house is some thirty miles south and, while my father's businesses are diverse, he has few holdings within the city that command his attention. As such, I've had little opportunity to spend time in the capital."

Franklin fixed me with a surprisingly serious look. "Then you should *find* time, Monsieur Gruel. Paris is a jewel in the crown of the world's great cities. One does not simply 'see' Paris. One *experiences* it. It has an energy that is quite singular—very different from London, or from Boston, where I was born...or from Philadelphia, where I make my home."

My only memories of Paris were of narrow, twisting streets that smelled of horse manure, but I did not pursue the point. Instead, thinking now of my mission for the king, I said: "I would like to hear of America. Of course, if you feel tired, my inquiries can certainly wait..."

"Foolishness!" the old man exclaimed brightly. "I don't deny answers to young men with questions. Ask me what you will, my good host. I am at your service."

"Then, sir," I said eagerly, leaning forward in my chair. "Tell me about America. Tell me about your fight against the British and about your battles and about this General Washington, of whom we hear so much. He is called the greatest soldier in the New World."

Franklin smiled patiently. "I'm afraid that I am no soldier and so cannot rightly judge the respective merits of one fighting man over those of another. However, I have known General Washington and can say with confidence that he serves his calling with most outstanding capacity. Tall and strong and resolute, he is possessed of an inner fire that is quite inspiring. He won the confidence of a Continental Congress that was not at all committed to the notion of independence. He won that confidence by saying little and doing much and by simply *being*...by standing there with such pride and conviction that the old women in Congress had no choice but to follow his banner. Most remarkable.

"However, I must also say that, personally, I find him an infernally *serious* fellow. I do not believe that I have ever seen him smile. Still and all, America has been fortunate to have rallied to its cause some truly wise and courageous men, General Washington among them."

"And you, Dr. Franklin," I said. "The talk throughout Europe is that, if General Washington is America's fearsome fist, *you* are its noble heart."

Franklin chuckled. "How poetic. Did you come up with that yourself, Monsieur?"

"I hope I haven't been presumptuous."

"Quite the opposite. I rather like it. To be honest, however, I am simply a messenger...more a tongue than a heart, I should think. I travel abroad to spread the word of our struggle, and to solicit what sympathy I may."

"And arms?" I asked, a bit too quickly. "To solicit arms as well."

Franklin regarded me in gentle silence. I suddenly knew that I had overstepped myself. A nervous flush of color filled both my cheeks.

"May I show you something, Monsieur Gruel?" Franklin asked at last.

"Of course," I said.

From the pocket of his coat, the old man slowly withdrew a long envelope. He took from it a folded sheet of paper, which he handed to me.

"Do you read English as well as you speak it, Monsieur?" Franklin asked.

I nodded slowly, unfolding the document in my hands. It was a printed manifesto, a statement of political standing and doctrine, an argument in favor of making war. It began:

When, in the course of human events, it becomes necessary for one people to dissolve the political bands which have connected them with another, and to assume among the powers of the earth, the separate and equal station to which the Laws of Nature and of Nature's God entitle them, a decent respect to the opinions of mankind requires that they should declare the causes which impel them to the separation.

We hold these truths to be self-evident, that all men are created equal, that they are endowed by their creator with certain inalienable rights, that among these rights are life, liberty and the pursuit of happiness. That to secure these rights, governments are instituted among men, deriving their just powers from the consent of the governed...

There was more, much more, and I did not read it all, not wishing to leave my guest unattended for so long a period of time. When I looked up from the paper I found an indulgent smile upon Dr. Franklin's lips, but hard conviction in the set of his eyes. "You mentioned the heart of America, Monsieur Gruel," he said softly. "*That* is its true heart, more so than any one man, or any hundred. *That* is the cry of an entire continent to be free."

"Indeed, sir?" I asked. "And are you the author of this document?"

"I am not," Franklin admitted. "Although I take some pride in having had a hand in its creation. Its author is a Virginian by the name of Thomas Jefferson, a young man of vision and considerable skill with a pen. I suspect that I was not asked to write the document myself because my colleagues in Congress feared that I might be tempted to hide a joke in it." He chuckled softly.

"You state...or rather, Monsieur Jefferson states...that a government rules only by the consent of the governed. But does not an anointed king rule by divine right?"

"My dear Monsieur," Franklin said. "That is a question I expect to be asked rather frequently during my stay in your country. I shall offer you the same answer that I intend to offer all the rest. God decides over whom a king shall rule and how long the tenure of that sovereignty may last. Right now, a war is being waged to determine what God wants of us, as surely neither side can prevail without His divine assistance. If the British win, then we shall know that our Lord has favored King George. But should the victory come to *us*..." Franklin winked. "...then we shall know something else altogether."

"Dr. Franklin, *are* all men created equal?" I asked.

"Without any doubt at all, Monsieur," Franklin replied seriously.

"Be they aristocrat or merchant?" I pressed.

"Be they pauper or king," Franklin said.

I fell silent, looking thoughtfully down at the paper in my hands. Finally, I said hesitantly: "May I borrow this, so that I may read it through?"

"I would have it no other way," Franklin replied. "Now, however...with a full belly...I must ask your leave to retire for the night. My compliments to your cook. The soup was excellent and the rum finer still. I assume you keep a wine cellar?"

"Of course," I said.

"Splendid. I look forward to sampling some of your vintages." He stood, leaning heavily on his Crabtree stick as I rang the bell for Monsieur Jogues. "I enjoyed our talk, sir," Franklin said to me as the caretaker opened the drawing room doors for us.

"As did I, sir," I replied, escorting the American to the foot of the central staircase. "And thank you for the loan of your document."

"I look forward to your critique," Franklin replied. "Perhaps over breakfast tomorrow?"

"Of course. Monsieur Jogues will show you to your room. Goodnight, Dr. Franklin."

"Monsieur Gruel," Franklin said as he began to slowly climb the steps. "I wonder if I might impose upon you for one last favor tonight?"

"I am your servant, sir," I said.

"Do me the honor of addressing me as 'Ben.'"

The Franklin Affair

I stood stock-still, speechless. Monsieur Jogues stopped halfway up the staircase and looked back at us, surprise playing on his elderly visage.

"I apologize if I have shocked you," Franklin added with a smile. "But if I am said to have any religious leanings at all, it is in the ways of a Quaker. As such, I make little distinction between classes. I ask you to do this and, by doing so, to make my stay at La Barbarie all the more comfortable."

"I...shall do so, doctor...Ben. In return, I must insist that you call me Henri."

"With great pleasure," Franklin replied. "Goodnight then, Henri."

"Goodnight to you...Ben."

I returned to the drawing room, settled myself down once again upon the sofa, and took a long, calming draught of warm rum. Then slowly, almost reverently, I read the whole of Dr. Franklin's document.

A declaration of independence.

Chaumont and Father Hilliard had been right. Youthful and naïve as I might be, even I could not fail to recognize the dangers implied therein.

Yet, dangerous or not, I found myself filled with great admiration for the old man who had, this night, become my guest and charge. For all my love of king and country, I somewhat regretted the notion of working as a spy against this fine gentleman. It occurred to me, with no little astonishment that, throughout our short association, Franklin had never ceased to address me as "Monsieur Gruel". I was not "Master Henri", or "Young Master", or even "Boy". I was the master of this house and his host and peer, despite my tender years. He had not even used my Christian name while beseeching me to employ his own.

...all men are created equal.

How ridiculous, I thought.

Chapter Four

"To the discontented man no chair is easy." - Benjamin Franklin

Sadly, Dr. Franklin and I did not share breakfast, as we'd hoped. The Mayor of Nantes came calling just after first light, before I had even fully dressed for the day. He presented an invitation to the American doctor that apparently proved difficult to refuse, and so Franklin was gone by the time Thérèse came to tell me what had occurred.

Whatever devilish conspiracy this charming, gentle old man may have had in mind was quickly and soundly crushed under the weight of his own popularity. On the 8th of December, as the winter storm passed and the day turned bright and crisp, he was called upon to accept the accolades of the entire community, and induced to give a brief speech in the town's central square. Hundreds of people came to welcome him, the great scientist and printer, the inventor of the stove and the lightning rod, the honorable author of wisdom and witticism. I managed to attend this chilly affair, though only just, as the town fathers did not feel obliged to inform me of the schedule. Thérèse came along with me, and together we witnessed Dr. Franklin being publicly eulogized by the Mayor and council. Speeches were made about Franklin and speeches were made about France, though no one mentioned the American Colonies' war against Britain. Through it all, Franklin occupied his chair, flanked by the various members of the city council, smiling indulgently and laughing when others laughed.

I wondered, given his poor French, how well he understood the compliments being paid to him.

At one point, as my eyes scanned the assembled crowd, I spotted Father Hilliard standing in the alcove of a closed apothecary. I motioned to him—foolishly, I admit, given our relationship—but he did not acknowledge me.

Finally, it was Franklin's turn to rise and approach the podium. The Mayor, who spoke English, rose with him, evidently to serve as translator. Franklin let his gentle gaze wander across the many faces. His eyes found mine, and a smile of recognition touched the old man's lips.

"It is difficult," he said, "on such occasions as these, not to permit vanity to consume me. My dear wife often warned me against the danger in taking too seriously the accolades of others, generous and sincere though they may be. Most people dislike vanity in others, however much of it they may harbor themselves, but I give it fair quarter whenever I meet with it. As vanity can often prove advantageous to the possessor and to others that are within his sphere of action, I therefore frequently thank God for my vanity among the other comforts of life. So, in that spirit, I accept your kind words with a glad and grateful heart, and thank you for so graciously welcoming me into your fold."

He waited patiently while the Mayor translated these words, which garnered a round of applause from the enthusiastic audience.

Franklin continued: "Special thanks must be paid to my hospitable host, Monsieur Gruel, whom I see amongst you on this cold afternoon. Henri, who has been kind enough to permit me such familiarity, is, despite his years, a capable and courteous gentleman...one who has kindly offered me the use of his home and his kitchen and, most especially, his wine cellar. Given the quality of your local wines, my good friends, that is one act of generosity which he may come to sorely regret!"

A ripple of laughter ran through the assemblage as

the Mayor dutifully translated Franklin's words

"If I may be so bold," Franklin continued. "May I ask those present to acknowledge Henri Gruel's hospitality with a cheer of hands?"

The applause went on for most of a minute. Taken aback, I stared about me at the townspeople, all of whom were regarding me with new admiration and respect. At the podium, Dr. Franklin wore a merry expression and a thoughtful smile. For the first time in my life, I began to understand one of my father's axioms: "A man is judged by the company he keeps."

From that day forward, I was never again treated by any citizen of Nantes as a boy trying to fill his father's shoes, but as a man and the master of my own house. Better still, the next time an event was arranged in Franklin's honor during his stay in Nantes—and there were many—I was the first invited.

Sometime later, as the day grew long and most of the townspeople, weary of the winter's chill, retreated indoors for the night, I encountered Dr. Franklin while on route to the Common Hall for a banquet, to be held in the American's honor. At the sight of me, the old man approached and hastily led me aside, making excuses to His Honor the Mayor and to Monsieur Pierre Penet, of Pliarne & Penet, who had been his escorts. Together, on the steps of the Common Hall, with a biting wind working its way into our garments, Dr. Franklin said: "So, Henri. I regret my schedule has delayed our further discussion. Have you found the time to read the declaration?"

"I have, Ben," I said, surprised by the ease at which I employed his Christian name. "It's an astonishing document. Tell me, are all those accusations made against King George accurate?"

"They and many more like them," Franklin replied with a chuckle. "The truth is that the document I lent you bears little likeness to the original draft penned by Tom Jefferson's skillful hand. Once the popinjays in Congress were finished with it, John Adams and I had counted more than seventy separate changes and the removal of near to three hundred and fifty words."

"Still, such charges!" I exclaimed. "If you'll forgive my saying so, Ben...your signature on that declaration is your death sentence."

"I know that well enough, Henri," Ben said, more seriously now. "As do the other men courageous enough to have lent their names. But, as I have told many a member of Congress: there's no turning back now. Either we all hang together on this matter..." He grinned mischievously. "...or we shall, most assuredly, hang separately."

Despite the dire nature of what he had said, I found myself laughing at his "gallows" humor. "Well, you're surely safe in France. From the tide of events today, I would be bold enough to say that you could run for constable and win handily."

"Do you think so?" Franklin asked. "Tell me, Henri, as you know my French is somewhat lacking. That one councilman, Monsieur LaBrie, did he not call me a 'fatted English pig'?"

I studied him for several moments, wondering if he might be playing a prank upon me. But he seemed in such earnest, that it bade me laugh anew. "Ben!" I cried. "He said that he should be pleased to *offer* a fatted English pig for your supper tonight! Monsieur LaBrie is our local butcher!"

"Well!" Franklin cried, a great hoot of joviality rising from him, so loud as to make the Mayor and Monsieur Penet, who waited impatiently from the Common Hall's open threshold, look over in annoyance. "It's best that I keep close to you tonight, I think. I'll have need of your language skills before this supper is finished, I'll warrant."

"I would be honored, sir," I said.

The days passed amiably and without conflict. My mission for Chaumont and Hilliard proved foolishly easy, as Dr. Franklin fell quickly into the habit of taking me everywhere with him, introducing me as his "host and translator". I saw nothing of either Chaumont or his clerical companion, and so was spared having to offer illicit information against my guest. Their absence did not surprise me. After all, I could hardly be called upon to inform on a man who had not a moment's peace with which to indulge in any devious conduct. In my youthful, but considered opinion, Dr. Benjamin Franklin was simply too public a man to make a worthy spy. I confess to feeling no little relief at being rid of the burden.

Then, on the afternoon of the 13th of December, as I was dressing for dinner, I found upon my writing desk a folded sheet of paper, addressed to me and sealed with a few drops of red wax. There was no signet or glyph of any kind embedded in the wax. Frowning, I picked up the parcel and turned it over in my hands. Then I rang for Thérèse.

"Did you come into my room today and leave this?" I asked.

"No, Master Henri," she said, with what I took to be sincere confusion. "Your door has been locked since after breakfast. My parents are out for the day. There is no way anyone could have come into your room. Perhaps my father or mother left it here last night, and you simply didn't notice it."

"Perhaps," I said, though I didn't believe it for a moment. When Thérèse had gone I broke the seal and unfolded the message. It was as brief as it was disturbing:

The time has come for you to earn your French honor. Dr. Franklin dines tonight with the Mayor and his wife at their home in the Rue Arlé. You will search Dr. Franklin's rooms and personal belongings.
Tomorrow, I shall visit on a pretext, and you shall avail me of your discoveries at that time.
Do not fail me.
Father H.

"Search his room!" I exclaimed aloud. "I'll do no such thing!"

The very idea filled me with a cold and bitter regret. Crushing the offending paper in my hand, I fell upon the bed, my face twisted in anger, my mind boiling with conflict. How could I violate the privacy of a man whom I had come to admire so greatly? Such a betrayal would be unbecoming in a host, let alone a friend.

But was Dr. Franklin my "friend"? I had known him only a few days. We had spoken, yes. We dealt quite well with one another, yes. He treated me as an equal, despite my youth, yes. But a "*friend*"?

I thought of the American declaration of independence, a copy of which I still had in my writing desk. I had been meaning to return it to the doctor for some time now but, with the busy schedule we shared, I simply had not found the opportunity. What harm would it do to take a moment to return it now? I could place it upon the desk in his room—better, inside a drawer, where it would be safer from prying eyes. Then, with the desk so opened, if my eyes should befall something of interest—

I shook my head angrily. Curse the promise that I had made to Chaumont and Father Hilliard! I had not then known this man as I did now. Who *was* this Hilliard? Surely no priest! What kind of priest left strange notes in locked rooms, without being seen coming or going? Clearly there was more to the fellow than Chaumont had led me to believe. Why *should* I ally myself with such obvious trickery?

But then I recalled King Louis, and my fancy of his royal command. I thought again of what France had asked of me, and of the declaration, and the dangerous things it proposed.

So, as twilight fell, and Dr. Franklin set out to dine with the Mayor and his wife at their home, I resolved myself to the task. With a grave spirit, I moved to the door of his room and listened to the empty house around me. The Jogues' would be out until quite late this evening. Thérèse was in the kitchen, busily cleaning the plates left after my own supper. There was no one else.

Slowly, acting with far more guilty caution than my task demanded, I used my master key to unlock Dr. Franklin's door. Then, with a heavy heart, I stepped across the threshold, and became a thief in my own home.

Chapter Five

"Never put off till tomorrow what you can do the day after tomorrow just as well." - Benjamin Franklin

Franklin insisted on his privacy. As such, Madame Jogues was never permitted to enter his room, not even to clean. She had protested this matter to me more than once, and I had approached Dr. Franklin with the idea of letting Madame borrow his key just long enough to straighten things up a bit, to air out the room and make sure he had enough logs for his fire. Franklin, smiling, had politely refused. "You are a novice to matters of political protocol, Henri," he'd told me gently. "I am in France to serve as an ambassador of sorts. As such, I am entitled to a degree of sanctity wherein my personal effects are concerned. I assure you that the integrity of your property will be studiously maintained, my good host. I am quite capable of making my own bed, and when I find myself in need of firewood or the attentions of a feather duster, I can always ring for Madame, myself." I had passed this news onto Madame Jogues who didn't care for it, but accepted it nonetheless.

"No *man* can keep a room clean for long," she had grumbled. "When the doctor is gone we shall open his door and find the windows blind from soot and the floor gray with dust."

But this was not the case. Franklin's room was quite proper. In fact, immaculate might not be too strong a

The Franklin Affair

word to describe the state of things. The bed was made. The floor was swept. The windows had been recently wiped and dried. Even the fireplace had been shoveled out—the ash bucket filled and closed. Whatever else Benjamin Franklin might be—a spy or a rabble-rouser—he was certainly not a slovenly houseguest.

I went to the writing desk and found it uncluttered, the quill in its bottle and the blotter clean and dry. The only drawer was locked, but this did not deter me. For this room had been mine as a boy—or a *younger* boy, anyway. I had slept in this very bed during the long, leisurely summers that the Gruel family had spent in Nantes during happier times. I knew this desk, was as familiar with it as with any of my childhood toys, and knew also that the lock on its drawer was loose, and would respond to a particular touch.

I slipped the tip of a small knife into the crack between the drawer and the desk frame. Twisting the point of my villain's tool left and right sharply, I felt the lock give way and the drawer slip obediently open in my hand. My elation was tempered by a fresh wave of guilt. Part of me had been hoping this old trick would fail, giving me an excuse to abandon my task.

In the drawer was a leather-bound journal, half-filled in Franklin's elegant hand, and two sheets of yellowing paper. The first was a letter to someone called Sally, half-finished and clearly authored by Franklin, himself. The second, however, bespoke another man's hand. The style was more delicate, and the lettering more precise. The paper bore no crest or watermark, but was of a higher quality than the other sheet and smelled faintly of a man's perfume. The note was dated the 5th of December, the very night that Chaumont and Hilliard had enlisted me as their spy.

Dear Ben,

Greetings old friend! Allow me the honor of becoming the first of my countrymen to welcome you back to France. I believe, as you do, that there is much our re-

spective nations may do to lend aid to one another. I have left this letter in the care of a messenger, with instructions to present it to you upon your ship's landing. No reply is needed, as I am already en route to Nantes by the fastest possible means to meet you and to bring you to Paris. Everything is being made ready for your arrival in the capital. Great excitement, both public and private, anticipates your coming, sir. With luck, we may ride the wave of your popularity right up to the palace doors at Versailles.

However, I must temper these optimistic thoughts with a sober warning. S is well aware of your arrival in France, despite all our best efforts to keep the matter secret. As fearful of your fame as we are dependent upon it, S has taken steps to ensure that your audience with His Majesty should never take place. The Fox has been placed in your path, Ben. Suffice it to say that you may be in great physical danger, and that this danger is what has induced me to ride with all speed to meet you in Nantes.

I implore you, sir: Accept no invitations to travel to Paris or anywhere else until I arrive. Keep your personal belongings secure and your door locked. Expect me no later than the 14th. My honor and my sword are at your service. As always,
Your Most Humble Servant,
Pierre-Augustin Beaumarchais

The Fox. I had certainly never heard of such a person. And who was this "S" who seemed so determined to keep Dr. Franklin from meeting with the king? I felt as if all this time I'd been wading in a pool of waist-deep water, cold and unfathomable, only to find it suddenly deepening beneath me with each step I took. Should I deliver these letters to Father Hilliard tomorrow? What would Dr. Franklin say when he found them missing? Should I take the time to copy them? What of the journal? I had yet to even look at that. With the letter of warning still in hand, I reached with tentative fingers for the leather-bound book.

Suddenly, I was seized from behind in a grip of iron and thrown to one side with such force that I was cast across Dr. Franklin's perfectly made bed, my head missing one of the four posts by a hair's breadth. Then, before I could right myself, I was set upon once more. Hands like the paws of a bear seized me by my cravat and drew me up onto my feet. At first, all my panic-addled mind could register was the fire of two green eyes and a man's mouth twisted in anger and outrage. A voice spoke, the face so close to mine that I could have named the man's luncheon menu.

"Where is he, thief?" the owner of the baritone voice rumbled, shaking me until my eyes rattled.

"Wha..." But even this poor reply was cut off as I was lifted completely off my feet and hurtled back against the wall. A portrait of my Aunt Sophie clattered to the floor beside me. From somewhere close by I heard Thérèse scream.

I looked up dazedly, and was met with the point of a saber, hovering scant inches from my nose.

"What is this?" Thérèse called from the open doorway. "*What are you doing?*"

"Call for your master, girl!" the swordsman bellowed. "I've caught a thief in the house, a well-dressed cutpurse, or perhaps worse than that!"

Thérèse's eyes met mine, and I felt a moment's gratification that she seemed every bit as frightened as I. "Sir," I said, with all the self-possession I could manage. "Let me arise and..."

Suddenly, and with blinding speed, the saber point pressed itself against the soft flesh just below my chin. "Move again, boy and I'll cut your throat. Girl! I told you to fetch your master. You! Tell me where Dr. Franklin is if you want to live to see the dawn!"

I took a long, deep breath. Then, mustering my courage, I said as slowly and deliberately as I could: "Dr. Franklin is dining with the Mayor this evening," I said. "And *I* am the master of this house."

The saber point remained as rigid as an iron bar, but the eyes behind them wavered.

"Thérèse," I said. "Would you be kind enough to tell this gentleman who I am?"

"Yes. He's Monsieur Henri Gruel, the master of La Barbarie," the blessed woman said instantly.

The man, whom I could now see was red-haired and possessed of eyebrows as thick as brushes, looked from one to the other of us before settling his gaze upon me once more. "You're only a boy! Certainly no master of such a house."

"The house is my father's. I was sent in his stead to serve as host during Dr. Franklin's stay."

This time the saber *did* waver. Then, slowly, almost reluctantly, it withdrew.

The man straightened. He did not offer to help me to my feet, and I did not ask. Thérèse made as if to come to my aid, but I waved her off. My knees seemed weak, but they supported me well enough.

"I..." the man began. Then he turned back and looked at the open desk, and at the letter that had flown from my hand during his assault. It lay atop the bedcovers, face up. His face darkened all over again.

"What manner of host reads his guest's mail, I wonder?" His tone dripped menace as he turned back toward me, his eyes filled with accusation.

I retorted: "What manner of visitor is it who comes uninvited into a house and lays attack upon its master? Some might call that robbery, sir."

He stiffened, and the point of his saber rose slightly, more from reflex than anything else, I thought. "My name is Beaumarchais. I have ridden these past three days from Paris to place Dr. Benjamin Franklin under my protection." His green eyes fell once again upon the incriminating letter on the bed. He snatched it up and waved it at me. "This is *my* letter to him, sent by special messenger. I came to this house because the merchant, Penet, said that this is where Franklin is staying. But instead of the great man, I find the front door ajar, the

The Franklin Affair

house deserted and you...*you*...going through Franklin's personal papers!"

I looked at Thérèse. "I was dumping the dinner ashes, Master Henri. He must have come in while I was around the side of the house."

"Surely, he had a horse," I remarked.

"I stabled my exhausted horse in the village and hired a driver to bring me up the road," the man said, his tone softening slightly. "I sent him away immediately. Your girl probably did not see the carriage."

"I did not," Thérèse confirmed.

"Still," I said. "You enter my home, uninvited? It matters little that the door may have stood partially open. By what right...?"

"By *this* right, boy!" Beaumarchais snapped, advancing and shaking his letter to Dr. Franklin under my nose. *Well, better that than his saber,* I thought sourly. "By my right and duty to protect the man you have under your roof. Who knew what an open door and an empty house might mean? For all I knew La Barbarie had been set upon by English spies, the household killed and Franklin either abducted or assassinated! So I drew my sword and came in. I went upstairs, to where I thought the bedchambers would likely be, and found you in the first room I saw. At first, I meant only to question you. But, as I approached you from behind, I recognized what you were reading..." He looked down again at the letter. "Now, I think Monsieur, it's your turn to answer questions. What right had you to be searching Dr. Franklin's room?"

"This is my father's house," I said. It sounded lame to my own ears.

"That may or may not be true," Beaumarchais said. "For the present, let me concede it. Do you think, as a genial host, your duties should include invasion and burglary, boy?"

"Stop calling me that," I said flatly.

"I'll call you anything I like, boy," Beaumarchais replied, smiling thinly. "Who's to stop me?"

"My husband," said Thérèse.

He looked at her. "Your husband?" Beaumarchais laughed. "And what, pray, is his role in this noble household? Butler? Brigand? Cutpurse?"

"He is Jacques-Donatein Leray de Chaumont." She spoke slowly, fixing him with a look more venomous than I would have believed her capable of producing.

Beaumarchais' eyes flashed. "Chaumont!" he hissed, looking from one to the other of us as if we had just removed our masks to reveal ourselves as demons. "I should have guessed! Listen to me, both of you! Listen and pay heed. Tomorrow morning...no later...I intend to have Dr. Franklin out of this cursed house, out of this damnable town and away from this pit of vipers. Chaumont you say! He may as well have *Stormont* himself as his landlord!"

Stormont? Who the devil was Stormont?

The saber came up again. "You will both leave this room. Fetch the constable if you wish, but I will not have either of you tampering any further with Dr. Franklin's belongings or his business. You may lock the door behind you and leave me here, or you may wait with me, but I shall not leave this place until the man I seek stands safely before me. Is that understood?"

Thérèse looked at me and I could see in her face that Beaumarchais' disdain for her noble husband had left her stunned and angry. It was a credit to her that she did not revile this brazen intruder, but instead directed herself to me, the master of the house. "Master Henri," she said. "What should we do about this business?"

I eyed Beaumarchais, who stood as proud as any statue. "Our guest has had a long journey," I said to Thérèse. "Fetch us some wine. And bring some cheese, too, if you would. We may be here a while."

Chapter Six

"Any fool can criticize, condemn and complain...and most fools do." - Benjamin Franklin

I thought he would split his sides.

Franklin laughed until tears ran down his face, until he clutched his ribs and sputtered and spun around like a dancing child. His cheeks grew very red and his Crabtree stick clattered noisily to the floor. Finally, his chest heaving from taking in great gulps of air, he clutched the door jamb for support, his other hand covering his heart in mock astonishment.

"Well, such an impasse as this I have never seen!" he cried delightedly. "The Great Pierre Beaumarchais faced down by the Master of La Barbarie, and over cheese and Madeira, no less!"

Beaumarchais sat at the writing desk. The letter had been replaced, the drawer shut, and the chair turned so that he could sit with his back protectively against it, lest it should slide open again of its own accord. I sat on the bed. I had asked Thérèse to position the sideboard between us, so that we could share it as civilized men might share a table. Upon it, she had placed two goblets, a bottle of wine and a board of cheese.

Franklin had come two long, silent hours later, during which time Beaumarchais had done little but glower at me, sip his wine and nibble at squares of Brie. At one point, he actually forgot himself and remarked that the wine was excellent. The lapse had not lasted long.

With embarrassment and a certain child's, dread, I'd listened as Thérèse had opened the front door for the returning American doctor. There had been a long silence, during which time I'd assumed Madame Chaumont to be struggling—given the language barrier—to avail Dr. Franklin of the circumstances. Then the old man had come hurrying up the staircase, despite his age and the discomfort of his gout. Apparently, the sight of us had not disappointed him.

"Well, Henri, I see you have made your newest guest comfortable from the first! Madeira!"

"It's actually a merlot," I said quietly.

"Ah! Well, that does nothing to lessen the humorous effect. And you, Pierre! How are you, my good fellow?"

Beaumarchais, to my astonishment, smiled with what appeared to be genuine affection. I found it a bit disconcerting. I'd already resigned myself to despising this man. "Ben, I do believe you're drunk!"

"That accusation may be somewhat harsh," Franklin replied with feigned offense. "I was sampling some of the local vintages. They are quite excellent. If you can find it in yourself to forego Fox hunting long enough to relax, you might..."

"Relax, is it?" Beaumarchais cried, scowling. His now familiar bluster had returned. "Do you have any notion of what I found when I came in here?"

"Of course I do," Franklin replied. "You found Henri here fixing my desk drawer."

"What?" Beaumarchais and I said together.

"I had complained that the lock simply refused to catch properly," Franklin continued, talking amiably. "And I recalled the concern that you expressed in your letter, so I asked Henri to please see what he could do to secure the mechanism while I was away at dinner. He would have done it sooner, you understand, but I have had such need of his translation skills since coming to Nantes. Tonight, however..."

"Hold a moment." Beaumarchais said. "I found him

reading one of your letters!"

"Well," Franklin said, drawing out the word. "I can forgive a young man's curiosity. In fairness to him, I did not actually say that anything in my drawer was, strictly speaking, private. Did I, Henri?"

"No...you didn't," I said, feeling as if I was suddenly walking through a fog.

"So," Franklin said, clasping his hands together. "Is there any more merlot?"

"Just wait! Just wait!" Beaumarchais said, rising to his feet. "But what of the woman? Thérèse? Her husband is Leray de Chaumont!"

"So he is."

"You know Chaumont's position regarding your mission to France!"

"Of course, but this does not make Thérèse any less lovely, does it?" Franklin asked innocently. "Or Henri any less gracious a host."

Beaumarchais glared down at me. He wanted badly to challenge Franklin's words, to ask me why I had not recited this fabrication about insecure locks when first he'd caught me. Yet, how could he address this now, without calling Dr. Franklin himself a liar? It was a social quandary worthy of Machiavelli. "Ben..." he stammered.

"Pierre," Franklin said soothingly. "You really must step back and re-examine the situation with a less critical eye."

"Ben," Beaumarchais said again, this time with a smile. "You're doing it to me again."

"Is that all you can say after all these years?" Franklin replied. "Can you not spare a hand for an old friend?"

Beaumarchais came around the sideboard and embraced the old man as he might a father. I felt a sudden, inexplicable twinge of jealousy. This was then replaced with a curious mixture of relief and confusion. Evidently, I was not to be branded a thief and a spy. Dr. Franklin had not merely come to my defense against a man who was obviously his long-time friend, but had also fabricated a clever lie to explain my presence in his room! Once again I felt myself tumbling like a skiff upon a turbulent ocean, and what occurred in the next several minutes did nothing at all to relieve my *mal de mer.*

"So, Ben!" Beaumarchais said, holding the old man at arm's length and regarding him with a measuring eye. "You look none the worse for your crossing. When word reached me on the road that Captain Wickes had made port in Nantes a week overdue, with two captured British merchant ships and without *you* aboard, I redoubled my efforts to reach you. I wasn't at all sure my letter of warning would find its way to your hand. I'm pleased it did."

"Yes! Your poor, bedraggled messenger," Franklin moaned. "How that man fears you! Or rather, how he feared your wrath were he to return with your precious message undelivered! He found me before I left Auray by carriage, bound for Nantes. You see, my dear Pierre, I begged Captain Wickes to put me ashore in a boat, as I could no longer afford to wait for the weather to favor us with a right-blowing wind that could carry us the rest of the way up the river."

"Perhaps that was providence wearing ill fortune's masque," Beaumarchais said. "Vergennes suggested to me that Stormont might know of your travel plans, and may have communicated that information to The Fox."

Franklin raised a hand and glanced furtively in my direction. "We can talk of that business later, my good fellow. In the meantime, allow me to properly present my friend and host, Monsieur Henri Gruel. Henri, this is the estimable Pierre-Augustine Beaumarchais, master of the sword, playwright extraordinaire and student of all matters worldly."

Slowly, I rose to my feet, determined to make a show of confidence and decorum worthy of my station as master of La Barbarie. But I rose too quickly and upset the sideboard. The wine bottle tumbled over and before I could catch it, much of its remaining contents spilt across the lace coverlet and fell to the floor.

"Never mind that, Henri," Franklin said, chuckling. "There is surely no shortage of wine in France. Ring for Thérèse."

"Yes," I said, stammering like a schoolboy. "I..."

When I finally managed to recover myself, I found Beaumarchais regarding me with such a look of disdain that I felt my cheeks grow hot from humiliation. "Surely not The Fox," he muttered to himself. Then to Franklin, he said: "I've come to bring you back with me to Paris."

"Of course," Franklin said. When he saw me start to speak, he added quickly: "I must have Thérèse pack my belongings, naturally...after she has dealt with this unfortunate spillage. Henri, I know this is a terrible imposition, but might you find room in both your heart and your home to accommodate Monsieur Beaumarchais?"

I came around the sideboard more carefully this time, doing my best to appear mature and capable, despite the splotch of Merlot that stained my waistcoat. "I'm sure we can arrange something suitable," I said. *Perhaps in the stables,* I thought bitterly, *for a brute such as you.*

Beaumarchais must have read some of this in my expression, for he frowned and said sourly: "You're very kind...Sir."

"There we are!" Franklin said brightly. "All friends at last. Well then, now that this unfortunate misunderstanding has been appropriately dealt with, may I suggest that we adjourn to the comfort of the drawing room?"

"I'll ring for Thérèse," I muttered.

"No need." Franklin faced the open doorway. "Madame Chaumont? Madame?"

After a long, telling pause, Thérèse appeared at the threshold, looking most contrite. It took me several moments to realize that she must have followed Dr. Franklin up the stairs from the vestibule, and had been listening to us all this time. But to what end? Thérèse, as I've said, could not speak English. "We've had a spill, dear lady," Franklin told her in his poor French.

"Oh..." she said. Her eyes found mine. "Oh," she repeated.

"And please prepare the east bedroom for Monsieur Beaumarchais, who will be staying the night," I said.

"Yes, Master Henri." She turned to leave.

"One last thing," Franklin said. "Pierre, I wonder if you would be so kind as to give us this room...Henri and I...for the next few minutes. Yes? Henri, would you please ask Thérèse to show Monsieur Beaumarchais to the drawing room. We will follow along shortly."

Beaumarchais fixed me with a withering look as I translated Franklin's request. Then he followed Madame Chaumont down the corridor and out of sight. Franklin listened to their footsteps descending the staircase, a thoughtful, bemused smile playing on his face.

"A very eventful week," he said to no one in particular.

"So, Ben," I remarked. "It seems this is good-bye."

He turned and regarded me over the rim of his spectacles. "Is it?" he asked.

"You're to leave in the morning. Monsieur Beaumarchais made that quite clear."

Franklin chuckled. "Dear Pierre. I've not seen him these past ten years. A fine fellow, but with a flair for the dramatic, I'm afraid. He angers easily, I think, because he believes he looks his best when angry. But to answer you, Henri, I should submit that our association need not end with the dawn."

"How so?" I asked him, perplexed.

"I should like it very much if you would accompany me to Paris," he replied brightly.

I gaped at him. He waited patiently as I struggled to find my tongue. "I...what...?"

"You shouldn't look so surprised," he said. "I need a translator. Pierre's English is excellent, as you have seen, but he has too ill a reputation to make him useful in some circles. You, on the other hand, my dear boy, fit that particular bill quite nicely. You have youth, energy, and you have offended no one...save perhaps Pierre. A perfect choice!"

"Yes, but...my father..."

"You may write to your father. I don't believe he will mind. Come come, Henri! We're going to Paris! Eventually, perhaps even to Versailles to meet with the King of France! Surely that would turn the head of any adventure-minded lad!"

Turn my head it did! The notion of traveling with this man, of standing at his side to serve as his French tongue in situations both auspicious and mundane filled me with a thrill of excitement! My father had sent me here to serve as host, and to return when Dr. Franklin left La Barbarie behind him. Therefore, as Franklin's departure heralded my own, was this not simply a change of destination? I could send a letter to my father, informing him of the turn of events, and asking for his approval and blessing.

"Sir, you honor me!" I remarked eagerly. "I would be delighted to bear you company to the capital."

"I thank you," Franklin replied with a short bow. "Now let us join your newest guest in the drawing room, lest he think us up here conspiring against him."

At the mention of Beaumarchais, my demeanor darkened. "He'll be coming along with us," I said. It was a statement, not a question.

"Of course," Franklin replied.

"He won't very much care for my joining your travels, will he?" I asked.

"Not a jot," Franklin said, grinning. "Isn't that delightful?"

Chapter Seven

"A countryman between two lawyers is like a fish between two cats." - Benjamin Franklin

The next morning brought a flurry of activity as my household at La Barbarie prepared to close down. Most of the bedrooms would be shuttered against the cold, the furnishings covered to keep them free of dust. The Jogues' would stay on, of course, as caretakers, but with both Dr. Franklin and myself gone, Thérèse would have little reason not to rejoin her esteemed husband. The house would remain quiet until late spring, when my father and sisters came and took up residence during the warmer months.

Beaumarchais insisted upon as early a departure as possible. Dr. Franklin's revelation to him regarding my accompaniment had been met with a bitter outrage that had gradually simmered down to a rather sullen acceptance. He'd said little to me and had retired early, leaving Franklin to assure me that "Pierre is really a fair and decent fellow, and should come around before long."

I spent most of the dawn hours packing. My head ached, a reminder of a night spent in restless repose, my thoughts filled with rivaling emotions and conflicting interests. Dr. Franklin, however, appeared truly rested, his blue eyes bright with the morning's promise and the anticipation of our journey to Paris.

By eight o'clock, after a breakfast delivered by Thérèse's skillful hand, I bade Monsieur Jogues bring the carriage around from the stables, so that we might take our leave. We resolved to have Monsieur Jogues drive us down to Nantes and, from there, hire a proper traveling coach to carry us on the first leg of our journey to Paris. My father's carriage, being normally reserved for summer use, was too small and too open for a long winter's trip.

When Monsieur Jogues had loaded the last of our belongings into the carriage's baggage bench, he came to stand beside his wife and daughter. Dr. Franklin approached them, wrapped once again in his unembroidered coat and with his fur hat pulled tightly down over his ears. He took the caretaker's shoulders and delivered kisses to both his cheeks. "I thank you for the loan of your young master," he said as he moved on to Madame Jogues, who giggled prettily when Franklin kissed the back of her hand. "I promise to return him to you in the very best condition." Both caretakers gave him thankful smiles after I had turned Dr. Franklin's words to French.

To Thérèse, he offered a proper bow, touching her hand to his forehead. "Madame," he said. "My compliments to your noble husband. Please express to him my most bitter jealousies at his having won your fair hand before I had even the opportunity to offer protest to his claim."

Thérèse looked to me for a translation but, as she did, I saw a smile raise the corners of her mouth. In the moment that it took me to recite Dr. Franklin's flowery farewell in French, I was struck by a most singular revelation. Despite that which I had always believed, Madame Chaumont *did* speak English—or at least understood it! There could be no mistaking her expression. She conducted herself exactly as if she had grasped Dr. Franklin's flattery, but was determined not to reveal this fact.

I stood staring at her, as Beaumarchais muttered his hasty regrets and helped Dr. Franklin into the carriage. Then he turned and looked upon me with irritation and expectance. I continued to gape at Thérèse until she took notice and approached. "Is something wrong, Master

Henri?" she asked.

"I..." But words failed me. I had known this woman all my life. I had come to rely on her, to trust her without question, as I trusted her parents. Her subterfuge unsettled me deeply, and yet I could not find it within me to confront her. Finally, feeling betrayed, I said: "Please offer my compliments to Monsieur Chaumont."

"I shall," she said, offering my forehead a sisterly kiss. I took my place in the carriage. Monsieur Jogues climbed up onto the driver's bench and shook the reins. So, with a final wave from Thérèse, I left La Barbarie behind me. I would not again see my father's country house for many, many years.

"Do you think His Honor the Mayor will be awaiting us in Nantes?" Franklin asked thoughtfully.

"He has had no warning of your departure," I said, "But you may rest assured that, *if* he is waiting, it will be with the intention that one last tribute be paid to you before you leave."

"No more tributes," Beaumarchais declared, in a voice that would brook no argument. "No more banquets. No more accolades. I'm sorry, Ben, but I think it best if we leave Nantes behind us as quickly as possible."

"Oh, foolishness," Franklin retorted good-naturedly. "I think you mother me too much, my dear Pierre. But, for your sake, we shall comply. We can leave it to Madame Chaumont to make my regrets to the village fathers."

At Beaumarchais' insistence, we selected the stable yard furthest from the heart of the city, to better facilitate our discreet "escape". It was a large establishment, made fat upon the traffic through Nantes' thriving freshwater port on the River Loire.

To avoid the attention that Franklin's familiar face would generate, I ventured forth alone to seek out the stable master and arrange for a coach and driver

The transaction was conducted simply enough. As the stable master set out to prepare our new coach and horses, I made my way around the far side of the build-

The Franklin Affair

ing to instruct Monsieur Jogues to unload our baggage from my father's carriage. Set upon this task, I happened past a shadowed place between the master's house and the main livery stable.

Suddenly, a strong hand reached out from the shadows and took me by my shoulder, drawing me into the narrow walkway so abruptly and forcefully and I very nearly left both of my shoes behind. Before I could cry out in alarm, I was pinned firmly against the rough wood of the stables' outside wall and a hand was pressed to my mouth. I looked up, horror-stricken, into the glowering face of Father Hilliard.

"Don't utter a sound!" he commanded. Then, after several moments: "Do you know me now? Are you calm?" I nodded and he took the hand away.

"What...brings you here, Father," I stammered, feeling cold perspiration settle upon my brow.

"I followed you from La Barbarie," he said. "I wasn't expecting to see the carriage leave with Franklin aboard. What's the meaning of this?"

"Dr. Franklin...decided to leave for Paris," I replied hesitantly.

"Did he? And Beaumarchais? What has that flamboyant fop to do with this business?"

For a moment I simply stood there, as flustered as any simpleton, struggling to sort out my feelings in this matter. Father Hilliard seemed to sense my indecision, for he drew himself closer to me and looked down upon me with a face as stern as any schoolmaster's. "Remember whom you serve, boy," he said darkly.

"I remember," I said quietly.

"Then speak! What is Beaumarchais' place in all of this?"

"He came to escort Dr. Franklin to Paris."

Father Hilliard's frown deepened. "Indeed? I was not aware that the two men knew one another. So it is at his insistence that the American departs Nantes like a thief in the night?"

I nodded mutely.

"And the old man's room? Did you search it as I

bade you?"

I nearly confronted him and demanded to know how he had managed to spirit his written orders into my locked bedchamber. But the sight of him proved so daunting that I confess my nerve failed me. Instead I only nodded like an obedient child.

"Well, then? What did you find?"

"There was a letter to someone named Sally," I said. "Unfinished."

"That's his daughter," Hilliard remarked impatiently. "Go on."

"There was a journal, but I had not the time to read it. Monsieur Beaumarchais discovered me in Dr. Franklin's room and put a stop to my...activities."

"Was there nothing else, then?" Father Hilliard demanded.

"There was a letter, penned by Monsieur Beaumarchais and delivered to Dr. Franklin by messenger when he landed at Auray. It warned Dr. Franklin that someone called 'S' may have sent someone else called 'The Fox' against him."

"The Fox!" Father Hilliard exclaimed. Suddenly his hands were upon me once more, full of bitter earnest. With a hard shake he said: "Tell me about this letter? Does Franklin know the identity of The Fox?"

"I...I don't believe so," I said, gasping. "It was a letter of warning, sent to herald Monsieur Beaumarchais' arrival in Nantes. He is resolute in his intention to escort Dr. Franklin safely to the capital."

Slowly, Father Hilliard released me and stepped back. "Why have *you* come along this morning?" he asked. "What is your business here? Did Franklin bring you simply to arrange the transportation for himself and Beaumarchais?"

"No," I said anxiously. "Dr. Franklin has asked me to accompany him to Paris...as his translator."

Father Hilliard started. Then, for the first time since I had met this mysterious and unsettling man, a genuine smile cast itself upon his pale, thin lips. His placed his large fists upon his hips and uttered a short, bemused

The Franklin Affair

laugh. "Well now!" he exclaimed. "It seems that you have fallen in well with the American doctor! Tell me, my little mouse, do you fancy the old man?"

"I..."

"Yes, of course you do," he said. "And why shouldn't you? Franklin can charm the fangs from a serpent." The uncharacteristic smile gave way to his usual glower. "But remember this, Mouse: that old man is dangerous. Not just to France, but to all of Europe. He stands for a nation of outlaws and rebels, and he will do anything...*anything*...to further his unholy cause. In the King's name I charge you with this mission: stay with Franklin and serve him, as he would have you do. But watch and listen. Chaumont and I will be in Paris to hear what you discover. Chaumont you shall see quite openly, in his role as an advisor to the king. But I shall limit myself to the shadows. Do not endeavor to seek me, Mouse. When the moment grows ripe, I will come to you. Understand me?"

"I understand you," I said.

"Off with you, then. Remember what we have said here. Go...before you're missed." Then, with an unkind shove, he sent me stumbling out into the harsh winter's sunshine. I stood in the dust for several moments, blinking stupidly against the glare. When at last I risked a look back, there was no sign of the priest.

Slowly, wrapped in a cold blanket of uncertainty and regret, I returned to my father's carriage. In my absence, the new coach and horses had been readied. Monsieur Jogues was busily conducting our baggage from one carriage to the next. The new driver, a young man wrapped in a long coat and scarf, tipped his hat to me as I approached.

"Is...all prepared?" I asked the stable master.

"It is, young sir," the man replied. "I came out to pay my respects to Dr. Franklin. I had no idea he would be a passenger on my coach. Such an honor!"

Franklin smiled at me from behind his spectacles. It was a look of such kindness and genuine affection that it left me feeling half-sickened with guilt. I returned the smile as best I could and then slipped past him to climb up into the new coach. It was a decision that I immediately regretted.

"And just where have *you* been, boy?"

Beaumarchais, bundled up in his fine wool coat, greeted me with a stare filled with hot suspicion. Something in my face must have fed this flame because he suddenly leaned forward. "I asked a question of you, Master Henri!" he said sharply.

"I happened upon the village priest," I said, managing to keep my tone level. "We spared ourselves a few moments to chat."

"Did you tell him that Franklin is leaving Nantes?"

"He asked what news there was of Dr. Franklin," I said. How smoothly the falsehood came to my tongue. "Would you have had me lie to him?"

"I would have you not be here at all! But, as you are, I must remind you that Franklin's life may well be in serious jeopardy, jeopardy that is in no small way heightened by your freely discussing his movements with anyone who asks!"

I sat back upon the cushioned bench, feigning anger at the chastisement, but secretly relieved that my deception had garnered such ready belief. "Dr. Franklin has been here for more than a week, Monsieur," I said quietly. "He has been dined by every noble house within ten miles. I know...for I accompanied him on most of these occasions. Courtesy and genuine welcome have met him at every door. Where, then, are these assassins you fear?"

"There are always assassins, boy," Beaumarchais replied. "And they keep their own counsel as to when and where they shall strike."

"Like The Fox?"

He cursed me with a withering look. "You do yourself little service by mentioning that appalling invasion. Franklin may have settled that account by calling it 'curiosity', but to me it smacks of intrigue. Mark me, boy!" His tone was reminiscent of Father's Hilliard's. It made for an unsettling parallel. "If I ever learn that you have,

The Franklin Affair

in any way, betrayed that great man's faith in you...if you ever do or say anything to bring him the slightest harm...I shall open you from your chin to your navel. Be quite clear on that, Monsieur Gruel!"

"I'm clear," I said, trying to convey a measure of bravado that I did not feel.

Beaumarchais fixed me with his eyes for another moment. Then he wordlessly pushed past me and exited the carriage, sending it rocking on its thorough-braces (for my readers who may not recall, these were the leather straps upon which the body of the coach rested, in the times before springs).

Less than a minute later, the door opened again and Dr. Franklin entered. With a smile and a sigh, he placed himself upon the facing bench and rested his walking stick upon the cushions beside him, turning it so that it pointed roughly westward, toward his beloved America.

"We shall be departing shortly," he told me. "Pierre is settling our affairs with the stable master. Our driver's name is Antoine. Do you know him?"

I slowly shook my head.

"Well, it is two days to Le Mans," Franklin said. "By then, we should come to know him well enough, I'd fancy. He seems a kindly young fellow."

"I'm sure he would be most honored by any attention paid to him by so noble a passenger."

"Well said, Henri," Franklin replied with a chuckle. "And I could not agree more. But, what's this? You appear...unsettled." His smile faded. He said, with some annoyance: "Did Pierre say something to upset you? I've already spoken to him once on your account. If I need do so a second time..."

"I am well," I said, endeavoring to sound sincere. "It's only that...Ben, do you ever find that life can become terribly...*complicated?*"

"My dear young fellow," Franklin replied, his usual bemused grin returning. "Without its complications, I should think life a most tedious affair. Savor complexity, my boy! It is the spice in the soup, the honey upon the bread and the splash of rum in our cup of mortal tea!"

Chapter Eight

"Three may keep a secret, if two of them are dead." -
Benjamin Franklin

The journey to Le Mans was spent in close quarters, the three of us struggling to keep warm as the carriage bounced uncomfortably beneath us. Antoine drove his horses hard in an effort to reach each day's scheduled lodging within the shortened span of a winter's daylight. This made for an arduous journey, one rendered none the lighter by the emptiness of the road, and the ever present fear of highwaymen.

Dr. Franklin was the only one amongst us to speak with any frequency. Beaumarchais seemed content to simply brood, and many times I noticed him regarding me with a barbarian's scowl. This left me in a less than gregarious mood, and so it was an effort to lend polite attention to Franklin's queries about my family and my childhood.

"I am the youngest of eleven children," I told him as our journey wore on. "Six boys and five girls. My eldest brother, Gaston, manages my father's business affairs for him. He is twenty-three years my senior. All of my other brothers died for France in the Seven Years War."

"A tragedy," Franklin said with heartfelt sympathy. "And your sisters?"

"Four are married. Two have children. The fifth joined a convent."

"And your mother?"

I looked up at him. "My mother died while giving birth to me," I said quietly.

"Henri, I'm sorry."

"My father raised us alone, with my eldest sister, Helene, to act in a mother's role. I never missed having a mother of my own...not really. It was a large family, you understand."

"Yes, I do understand. Quite so, in fact." Franklin placed a grandfatherly hand upon my shoulder. "I am also born to a large brood, seventeen in all. I, too, was my father's youngest son...though not his youngest child. I remember thirteen of us sitting at one time at his table. The rest of the seventeen met various unhappy ends, I'm afraid."

"My sympathies, sir," I said.

"I daresay my tribulations are no better or worse than your own, Henri. As we grow older, and the losses in our life count one upon the next, we are given to feel a bit like a wheel of Swiss cheese, for the number of holes that fate has left in our heart." Franklin saluted me with a covered mug of rum. "Still, the good Lord is generous, for He gives us the means with which to celebrate life, rather than to mourn it!"

No mention was made of The Fox or of Franklin's mission to France. On the few occasions when I endeavored to broach these subjects, my efforts were firmly stifled by the menace in Beaumarchais' hard, suspicious eyes.

It was the 17th of December when we reached Le Mans. The night was overcast and threatened snow. Antoine stabled the horses and found us lodgings above a local tavern. So crowded was the inn that the three of us were forced to accept a single small room, and one without a hearth. To keep warm, it would be necessary for us to share a single bed, an uncomfortable prospect that I think none of us much fancied, and so we stayed up quite late into the night, drinking warm spirits in the tavern. This proved ultimately advantageous to my mission, as my two companions—with some rum to warm their bellies and loosen their tongues—began to speak in earnest of matters of political import.

"When do you expect we will make Paris?" Franklin asked Beaumarchais.

"Two days," was the reply. "No more than three. This weather makes for the most damnable traveling." Beaumarchais, who had drunk more than the both of us combined, appeared flushed and a bit hazy in the eyes. He kept treating me to strange, sidelong glances.

"I wrote to Silas and asked him to expect me sometime before Christmas," Franklin said. "Where do you think he will put me up?"

Beaumarchais barked out a laugh. "Ben! Whether you know it or not, all of France has awaited your coming. Do not think for a moment that your reception in Nantes was in any way unique. Paris will be the same, only much more so! I hear it said that every noble house has approached Monsieur Deane with offers to play host to you during your stay. You shall have your pick of them!"

Franklin grinned mischievously. "Poor Silas. I wonder how many such offers were made to *him* when *he* first came to France?"

"Not many, I fancy," Beaumarchais replied with a drunken chuckle.

"I beg your pardon, Ben," I said "But...if I may ask...who are Messieurs Silas and Deane?"

Franklin smiled. "'Tis not two men, Henri, but one. Silas Deane is my colleague in Paris. He is, like me, a commissioner to France, charged with extolling the virtues of the American cause against the British. There is one other: Arthur Lee. But he is currently in London, ever-faithfully negotiating for a peaceful British acceptance of American independence."

"No longer," Beaumarchais reported. "Before I left Paris, I heard tell that Lee had informed Deane by letter of his intention to join you both in France. I don't believe he cares for your coming abroad, Ben."

"Arthur enjoys the footlights, and fears my reputation may dim his own."

"So...there are *three* commissioners," I said. "This I did not know. And Monsieur Deane has been in Paris, set to this task for how long?"

"Close to a year," Franklin replied. "He has, by all accounts, worked quite diligently, and has enjoyed considerable success...with no small thanks to Pierre here. However, he has so far failed to gain *open* support from the French. In other words, while King Louis and his foreign minister, Vergennes, are pleased to provide us with secretive aid, they remain reluctant to admit their support of the American cause before their fellow European nations. This is why I have come. Congress hopes that the French will be better disposed toward me, if only by virtue of my name and humble history."

"Humble?" Beaumarchais said, laughing. "The three commissioners indeed! Beside you, the two of them make as loud a noise as a mouse beside a lion."

Franklin raised his eyebrows. "In all my life, my dear Pierre, that may be the only time anyone has ever compared me to a lion!"

"Deane is not without his virtues," Beaumarchais elaborated. "He is a friendly fellow, quite loyal and extremely talkative. However, I'm afraid that he lacks a certain..." he frowned, hunting for the right word with his drink-addled mind. "...charisma, if you take my meaning, Ben."

"I do, as I'm sure Henri does."

"Indeed," I said. Then, most unwisely, I added: "So Monsieur Silas Deane is the 'S' of which I read in your letter, Monsieur Beaumarchais?"

Beaumarchais' expression darkened. Suddenly his large, trembling finger was in my face. "As I have said to you before...you would do well not to remind me of that 'boyish curiosity'. Ben has taken a fancy to you and, for his sake, I tolerate you as best I may. But do not think to press that point too far!"

"Pierre," Franklin said, gently but firmly. "Please

calm yourself. Henri has asked a question. Would you have me ignore a young man's healthy interest in the ways of the world?"

"I would," Beaumarchais grumbled. "Though I don't for a moment believe you shall heed me."

"Indeed not. Henri, the 'S' in Pierre's letter referred to Stormont...David Murray Viscount Stormont, to be precise. He is the British Ambassador to France."

"He's a spy master!" Beaumarchais spat. "A filthy blackmailer and assassin."

"Lord Stormont has never been directly connected with any intrigue within French borders," Franklin remarked.

"He's slippery, I'll grant you that," replied Beaumarchais. "Yet he is well known to command a considerable spy network throughout King Louis' domain. Worse, he gives orders that see good men killed at the hands of The Fox."

Ah! I thought, feeling my momentary elation dampened by a now familiar stab of guilt. I looked at Dr. Franklin, who returned my gaze with open sincerity on his broad, expressive face. "The Fox?" I asked, endeavoring to sound both naïve and earnest. "The letter mentioned him also. Who is The Fox?"

"The Fox," Franklin replied, regarding me thoughtfully. "He is an assassin, Henri...a British agent of unparalleled skill and cunning. No one knows how long he has operated in France...many years, I should think. No one knows who he is..."

"...but he has killed more than two dozen men of rank and influence," Beaumarchais concluded hotly. "He has also managed to pass ruthlessly damaging secrets to the British, and may have been more than somewhat responsible for France's catastrophic loss during the last war."

"Indeed!" I said to the playwright, aghast. "And you fear that this assassin may be after Ben?"

"I more than fear it. I was present when Stormont came before the king. He was red-faced with outrage,

The Franklin Affair

having heard that Dr. Franklin was en route to France to join in Silas Deane's effort to secure French aid for the American war effort. He made all sorts of entreaties and threats against Ben, insisting that something *must* be done to...how did he put it?...'remove this ungrateful incendiary from the tide of events.'"

"Ungrateful?" Franklin remarked with mock offense. "Who's ungrateful?"

"The Comte de Vergennes, the king's foreign minister, was in attendance," Beaumarchais continued. "After the royal audience, Vergennes and I took Stormont aside in an effort to placate him. I fear that I was of little help in that effort. I despise that English rogue and always have. I'm rather afraid that my animosity displayed itself in my conduct toward him."

"Pierre, my friend," Franklin told him. "You are as frank and honest as any man I have ever known. You make your friendship quite plain, and your disdain equally obvious."

"Perhaps, but Vergennes plays a more subtle game than I where politics are concerned. He urged Stormont to take no action that would damage the peace that now exists between Louis and George III. But Stormont was adamant. Forgive me, Ben...these are his words, not mine: 'Mark me, Gravier...' The scoundrel had the audacity to address the comte by his birth name! '...if that traitor sets one foot upon French soil, I shall see that he never leaves it!' Then he stamped off, leaving his threat to hang heavily in the air behind him."

"Pierre," said Franklin. "I do believe you may be letting your sense of drama gain the better of you."

"He said what he said," Beaumarchais insisted. "He meant The Fox and none other. That's why I came out here, Ben. No one knows what this man looks like. He could be our driver, or that barkeep over there..." He paused and fixed me with a withering look. "...or even a boy of some sixteen years."

"Surely not!" Franklin said with a laugh.

"Then such a boy could be made to serve him,"

Beaumarchais pressed, keeping his eyes trained upon me.

"Can this be, Henri?" Franklin asked me, his voice filled with such innocent mirth that it tugged at my already beleaguered heart. "Can you be Stormont's spy? Can you serve The Fox?"

"I..." I began, but the words caught in my throat.

"Have no fears on this score, Pierre," Franklin said, smiling. "Henri has always been as sincere with me as I have been with him. Isn't that so, my boy?"

"It's so, Ben," I said, and the weight of the lie was like a stone upon my chest.

"Well, unhappy though the thought of our cold, crowded accommodations may render me," Beaumarchais remarked after a long pause, "I think it best we retire for the night. We must ride out early if we hope to make Paris in two days."

"Come then, gentlemen!" Franklin declared, rising. "Let us find our small crowded bed. It will help teach us to better cope with our small, crowded carriage!" Then he laughed and took a long, last swallow of spirits before marching away from the table, weaving uncertainly through the busy tavern hall. After a moment spent glaring once more at me, Beaumarchais took after him.

I sat alone at our small round table, with the raucous laughter of the tavern's patrons filling my ears. Then, after a long, unhappy draught of ill-tasting rum, I followed behind the two men who were my companions—and my betters.

Chapter Nine

"Some are weather-wise, some are otherwise." - Benjamin Franklin

The next morning we said farewell to Antoine, who was kind enough to negotiate with a local stable master for a coach that would carry us the remainder of the way to Paris. Maurice was the new man's name, a tall gaunt fellow who smiled frequently but spoke little. The coach we obtained in Le Mans was larger than the last, and Maurice provided us with hot coals with which to battle the chill. We prepared to depart amidst a great curtain of falling snow, which had already settled upon the road to a depth of half-a-foot. Maurice cursed mightily as he slipped and stumbled, trying to affix the stable master's two horses to the new carriage. At the sight of Franklin, our new driver most humbly apologized, but the American doctor, ever gracious, replied: "Never fear, my fine fellow! Damning the weather is a bit like striking a stone with a piece of timber. No one is the better for it, yet none suffer over it either."

The night had been passed in reasonable comfort.

Franklin had insisted on sleeping in the middle, denying the attempts of both Beaumarchais and myself to offer him the edge of the bed. He claimed that he would be all the warmer for lying between us, but I suspected that he secretly wished to place himself firmly between the playwright and myself—lest Beaumarchais take it into his head to strangle me as I slept.

Everyone's repose was fitful. Franklin snored so as to make the windows tremble, and Beaumarchais murmured indecipherable mysteries into his pillow. For myself, I spent my time poorly, caught between dozing and empty hours of wakefulness, struggling with my own mission and with the conflict that my duty to king and country had inspired within me. More than once, I resolved to confess everything to Franklin upon the morrow, only to reject such folly and remind myself impatiently of where my true loyalties must lie. With the dawn, I saw sadly that I could do naught but continue as I had been, and pray that circumstances would soon free me from this ill-fitting burden.

On the road toward Paris, Beaumarchais said blessedly little. I could readily see that his head troubled him from his over-indulgence the night before. Franklin, however, chatted like a fishwife, revealing to me much of his life, his adventures, and the wondrous inventions that had earned him his fame.

"I watched the key glow, as soft and pretty as a candle flame behind a curtain of cheese cloth," he said wistfully. "The kite was, of course, in terrible straits, and the storm still raged overhead. Nevertheless we stood there, winsome child and foolish father, staring at the strange little miracle wrought by wire and lightning.

"My son William asked me what we should do about the key. I said that I thought I should touch it, though only just, and see whether or not it was only light that stayed with it...or if some of the elusive electricity remained there as well."

"And so you touched it?" I asked, captivated.

"Oh I did, indeed!" Franklin declared.

"What happened?"

"Well, let us say that the electricity *was* there...a portion of it, at any rate...trapped within the iron of that key. When I touched it, however, it came forth with the bite of ten dogs! I was cast right off my feet, and found myself in a heap upon the floor.

"You see, Henri, all lightning seeks the ground, and

The Franklin Affair

that which remained in the key was no different. It stayed there, imprisoned, hoping that something would come along to carry it the rest of the way to its destination. And something did. Oh yes! That something was myself! I touched the key, and the lightning took its chance and traveled through my arm, down my back, along my legs and down into the ground through the soles of my shoes! A most tremulous and exhilarating experience, and one I should not care to repeat!

"But the experiment had served its purpose. It proved beyond doubt that lightning sought the ground and that, if one could *help* it to satisfy this goal benignly, then one could prevent that same lightning from finding a roof or tree instead. I fancied that a shaft of iron might do the trick. As it happened, this was the case."

"The lightning rod!" I exclaimed.

"Exactly so."

"Brilliant, Ben! Absolutely brilliant!"

Franklin waved my compliment away with an impatient hand. "Brilliance is a thing of the moment, more swift and fleeting than any lightning bolt. I prefer to think of what came to me that day as a fool's inspiration. For the good Lord must surely have looked down upon this dolt with his hair all askew and his son tearfully begging to know if he still lived, and He must have said to Himself: 'Such a man as this deserves some small reward for surviving such idiocy.' And so he gave me my flash of 'brilliance'."

"You jest, sir," I said, laughing.

"Frequently," he replied.

"Tell me, Ben, did your son William grow into a man such as yourself? Intelligent and gifted?"

Franklin's face fell. "My son and I...are not in touch at the present time. We find ourselves on opposite sides of a war, you see. He was, at one time, the Royal Governor of the colony of New Jersey. He has since been taken prisoner by American forces, and is currently under guard in Connecticut."

"Oh!" I cried. "Sir, forgive me!"

"No, nothing to forgive. You did not know. How could you? He is unharmed in Connecticut, and will remain so. I have seen to that. But our estrangement is one of the reasons I had wished to bring Temple, William's son, along with me to France...to get him well away from his loyalist mother."

"It's a pity he took ill."

"Yes, it is." He looked upon me in earnest. "My boy, mark me well. Do not turn away from your father. And when, in time, you come to have a son, let him not turn away from you. There is no sorrow like the loss of a child. I know...for though I have lost my dear wife to a stroke, it is still for want of William that I feel the most bitter regret."

Very quietly, I said: "I will remember that, Ben."

I was about to say more, perhaps to ask after the old man's daughter, Sally, whom he favored and to whom had been addressed that half-finished letter I'd discovered while playing the thief in Franklin's bedchamber. But then our coach came suddenly to a loud, rumbling halt. It was so abrupt that we were cast about on our seats like rag dolls. I heard Beaumarchais utter a startled cry as I was dashed to the carriage floor with Dr. Franklin atop me.

"What has happened?" the old man asked. Then, more loudly, so that our new driver might hear him: "Maurice! Maurice! Have we crashed?"

Then we heard a man's muffled words float through the coach's thick planks: "Stand and deliver!"

"Oh my," said Franklin, pulling himself awkwardly up onto the bench. He looked down to me for a translation, but I could tell that the speaker's tone had already revealed his intent.

"Highwayman," I said in English, and I admit that my voice caught a bit in my throat.

Beaumarchais leapt to his feet and found the hilt of his sword. Franklin reached for him, staying his hand.

"You in the coach!" came the voice from without. The accent was provincial, but educated. Highwaymen, I

The Franklin Affair

knew, were often displaced merchants, their livelihoods lost to ill fortune or ill management, who took to stealing to offset a winter's starvation. "Come out now or find yourselves another driver!"

I translated for Franklin, who then whispered sharply to Beaumarchais: "Think of Maurice! Make no move against this man!"

"Ben!" Beaumarchais replied sharply, his eyes and manner suddenly keen. The crisis of the moment had evidently cleared his head more surely than any tonic. "This man will rob us, take the carriage, and likely leave us out here to die in the snow!"

"It may be so," Franklin replied gravely. "But I'll not have an innocent driver's blood on my hands."

"Last chance!" the highwayman called. "Shall I count to five?"

"We're coming out!" Franklin called after I had hastily turned the thief's words to English. "Stay here," he said to me, speaking in an uncharacteristically authoritative tone.

"You'll need my language skills!" I retorted.

"Pierre can translate for me with this fellow. It's plain enough what he wants in any case. I will not have your death on my conscience. *Stay!*"

Opening the door and holding his hands in plain sight, Franklin stepped unsteadily down from the coach and into the snowy afternoon. Beaumarchais turned and regarded me, his expression unreadable. Then he followed the American doctor out into the cold.

"Are you alone then?" I heard the highwayman ask. "Just the two of you?"

"Just the two of us!" Beaumarchais called back. Take our gold, but leave us the coach, lest we freeze!"

A laugh, hard and bitter, filtered through the curtain of snow beyond the coach's open door. "Surely two such rich men as yourselves will be made warm by the fat on your bones. The coach is mine, as are your belongings. If you cooperate, I shall leave you your lives...and for this you should call me generous!"

A terrible anger rose within me, swiftly eclipsing my fear. Dr. Benjamin Franklin was out there, and this brigand intended nothing less than to abandon so great a man to the winter's ill mercy, all for the sake of a coach and a few livres.

My eyes fell upon Franklin's stout Crabtree stick, which, in his haste, the doctor had forgotten.

I admit now that I acted more out of anger and instinct than a man's reason. I took up the stick and went to the carriage's opposite door. This I opened slowly revealing a day rendered white by falling snow. Moving carefully, so as not to alert the highwayman with the bouncing of the coach's thorough-braces, I stepped down into the foot of powder that covered the roadway. Then, stick in hand, I made my way up toward the unsettled horses.

"Keep the old man where he is!" I heard the highwayman demand. "You! Empty your purse and your pockets! Bring everything to me! Hold nothing back now, unless you want a ball in your gullet!"

I ducked down and moved around the front of the horses, which shuffled and stamped nervously. Crouching low, I peered around the tremulous foreleg of the leftmost steed and saw Beaumarchais busily, angrily, fishing his money purse from the inside of his heavy woolen coat. Franklin and our driver, Maurice, stood side by side at the edge of the road, doing the same. Before them, with his back to me, was a thin fellow in a heavy cloak. A sword hung sheathed at his belt and his right hand held a raised pistol.

Fear rose up within me anew, a child's terror that I quickly swallowed as I stepped slowly and silently out from my concealment, approaching the brigand from his rear right flank. He wore a thick, unkempt beard, and the one eye that I could see was filled with a cruel, predatory calm.

Franklin spotted me, but made no sound. His eyes widened and thought I saw his cold-reddened face grow suddenly pale. Maurice had not yet seen me, as the

The Franklin Affair

highwayman's bulk stood between us.

Beaumarchais dropped a leathern purse onto the snowy ground. The highwayman's hungry gaze fell upon it, and then looked with lustful avarice at Franklin's heavy trunk, which remained fastened to the side of our carriage—the carriage with which he intended to abscond. The Declaration of Independence was in there, I thought, and the notion of such a document becoming kindling for a thief's hearth did much to fuel my courage. I approached the cloaked brigand and raised Franklin's walking stick high over my head.

Then, quite suddenly, Maurice cried out: "Look there!"

The villain turned toward me. His face was concealed beneath a thick scarf, but I could see his eyes well enough; they shone with surprise and outrage. He brought the pistol to bear upon me.

Shrieking like a savage, I stuck downward with the stick. Necessity guided my aim. I heard a cry of pain, and looked to see the pistol upon the ground and the highwayman clutching at his wounded wrist. "Beaumarchais!" I exclaimed, trying to keep the panic from sounding in my voice. "Have at him! *Have at him!*"

The playwright moved with astonished alacrity. Drawing his saber, he advanced toward the highwayman, who met him with his own blade in hand.

They came together there in the road, between Dr. Franklin, Maurice and myself. The highwayman fought fiercely, fueled by his desperation, but Beaumarchais parried each thrust with deadly precision. The combat carried them toward the rear of the carriage, with Beaumarchais making a slow, calculated retreat. I watched his eyes as he fought, admiring the way he gauged his opponent's every strike, matching him steel against steel, the noise of the duel floating dully through the snow-riddled air.

Then, with a smooth, swift motion, Beaumarchais parried a final time, turned and came up under the highwayman's outstretched arm. The point of his saber drove deep into the villain's side, piercing his heart. The man groaned, stiffened and fell dead upon the ground, his blood mixing with the powdery snow.

Franklin crossed to me, leaving Maurice standing at the roadside. He came up and, to my surprise, embraced me, clutching me to him with fevered relief. "I told you to stay in the coach!" he scolded, and I looked up into eyes that shone with frightened tears. "You'll do as I tell you, Henri, if you wish to stay in my service. Do you hear me? Do you hear me...you wonderful, courageous boy!" Then he pulled me to him anew.

"Maurice!" Beaumarchais called. "Help me drag this damnable fellow off the road!"

Franklin released me and turned suddenly. "Pierre! No!"

Beaumarchais looked up at him. "What?"

"Maurice warned the fellow as Henri was about to strike him!"

I saw our driver's face grow fearful. "Sirs! I did no such thing. My warning was meant for the boy!"

"This is no weather for even a thief to venture out in," Franklin insisted. "There are too few travelers this day to make risking such cold a worthy pursuit. Pierre, I tell you this business was arranged beforehand! It is the only explanation for this ambush. Maurice made certain this highwayman knew where to lie in wait for us!"

Maurice looked from one man to the next. Then he made a sudden, desperate snatch for the highwayman's pistol, which lay in the snow beside one of the carriage wheels. Beaumarchais was far too swift for him. He caught the driver by the collar of his coat and spun him around, driving him up against the side of the coach. Then he pressed the point of his saber against Maurice's bobbing Adam's apple. "Speak plainly or die," he said in a tone so filled with menace that it sent a shiver up my spine.

"I tell you..." Maurice began, but then the tip of Beaumarchais' saber split his skin and he cried out. "Yes! Yes! I was paid to bring you here. I was told that there would be trouble, but that I would not be harmed!"

"And who told you to expect us?" Franklin asked, coming closer.

"I was...approached...the day before your arrival from Nantes," Maurice stammered. "It was an Englishman."

"The Fox!" Beaumarchais exclaimed.

"Unlikely," said Franklin. "The Fox is more subtle than this. Stormont perhaps...or one of his agents."

"They meant to strand us out here!" I said.

"They meant to kill *me*," Franklin corrected. "And make it seem that I had fallen victim to a faceless highwayman. Is this not so, Maurice?"

Slowly, and with obvious terror, the driver nodded. "Please, sirs. I was in need of money. The winter is hard on men of my trade. My children..."

"Your children would do well to find a less villainous father!" Beaumarchais spat. His sword arm drew back.

"Don't kill him, Pierre," Franklin said.

"What? Ben!"

"We could take him back to Le Mans," I suggested. "Turn him over to the constable..."

"I'd be hanged!" Maurice wailed.

"Better than you deserve!" Beaumarchais exclaimed. "But we can't spare the time. Already the day grows late. We would never reach Le Mans before nightfall. We must continue forward!"

"Then we'll take him as far as Chartres," Franklin said. "We can inform the local authorities of what has happened and hire ourselves a new coach and driver."

"It will delay us," Beaumarchais said.

"There's no helping that," Franklin told him firmly. "Pierre, I'll not have cold-blooded murder sing me to sleep tonight."

"We shall have to keep him in the coach with us, then," the playwright said. "We surely can't trust him to drive. Who will take the horses?"

With a voice far braver than its owner, I said. "*I*

shall."

Franklin looked hard upon me.

"Well, how can it be otherwise?" I continued. "Monsieur Beaumarchais is needed to guard our prisoner. You certainly cannot drive the coach, Ben...not with your gout. So it must be me."

"But can you handle this team and carriage all the way to the Chartres? It must be fifty miles."

"I know not," I admitted, already feeling the bite of the cold wind that through my coat. "But I'm certain we could manage my father's estate in Nogent-le-Rotrou. That can be no more than fifteen miles."

"Yes," Beaumarchais said after a moment's rumination. "He's right, Ben. Right now, it's our safest course."

Franklin frowned at me. Then reluctantly he nodded. "Very well, Henri. It seems we shall be paying a call upon your good father. Given our sharp pace these last few days, we may even arrive there before your letter to him does. Won't that make for a charming surprise! Go and fetch yourself blankets from the carriage. I'm sure Maurice will happily donate his coat and scarf. They look warm. Henri, you *can* drive a coach, can you not?"

"I can," I said, though this carriage was a good deal larger than the one my father employed, and upon which I had served as driver on no more than two occasions. Also, I had never before driven in weather such as this. But there was nothing to be gained by uncertainty now, was there?

"Then let's be on our way, Ben," Beaumarchais said. "The day is cold and will only grow colder. You!" He glowered at Maurice. "Your coat and scarf."

"Sir!" our former driver wailed piteously. "I'll freeze in the coach!"

"Your fear will keep you warm. I promise!"

So it was that I took my place upon the driver's bench, wrapped in a coat many sizes too large for me and with my head bandaged in Maurice's thick scarf. Franklin reached up and took my hand, concern and gratitude in his eyes. "If you grow weary, stop the carriage and come in to get warm. We'll have rum handy. But we're out of coals..."

"I'll be fine, Ben. Go into the coach so that we may be off."

He nodded. "You're a fine man, Henri Gruel. A very fine man."

I was glad the scarf concealed the flush of pride that warmed my cheeks.

Moments later, the old man was secured in the carriage and Beaumarchais appeared, clutching Maurice, who was bound at the wrists and ankles with heavy rope. The playwright looked up at me with eyes more respectful than any he had previously offered. "As you can see, I've put some extra horse rope to good use and bound this villain. I think you might be able to guard him now. There's no need for you to risk the cold this way. I will take the reins."

I looked down upon him. Every inch of me wished to abandon this folly, and find what warmth I may within the coach. But my traitorous tongue replied: "No, Monsieur. Dr. Franklin is too precious a passenger to risk simply for the sake of my comfort. Should the brigand somehow free himself, he might strike us both down without you even knowing. It's best that we keep things as they are."

Beaumarchais seemed to consider this. Then he nodded. "I was wrong about you, boy," he said. "How can I make amends?"

"For one," I said, a bit irritably. "You can stop calling me 'boy'. I have a name."

"Indeed you do, Henri. I apologize."

"Apology accepted, Pierre."

He stiffened a bit at my free usage of his Christian name. Then, quite surprisingly, he grinned up at me. "Take the road slowly," he said. "Rap upon the bench should you encounter trouble."

"I shall."

Then they were gone, sealed up in the carriage, and I was alone with the horses and the snow and the biting cold.

Chapter Ten

"Think of these things: whence you came, where you are going, and to whom you must account." - Benjamin Franklin

"Dr. Franklin...if you'll forgive me, sir...I find myself skeptical of your ability to properly look after my son, especially given the fact that, when you arrived at my home less than a hour ago, it was he, half-frozen and weak from exhaustion, who held the reins of your carriage!"

"Father..." I pleaded miserably. My face was tipped over a large bowl of hot chicken broth. The warm steam was like a balm to my chapped and reddened skin. The drawing room around us was bathed in the glow from the hearth, making the three men's shadows dance like phantoms upon the wall.

"Surely, sir, it is not your intention to employ my youngest child as your coachman."

My sire, Bathelemy-Jacques Gruel, was in ill temper. He had been so ever since our inauspicious arrival at the Gruel Estate in Nogent-le-Rotrou. This home was much larger and lacked the provincial simplicity of La Barbarie. The entire south border of my father's lands was marked by a high stone wall with but a single gate, and this gate bore upon it the Gruel family crest: a dragon and a griffon in conflict upon a checkered field. The sight of it, after so many hours of hard riding through

The Franklin Affair

falling snow and a bitter wind, had drained me almost to the point of collapse. Upon reaching the house and feeling the carriage wheels clatter to a stop beneath me, I had swooned upon the driver's bench, barely feeling the strong hands that drew me down and into the warmth of my family's ancestral home.

The Gruels are not members of the aristocracy. We do, however, boast both long tradition and substantial means, and, as such, command respect very nearly equal to that of titled gentry. My father, the sixth Gruel to command the fortunes of a successful shipping and trading business, was as proud and noble as any landed baron, and quite well regarded in the lower circles within the French Court. He tended to frown upon anything that might lessen his family's status or reputation. Having his son deliver two strangers to his door, whilst planted, half-conscious, atop the driver's bench of a carriage in winter, was exactly the sort of thing to rankle him.

"Monsieur Gruel," Dr. Franklin said, his manner apologetic. "I owe your son a debt that I cannot possibly repay. He quite single-handedly...and against my expressed wishes, I should add...came to the rescue of Monsieur Beaumarchais and myself, when we were set upon by a highwayman and his henchman, who turned out to be our driver."

"I have sent for the constable," my father said. "In the meantime, your prisoner shall be made quite comfortable under the watchful eye of my chief steward."

"My thanks, sir," Franklin said. "The fact remains that, even with this foul plot thwarted, we were in dire straits. We had no driver...at least none that we could trust. I, as you can plainly see, am no man to run a team of horses and my companion, Monsieur Beaumarchais, had a prisoner to guard. Henri volunteered for the harsh duty of bringing us to your door. Twice then, he has earned my undying gratitude. My congratulations to you, sir...you have raised your son into a courageous and resourceful young man."

"Indeed, sir," Beaumarchais added. "The boy has the heart of a bear. Make no mistake."

I looked up, astonished. It was the first time I had ever heard the playwright compliment me. Our eyes met for a brief instant. His expression was as stone.

"Yes..." my father said, regarding me thoughtfully. "I thank you gentlemen for your words, of course. However...under the circumstances...I think it best that Henri part from your company. He is obviously in no condition..."

"No, Father!" I cried suddenly, finding my feet so quickly that I nearly spilt my broth.

"Henri..."

Wrapping myself more tightly inside my blanket, I approached my sire. He was not a man of height or girth, but still stood easily a head taller than myself. As I looked upon his face I could read his concern, etched in with the lines of grief that had marked his features since the deaths of my brothers in the war. For a moment, I made as though to speak, then thought better of it and turned instead to Dr. Franklin.

"Ben, may I ask that you and Pierre give us this room? I'm sure my father's steward will gladly see to your needs."

Franklin regarded me with smiling eyes. "Of course, Henri. Come, Pierre." He bowed to my father and then the two of them departed. I waited until I heard the snap of the door latch.

"Now, Father..." I began.

"Henri," he interjected. "What *is* this business? I sent you to Nantes to serve as host, simply as a favor to my old friend Penet."

"Things have gone well beyond that, Father," I said. "As you may readily see."

"I know of this Dr. Franklin, Henri. He is a man of singular intellect, and as shrewd a gentleman as any you are likely to meet. He has come to France with very specific intentions. I made you aware of that before I sent you to La Barbarie. He is, by all accounts, an honest

The Franklin Affair

fellow and a good and noble personage, but his goals and France's may not be the same. Also, as this business with the highwayman would indicate, he is by no means a person with whom to associate oneself...if one wishes to remain safe from harm. I have already lost enough sons. I have no wish to lose you as well."

It was then, as I looked upon him, that I grasped the depth of his dread. He was seeing, with his imagination's eyes, yet another coffin—another gravestone to be erected in the family cemetery.

"I have no wish to further burden you, sir," I said gently. "But there is another side to this business of which I feel you should be made aware." Then I told him, step by step, of the events that had caused me to be seated atop that carriage in the dead of winter. I left nothing out, beginning with the visit from Chaumont and Hilliard, and ending with the highwayman's attack upon our coach. He listened attentively, but with growing unease and, when I had finished, he took to pacing the length of the drawing room and wringing his hands.

"What you tell me, Henri," he said after some thought, "does nothing to lessen my belief that you and these men should part company at once."

"But what of my mission for the king, Father?" I asked, aghast. I had been sure that, once he understood the import behind my actions, he would see the necessity of my continued pursuit of them.

"I know nothing of a mission for the king, my son, and neither do you. There is only your mission for Chaumont and this priest."

"You think Monsieur Chaumont lied when he claimed that he came to me with the king's blessing?"

"Chaumont is a friend, Henri," my father replied. "His wife, Thérèse, spent many years in my employ. It was at La Barbarie that the two of them met...while Chaumont was staying there as my guest and doing business with Monsieur Penet. I have known the man for many, many years and have always considered him an ally. His high position in government and his close association with the king have proven advantageous for me on more than one occasion. However, while I admire Chaumont...and even trust him to a point...I cannot say with certainty that he would not do whatever was necessary to achieve his ends."

I felt my knees weaken, and I slowly slid down onto a nearby chair, lest I topple onto the floor in a faint. Chaumont lied? And Hilliard, what was *his* place in this strange business?

"Henri, stay here with me," my father beseeched. "This intrigue and danger can wait for the attentions of an older man, not a boy of only sixteen years."

"And what of Dr. Franklin, sir?" I asked quietly.

"What of him? He has Beaumarchais to guard him. I know of that one also: flamboyant and quick to anger, though I'm told he has the king's ear. He's also a superior swordsman, and would make anyone a fine bodyguard."

I raised my head and looked upon my sire. He stood before me, so proud—even regal—in his powered wig and fine silver buttons. He was my only living parent, and I one of his only two remaining sons.

"Father," I said. "How is Gaston?"

The question seemed to startle him. "Your brother? He is well, last time I heard. He is in the West Indies, as you know, seeing after our sugar plantations on Santo Domingo. He won't be returning until the summer."

"He and I are the only ones left," I said.

"All the more reason not to risk you in this affair. Stay here, Henri."

"And do *what*, Father?" I asked. "Live the life of the spoiled youngest child? I have not Gaston's head for business. We both know that. Neither am I a fighting man. So where is my place in this world? Why did you select me to represent you at La Barbarie? Was it not because you *wanted* me to encounter Dr. Franklin, a man whom I know you hold in high regard? Did you not hope that I would learn from the experience...perhaps show some aptitude for political matters?"

The Franklin Affair

A small, proud smile touched my father's lips. "You've grown a bit these past weeks, Henri."

"There is more growing to be done, Father...and it cannot be done here."

"Henri..."

"Please, father. I *must* follow Dr. Franklin. I *must* see where this path will take me. He's as good and wise a gentleman as I have ever known, and there is so much he can teach me."

"What of the *danger*, Son? Think of that."

"You told us all once that *life* is dangerous, and that anything worth having was worth risking oneself for. Do you recall those words?"

"I recall them," my father said bitterly. "That naïve, esoteric philosophy has already cost me four sons."

"That does not make it any less true."

"There is duplicity here, Son. I know not how much, or who in this strange drama is the greater liar, but I trust not any of the players. You have little experience with such men, Henri."

"Then I must earn that experience, Father." Then, after a moment, I added: "I am of the firm belief that, whatever his motives, Dr. Franklin would not allow me to come to harm."

He regarded me thoughtfully for several moments. Finally, he said, in an even voice: "I can forbid this, Henri."

"Yes, sir," I replied, matching his tone.

Slowly, he turned and walked to a sideboard, which stood against the far wall between two tall bookcases. With a key from his pocket, he unlocked the cabinet and withdrew a sheathed blade. This he handed to me, placing it in my hands as if he were passing unto me the Holy Grail.

I had never before seen this weapon. I could not recall ever having witnessed my father open that sideboard. Carefully, I took hold of the sheath, which was crafted of soft, supple leather, and drew forth its blade. It was more dagger than sword, perhaps ten inches long, and polished to a mirror's shine. The hilt was leather-wrapped and adorned with our family crest, etched in gold leaf upon the pummel. "You've never shown me this before," I said, looking up.

"It was my grandfather's, and his father's before him. I cannot, with honesty, say how long it has guarded the Gruel fortune. There is a story...one I have never shared with you children because I feared it would pique your interest and send you scuttling around seeking a way to violate my sideboard. The tale is this: that your great-great grandfather, Augustin Gruel, fought for France against the English and took a lead ball to the chest for his trouble, but that the ball did not penetrate his flesh, because *that* blade was sheathed above his heart. I know not how much truth there is to this, but you can readily see the tear in the leather wall of the sheath, and the barest dent in the smooth face of the blade."

And so I could. The sheath had not been pierced precisely. It appeared to be more a pucker or indentation. The blade within bore a similar mark, not deep—but undeniably there.

"I want you to take that with you, Henri," my father said. "I want you to bear it upon your person always. The legend states that the Gruel who carries it shall come to no harm."

"If so," I said, captivated, "then why did you not offer this blade to one of my brothers?"

It was a cruel question, and one that bespoke my unthinking youth. I saw my father flinch, and watched his eyes close as he wrestled anew with his grief. When he opened them again, the sadness that bore itself upon his face nearly cost me my heart. "*Which* son, Henri? Would you have had me offer this magic...if magic it is...to one of your brothers, and nothing to the rest? So I chose to keep silent, and as payment for my sense of fairness, I lost all four of them. I shall not lose you as well. You must take the dagger and swear to keep it with you always. That is the price I charge for my blessing in this matter."

"I swear it, Father," I said, most reverently. "On the souls of my brothers, I swear it."

He smiled grimly. "Poetic as always, Henri. Go then and fetch back Dr. Franklin and Monsieur Beaumarchais. We shall tell them the happy news together."

As I stood and made for the door, he stopped me with a final question. "Henri," he said hesitantly. "What of Chaumont and Hilliard?"

"I don't know, Father," I replied honestly. "I shall have to wait and see what transpires. I can tell you this though: of the many things I hope and expect to do in Paris, one of the very first will be to decide...to finally decide...which side I am on."

Chapter Eleven

"Genius without education is like silver in the mine." - Benjamin Franklin

What shall I say of Paris that has not been said before? It was and is the quintessential city: a center of learning and arts, a seat of government and a cornerstone of civilization, dating back more than a thousand years. I had last been there when, at the age of thirteen, I had accompanied my family into Paris and had witnessed, along with thousands of others, the coronation of King Louis XVI in 1774. In the expensive celebration that had followed, my father had treated us all to a fine supper and then to an open carriage ride along the Seine. It had been one of the few times in my childhood that I could remember hearing my father laugh. Such are the wages of grief.

Dr. Franklin, Beaumarchais and I finally arrived in the city late on the 20th of December. The snow had thankfully stopped, and the sky grown clear. It was well past sunset when my father's carriage, with one of his men at the reins, navigated the lighted streets of the West Bank of the Seine, making its way toward the great river, herself.

Our previous coach, with its horses, was safely stored at my family's estate, with my sire's promise to contact the owners and arrange for its return. Maurice had been surrendered to the constabulary at Nogent-le-

The Franklin Affair

Rotrou. Our testimony in the matter had been collected, with polite deference to our timetable, and we had been allowed to depart promptly, with the assurance that local justice would settle our account with the highwayman's surviving accomplice.

"Tell me again the name of the hotel, Pierre," Franklin said as he gazed out the carriage window at the passing streets.

"The Hôtel d'Entragues," Beaumarchais said. "In the Rue de l'Université...here, on the West Bank. It's an old establishment and quite well respected. Deane makes his home there."

"So," Franklin said jovially. "I am to share a bed with Silas, am I? Won't that be cozy?"

"You shall have your own rooms, of course!" Beaumarchais replied with a smile. "It is *Henri* who will have to share your colleague's pillow."

I looked up, horrified, only to have both men suddenly bellow out great roars of laugher. I felt my cheeks grow hot. "How fortunate I am to have such distinguished entertainers," I muttered.

Despite the late hour and chill night air, the streets were busy. I witnessed men and women in motion all around us, passing before and behind our carriage as it maneuvered down the narrow streets and eased its way ever deeper into the lively metropolis. More than once, as we passed an establishment, I heard music playing, and the sound of laughter and applause. In a particularly singular incident, a young, heavily painted woman approached our carriage as it stood waiting at an intersection for another to pass.

"Out for an evening's entertainment, messieurs?" she asked, in a tone which I can only describe as provocative.

"Not your sort," Beaumarchais replied impatiently. "Let us be."

"The boy perhaps?" she asked, fixing me with a look so predatory that I felt my throat close up.

"He least of all. Off with you!"

She left us then, muttering a guttural curse.

Franklin seemed positively delighted by the exchange. Beaumarchais looked annoyed. I felt only an odd sense of otherworldliness, as though I had stepped through some portal and into a realm far removed from that which I had always known.

We found the hotel some minutes later, nestled in amongst others of its kind, with its back to the river and its frontage brightly lit with oil lamps. The Hôtel d'Entragues was a four-story structure of marble and gray stone. Small gargoyles lined the roof, staring down upon us from ornate parapets. An elegant flight of steps, carpeted in red linen, despite the recent snow, provided access to a set of doors fashioned of dark wood and brass.

As our carriage clattered to a halt on the stones outside the threshold, several men in stylish servant's garb emerged, accompanied by a woman wrapped in a long hooded cloak the color of spilt blood. She approached the carriage, surrounded by her entourage, and stood patiently at hand as my father's driver stepped lithely down from his bench and opened the door.

Dr. Franklin made it a point of exiting first. He climbed precariously down from the carriage, waving away any offer of aid from the driver, and stood before the woman with his walking stick clutched firmly in one hand, and his fur cap in the other.

"Sir," the woman said. "Have you the honor of being Dr. Benjamin Franklin?" Her English was excellent.

"Madame, I have that honor," Franklin replied, smiling. "But it pales beside the privilege of making the acquaintance of such a lovely and gracious lady."

The woman smiled as Franklin bowed smoothly. "You flatter me, sir," she said. "I am Madame Devereux. I keep this hotel and manage it. It is my privilege to serve as your hostess during your stay under my roof. These gentlemen are my valets. They shall see to your personal belongings and to the belongings of your companions."

"You are as kind as you are fair, madame."

She was not a young woman, I observed as I followed Beaumarchais from the carriage, but somewhere in her middle years. Her pale face, what I could see of it under her deep hood, was delicately featured, with full lips and eyes as green as summer's grass. As Franklin introduced us, she approached and offered me a delicate hand, bejeweled with many fine stones, which I accepted and held briefly—as I had always been taught.

"Welcome to the Hôtel d'Entragues, young Monsieur. I hope your stay will be enjoyable."

There was something in her eyes, something reminiscent of the young woman who had approached us in the street, and yet was somehow wiser and more elegant than she. Whatever it was, it lent with it a muddling effect, which left me as tongue-tied as a three-year-old child. "I...thank you, madame," was the best I could manage.

Beaumarchais did far better than I, taking Madame Devereux's hand in his own and holding it briefly to his lips, fixing her with a look of such gallantry and *panache*, that it drew from her a slightly embarrassed smile. "Madame Devereux, it is a most heartfelt privilege to see you again. You grow more lovely each time we meet. I do believe that, had you been born some centuries past, your face might have set the Greeks against Troy more quickly than Helen ever could."

She laughed and stood on her toes to kiss him lightly upon the cheek. "As charming as always, Pierre. Come gentlemen. There's warmth and good food within, though I must warn you, Dr. Franklin, Paris has been expecting you. My lobby is far from empty!"

The hotel was grand indeed—a polished tile floor, sculpted columns, and the finest of chandeliers, tapestries and other accouterments. The reception area, as Madame has indicated, was filled beyond its capacity. Some two hundred people closed around us as we passed through the doors, with Madame Devereux leading the way and her valets left behind to retrieve our personal effects. Our hostess paused in the center of the room and raised her delicate hands high above her head. "Mesdames and messieurs!" she called out to the expectant assemblage. "May I present Dr. Benjamin Franklin!"

A great cheer traveled through the crowd as Franklin moved among them, wearing his simple fur cap and wrapped in his unadorned brown overcoat. "Who is this old peasant who has such a noble air?" I heard a woman ask her companion. "Can it be Franklin, himself?"

"A gentleman of simple tastes," her companion replied. "See how he moves amongst us, smiling at one and all! A great man indeed!"

"The man who gave us the lightning rod!" someone exclaimed.

"The greatest mind in the New World!" another declared.

"Look how he smiles at everyone! See the kindness and wisdom in his eyes!" remarked a third.

So complete was the obstruction generated by the adoration of the assembled well-wishers, that it took some minutes for us to make our way to the concierge desk. Once there, Madame Devereux took command of all proceedings, providing us with a suite of rooms on the hotel's second floor, accommodations adjacent to those of Monsieur Silas Deane who, in the lady's words: "has graced us with his presence for quite some time."

Dr. Franklin signed his name to the book of guests. Then, as we were escorted up the grand central staircase, the old man spared a moment to address the crowd. As it became apparent that he would speak, the assemblage drew suddenly breathless and still. "My friends," Franklin said loudly, leaning upon his Crabtree stick. "Your welcome warms an old man's heart. I beg the Lord that I may prove myself worthy of such open respect and affection...and desire you all to know that your good wishes are returned upon you tenfold! Good night!"

The applause that rose up from the lobby was deafening.

The Franklin Affair

The rooms into which we were ushered were spacious and opulent. There were three bedchambers, one for each of us. Our bags were opened and our belongings removed and stored away as conscientiously as if they were holy relics. Dr. Franklin was given the largest chamber, Beaumarchais the next, and I the last.

Finally, the madame ushered her valets from the suite and stood alone with us in the well-appointed sitting room.

"Your care and comfort has, from this moment, become my most urgent priority, gentlemen," she said, looking particularly at Dr. Franklin, who seemed to drink in her attentions as though they were a fine wine. She had long since removed her coat and hood, revealing a dress of blue linen with pearl buttons and lace trimming. Her dark hair was carefully styled, built up upon her head in the manner of women of high birth. Small diamonds hung from her ears. Her face, though no longer young, was striking and handsome. Her smile seemed to rise from the depths of her soul.

"Madame, you mean to spoil us!" Franklin exclaimed in mock protest.

"Indeed I do, doctor. If there is anything that you may desire, at any time of day or night, you need only ring the bell there, or another like it in any of the bedchambers and I, or one of my trusted valets, will see that you have not long to wait."

"Thank you, madame," Beaumarchais said.

"Not at all. There is wine in the cupboard, as well as cheese and bread and fruit upon the table. I wish you a good night, gentlemen."

She left us then, allowing Beaumarchais to shepherd the door for her. I turned to see Franklin gazing after her with a bright, wistful expression upon his face. Beaumarchais went up to him and, smiling, placed a hand upon the old man's shoulder. "She has buried three husbands, Ben, the last of whom left her the deed to this hotel and the livres to run it."

"Lovely *and* a woman of means," Franklin noted.

"And well-known for her dalliances," Beaumarchais cautioned.

"Now Pierre, you know I was never one for judging a person by the rumors spread of them."

"Well, in this case, Ben...you may wish to be."

"And what's this business about you taking a room with us, Pierre?" Franklin asked, offering a change of subject. "Don't you keep your own apartment in the city?"

"I do, but until I am convinced of your safety, I shall happily stay here."

"Hardly necessary," Franklin remarked. "Still, as you will insist, I shall not say you nay. Henri, please break out a bottle of wine...Madeira comes to mind."

As I dutifully attended to this, there came a knock upon the door. I rushed to answer it and found myself met by two men. One was short and stout, with a nose like a beak. The other was taller, and of nobler bearing. The first man barely acknowledged me, but instead cast his eyes eagerly about the sitting room until they caught sight of Franklin.

"Benjamin!" he called, speaking English with an American's tongue. He shouldered past me and embraced the older man warmly. "I knew when the crowd took to cheering that it would be *you*. We've been expecting you for a week or more, ever since Beaumarchais insisted on riding down to Nantes to find you! How are you, old fellow? You look well! Where are your grandsons?" Then, as if the notion had only just occurred to him, he turned upon his heel and faced me. "This? Is this William Temple? He looks hardly at all like you or your son! His mother perhaps?"

"Silas," Franklin said, chuckling. "May I present Monsieur Henri Gruel, the son of Bathelemy-Pierre Gruel of Nogent-le-Rotrou. Henri, this gregarious fellow is one Silas Deane, my fellow commissioner here in France."

Confusion flashed across the gentleman's sharp features. "Henri Gruel, is it?" He turned back to Franklin.

The Franklin Affair

"What happened to William Temple?"

"Unable to accompany me, I'm afraid," Franklin replied. "Nor little Benjamin, either. I made the crossing alone—a long and lonely ordeal."

"Not so long and lonely that you did not see fit to order the captain to seize two passing British merchant brigantines, eh Benjamin?" Deane asked with a wry smile. "I've heard from Captain Wilkes. He believes the two ships, along with their cargo, should fetch between six and eight thousand pounds!"

"As much as that?" Franklin remarked.

"Our coffers can use the boost, I assure you," Deane said.

I turned back toward the door to find the second man, who was wigged and wore a coat of uncrushed velvet, smiling indulgently at Monsieur Deane. "Sir," I said. "I'm so sorry. Please do come in."

"Thank you, young man. How are you, Dr. Franklin? Monsieur Beaumarchais?"

"Most fine, thank you, Dr. Bancroft," the playwright replied.

"Weary from the journey," Franklin admitted.

"Of course," Dean said immediately. "How clumsy of me. I do apologize. Gentlemen, might I convince you all to join Edward and myself for breakfast? Our rooms are directly across from yours, though they are not..." He glanced about the room. "...as opulent as these accommodations. Your fame holds you in good stead, I see."

"We would be happy to breakfast with you," said Franklin. "And as for my fame...honestly, Silas, I think *you* must take some blame for that. Our reception below smacked of long planning."

"Not my doing," Deane replied with a great sigh. "All that was Madame Devereux's folly, I fear. When Beaumarchais rode off to fetch you, I informed her to expect you within days, and she set herself to the task of making of you a grand event. Your reputation in France...and in Europe, in general...is enviable, Benjamin. Our hostess simply wants it known that so great a man is choosing to stay under *her* roof."

Bancroft added: "A crowd has been filling the lobby for the past three days. Madame begged us for your description, so that she might compare it to that of each arriving guest."

"Flattering," Franklin chuckled. "How good it is to see you again, Edward! I trust Silas is not working you too hard."

"A labor to be enjoyed, Dr. Franklin," Bancroft replied. "And welcome to France."

"My thanks. You've met Henri? He is here to serve as my official translator. Henri, this is Dr. Edward Bancroft, Secretary to the American Diplomatic Commission."

"Your servant, sir," I said.

"And yours, young fellow. Congratulations to you! You will learn a great deal in the company of this gentleman."

"He'll learn how to treat gout and listen to an old man's whimpering," Franklin retorted. He turned to Deane. "Silas, I *am* weary, but before I retire, I must know the news. Has the third member of our triad, Arthur Lee, arrived yet from England?"

"No, though we expect him any day," Deane replied. Then, with a frown: "I fear that we may suffer conflict where Arthur is concerned. He resents your coming to France."

"So Pierre tells me," Franklin replied. "We will deal with that when the time is ripe. Now tell me: how goes the mission? Do we have an audience with King Louis, yet?"

Deane and Bancroft exchanged uncomfortable looks.

"What is it, Silas?" Franklin said, his manner suddenly serious. "In your last letter you assured me that the Comte de Vergennes had promised a further four ships loaded with war supplies."

"And so he had," Deane said. "Unfortunately...I... that is, we..."

"Gentleman," Franklin said, a bit crossly. "I am too

old to waste time over useless subterfuge. What has happened?"

"Washington was defeated on Long Island," Bancroft said gravely.

"And also at Kips Bay," Deane added.

An unpleasant silence settled over the room. I watched as Dr. Franklin's face paled slightly, and some of the light faded from his usually iridescent blue eyes. "Henri," he said finally, in as weak a voice as I had ever heard him utter. "Please bring wine for these gentlemen. Pierre, I suggest we sit for the rest of this."

I did his bidding while the four of them settled themselves upon the finely upholstered furniture that was nestled cozily around the raging fire in the hearth. Franklin and Beaumarchais each took armchairs, while Deane and Bancroft sat side by side upon the settee, their hands in their laps and their heads lowered. I poured wine for each of them, and one for myself. Then I passed the drinks around upon a silver service plate.

"Am I to understand, Silas," Franklin said, "that the comte withdrew his promise of arms over news of these British victories?"

"The ships are loaded and ready to sail," Deanne said. "But Vergennes has refused to grant them permission to leave port. Worse than that...I have received word from my sources within the French Foreign Ministry that Vergennes penned a letter to Ambassador Stormont, congratulating the British for their success at arms."

"Damn the coward!" Beaumarchais spat, quite venomously, I thought, given that he was describing a fellow countryman to three foreigners. "Ben, we still have Roderigue Hortalez et Cie to rely upon."

"Not without Vergennes' support," Franklin replied, frowning.

"Who is Roderigue Hortalez?" I asked earnestly.

Beaumarchais fixed me with a suspicious look, but his expression quickly softened. "'Tis not a who, but a what, Henri," he said. "Some time ago, at Ben's behest, I approached the Comte de Vergennes with the proposal of establishing a false company, through which the French government might funnel arms and livres to the American colonies. We called this company Roderigue Hortalez et Cie, and it has prospered in its task. Since its inception, more than two hundred thousand livres have been surreptitiously moved from the French treasury to the American coffers."

"Still, it's not enough," Franklin added. "Money is all well and good, but the war effort requires an ally willing to provide *open* support. Only then will the community of European nations take us seriously. Those four French ships, loaded with arms and bound for American ports, were to be the first overt, publicized gesture of France's commitment to our cause."

"Vergennes has no love for the British," Deane said. "He would enjoy nothing more than for France to face King George in battle—provided that King George's fleet is off somewhere, dealing with *us*. The news of these defeats has weakened his resolve. We *may* still receive quiet money, but he will not openly support us until he is convinced that General Washington can win against the British."

"He *can* win," said Franklin, with absolute conviction. "I have no fear of that. But to do so, he will need all the aid that France may supply."

"A trap of logic," Brancroft remarked. "Washington cannot win without the aid, and we cannot get him that precious aid without it being evident to Vergennes that he *is* winning."

Franklin fell into a thoughtful silence. All the other men in the room watched him, regarding him as if they were his pupils, and he, as teacher, was ruminating over a particularly vexing arithmetic problem. Finally, after more than a minute had passed, Dr. Franklin took up his wineglass, drew from it a healthy mouthful, savored it for a moment, swallowed, and then said thoughtfully: "Tell me, Silas. What are the chances of arranging a direct encounter between myself and the comte within the

The Franklin Affair

next day or so?"

"Just yourself?" Deane asked, looking disturbed. "I think it best that we wait for Arthur, and the three of us meet formally with Vergennes."

"And we shall certainly do so," said Franklin. "But first I desire a discreet, private encounter."

"Discretion may prove difficult," Deane said. "As you have seen from your welcome, you have been long anticipated in Paris. Lord Stormont is certainly aware of your arrival, as he has spies throughout the city. I daresay every move you make will be carefully watched."

"I am not so much worried about Stormont finding out, as I am about it becoming common knowledge amongst the Parisians," Franklin said. "Stormont may make a fuss about it, but what can he do, provided that the comte denies the meeting?"

"It will infuriate him," Beaumarchais remarked.

"Indeed," Franklin admitted. "But the ambassador's level of fury is not, at present, my chief concern."

"It is mine, Ben," said Beaumarchais ominously, "in my role as your protector."

"Then I leave it to you to worry on that account. I need to meet with Vergennes, and I need to do it before Arthur arrives. Otherwise, he will never allow me to do so without him."

"True enough," Deane sighed.

"Vergennes *may* meet with you," Bancroft said. "If only because he knows it will offend Stormont, something he enjoys doing when he believes it safe enough. However, I doubt that he will discuss with you the matter of the withdrawn aid."

"Arrange the meeting, if you will, Edward," Franklin said to Bancroft. "Do not write to Vergennes directly, however. I assume he maintains a staff? A secretary perhaps?"

Bancroft nodded. "His first secretary is a man called Gérard. Most of our correspondence with the comte has gone through him. I have met him and believe him loyal. We can trust his discretion."

"Most excellent," Franklin said brightly. "Then do this: inform the comte, through his first secretary, that I am at his disposal for the purposes of a discreet liaison...provided he acts quickly."

"And if he does not act quickly?" Bancroft asked.

"Then remind him politely of our proximity to Spain, or Austria, or even Russia," Franklin replied evenly. "Do this, and I guarantee you that I shall have my meeting within the week. And now, gentlemen, you must excuse me. The journey today has been long and arduous, and I hope to sleep well and dream of the fair Madame Devereux!"

Chapter Twelve

"He that goes a borrowing, goes a sorrowing." - Benjamin Franklin

The following morning we all enjoyed breakfast in the shared apartment of Monsieur Deane and Dr. Bancroft. Madame Devereux arranged for a superlative selection of eggs, ham, fresh milk and warm baguettes. Over the meal, the four men discussed the matters at hand, in particular, re-igniting the American effort to secure French aid.

"I sent a messenger to the Foreign Ministry at first light," Bancroft reported. "I hope you don't mind, but I took the liberty of wording the communiqué myself. Mr. Deane and I have dealt with the comte on numerous occasions over these past several months and I believe I know what will garner the most ready response."

"I have absolute faith in your skills with a pen, Edward," Dr. Franklin said, as he ate with his usual gusto. "This ham is quite splendid! I must make it a point to compliment Madame Devereux for the quality of her hotel's table."

"Vergennes is a spineless fool," Beaumarchais said angrily. "I know for a fact that he would savor nothing more than to see Britain fairly trounced in a war with America, but he fears King George's wrath if France were to offer open support."

"I hardly think so, Pierre," argued Deane. "The

comte is a cautious man, and he has your country's own interests to consider. France is still recovering from the Seven Years War, after all, though that conflict ended more than a decade ago. You have a new king...a young king...untested in military matters. Under the circumstances, I cannot say I blame Vergennes for his change of heart, especially in the face of Washington's defeats at home. To be honest, they trouble me greatly as well."

"Do they?" Franklin asked, looking up from his meal. "And you, Edward? Do the recent setbacks trouble you?"

"Dr. Franklin, they are more than simply setbacks. Washington's forces have been decimated. By the last report, he has barely four thousand troops, while the British forces number nearly five times that. We've also had word that King George has purchased the loyalty of between ten and twelve thousand German mercenaries to send to New York, under the command of General Howe. Sir, we are being overrun!"

"It is important to keep a cool head in such times," Franklin said. "I have absolute faith in General Washington. His force of will is indomitable."

"A cool head, sir?" Bancroft exclaimed. "Dr. Franklin, our cause is floundering. You know this as surely as I do. Are we to remain with a sinking ship? There is no greater advocate for American independence than myself, yet how I can deny this simple reality: that General Washington, for all his 'force of will', is weakening beneath the crushing weight of the finest army on Earth! Sir, we are losing! Perhaps we have *already* lost!"

Quickly, with his eyes averted, Deane said: "He has a point, Benjamin. Perhaps it would be best if we were to solicit Congress for our recall."

Beaumarchais sputtered, too outraged to find words. Franklin simply touched a linen napkin to his lips, took a sip of water and then folded his hands on the table before him. "Mr. Deane. Mr. Bancroft. Let me speak plainly. At home...right now...farmers are fighting for their very lives. They are abandoning their families,

The Franklin Affair

leaving their farms and fields to be pillaged and burned by British troops. They are condemning their families to a winter of starvation and despair. They are doing this because they believe that General Washington and the Continental Army *can* win...no matter what the British cast against them. More so, they believe that our forces *must* win, and they are prepared to meet their maker in an effort to see that this comes to pass."

"Benjamin..." Deane began.

Franklin held up a hand. "You sit here, in this warm room, enjoying this excellent breakfast, all the while worrying about our own necks. Sirs, you have not the barest notion of what it is to risk yourselves for your country. How *dare* you both sit there and express doubts and reservations! I shall not listen to it. You were sent here to fight for the American cause. You are *soldiers*, gentlemen...as certainly as is any Rhode Island militiaman. How can you expect to convince the French of American strength and American worth if you cannot convince yourselves? *Believe*, gentlemen...in our victory, in our right to independence, in our ability and intent to defend those rights. Believe to the end! Or don't presume to call yourself Americans!"

Bancroft rose to his feet, throwing down his napkin. "You forget yourself, sir! Mr. Deane and I have been here in Paris these many months, witnessing for ourselves which way the wind is blowing. Now you presume to condemn us for our lack of devotion to our cause! You say we have never risked ourselves. Forgive me, Dr. Franklin, but what risks have *you* taken? I've heard no tales of *your* heroics at Concord and Lexington, or Bunker Hill, or Kips Bay!"

"Brancroft!" Beaumarchais declared in outrage.

"Gentlemen, please," Deane said. "Edward, do sit down. We are all allies here."

But Bancroft kept his place. After a moment's worth of rumination, Franklin stood also, leaning heavily upon his cane. From his inside coat pocket he withdrew a folded sheet of paper, one that I recognized at once. This he fairly tossed at Bancroft, who stared down upon it as it landed beside his plate of food.

"Read it," Franklin said, in a tone that would brook no refusal.

Slowly, Dr. Bancroft took up the paper and unfolded it.

"Do you recognize that document?" Franklin asked.

"Of course."

"As well you should. Some one hundred copies were sent to you and Mr. Deane only two months ago. Is that not so?"

Bancroft slowly nodded.

"You were to distribute those copies to high-ranking members of the French court. Did you do this?"

"We did," Bancroft said.

"I'm delighted to hear it," Franklin said dryly. "Now I must ask you if, in the flurry of all that activity, you found the time to *read* the document, sir?"

Bancroft's scowl deepened. "I could hardly do otherwise."

"Quite so. Did you take note, then, of the names...there...at the bottom of the paper?"

"I did," said Bancroft.

"Do you see *my* name there, sir?"

"Yes, Dr. Franklin."

"I signed a warrant for my death when I added my autograph to that document. If the war is lost to Britain, my signature will undoubtedly place my neck in a hangman's noose for high treason. I have assumed that risk because I believe in what is written thereupon. We all believe in it...all the men who chose to lend their names to that most remarkable piece of paper. John Hancock...do you know him? He's a Massachusetts man, like you."

"I don't...I don't believe I've had the pleasure," Bancroft said in a small voice.

"Well, Hancock signed first, and signed his name quite large indeed. When someone asked him why, he replied: 'So that Fat George in London can read it with-

The Franklin Affair

out his glasses.'"

Slowly, swallowing against a dusty throat, Bancroft nodded. Deane sat beside him, pale and speechless. Beaumarchais was smiling a thin, bitter smile. Franklin's face remained carefully passive.

"Do you still want to go home, Edward?" Franklin asked.

"Sir, I..." Brancroft looked up. His face had become terribly flushed. "...I apologize."

Then he left the sitting room, disappearing into his bedchamber and shutting the door. For a long moment we all sat around the breakfast table, wrapped in an uncomfortable quietness. Finally, Silas Deane said: "It is sometimes easy to forget what's at stake in this business. So much of one's time is spent surrounded with finery and affairs of society that..." His voice trailed off, leaving us once again in the silence.

"Silas," Franklin said kindly. "It was not my wish to be harsh with you. I am not, by nature, an orator. If the good Lord sees fit to fill me with words of political import, I can only take it as a sign of his support for our cause. I meant what I said, however, that we are all of us soldiers in a rare and wonderful undertaking. It is necessary...even crucial...that we not merely act for that cause, but believe in it also."

"I felt as you do when I first came to France," Deane said unhappily. "I hope that the difficulties of the next several months do not dim your patriotic flame as they have Edward's and mine."

"Nonsense!" Franklin said, smiling. "Cheer up, my good fellow. I don't believe for a moment that your 'patriotic flame' has been dimmed. You have merely been hiding it under the bushel of your own insecurities. I have come, among other reasons, to see that this changes. Toward that end, I insist that we raise your spirits at once! I suggest we start with a friendly tour of the city. Henri, how does that sound to you?"

"Very well, Ben!" I said eagerly. "Should we ask Dr. Bancroft to join us?"

"Let him stew," said Beaumarchais.

"Edward will come around, I assure you," Deane said. "Until then, I suggest we leave him to his own devices. I, however, would consider it an honor to accompany you gentlemen on an excursion throughout Paris. Shall I ring Madame Devereux and ask that she arrange a coach?"

"Yes, do so, Silas," Franklin said. "Pierre, are you game?"

"I am," Beaumarchais replied. "If only to serve as escort."

"Escort?" Franklin laughed. "Surely you don't expect us to encounter a highwayman on the Rue St. Honoré!"

Beaumarchais said nothing, only rose from his chair and made for the door.

"Henri," Franklin said. "I shall remain and talk some more with Silas. Would you please be kind enough to fetch my coat and hat? The city awaits us!"

Our tour of Paris occupied most of the day. The carriage that Madame Devereux procured was a lavish and comfortable affair. The day was clear and a bit warmer than it had been of late, and so we were able to throw open the shutters and witness the streets of Paris, hidden though they were, beneath a blanket of snow. We began on the West Bank, riding through the recently completed Champs de Mars, before crossing the Seine. Here we were required to pay a toll, for all bridges across the river were owned and operated by private concessionaires.

On the East Bank, we followed the river in the opposite direction, eventually crossing onto the Île de la Cité, which split the Seine like a great stone driven into the historic heart of Paris. Here we saw Notre Dame, in all her magnificence—the great cathedral rising high into the clear, afternoon's sky and littered with doves. These delicate creatures were *everywhere*, filling the cathedral's parapets and resting upon its stone statues like feathered jewelry. The massive Palais de Justice had been recently ravaged by fire, but the Conciergerie was intact, its spires piercing the sunlit sky.

Finally, crossing the Seine a second time, we made our way back toward the Hôtel d'Entragues, passing the dozens of *quais* that lined the river. These small ports were busily loading and unloading all manner of goods and passengers. "It is difficult and expensive to transport anything over land in any bulk," Monsieur Deane explained to us. "And so produce and people are moved into the city most often by water." Witnessing this great flurry of activity awoke within me a curious and exhilarating sense of the world beyond that which I had known, of a place of great size and complexity, as diverse and particular as the most exquisite tapestry.

If my description of our tour appears grandiose, please remember that I saw all of this through a young man's eyes—a young man thrust into a depth of intrigue that I could only barely comprehend. To me, Paris was like a rose, a rare and wondrous bloom to gaze upon and to admire—but a rose not without its thorns as well. For along our route we saw also the squalor of the working classes. We passed, albeit briefly, through areas of the city where the streets were narrow and crowded with the hungry and the cold. Children begged, and each time they did, Franklin would throw small pieces of change out the carriage windows. He did this so often that his purse soon emptied and, to the chagrin of both Beaumarchais and Deane, he took to borrowing from them, in order to continue this charitable practice.

"'Give to everyone who begs from you,'" he said. "So says the Good Book. Come, Silas, don't look so cross. I have the means to repay you! Have I not just captured two British trade ships?"

Finally, we returned to our hotel, where Madame Devereux treated us to warm soup and wafers in the hotel's lobby. Here, Franklin's fame asserted itself. We could not long relax without someone approaching to wish him well, or to ask his advice on some esoteric point of science or philosophy. Dr. Franklin answered every question, greeted every stranger as though he were a friend, and regarded each new topic, no matter how trivial, as a most grave and serious matter, worthy of his attention.

So it was that we did not reach our rooms until well into the evening. Deane, whose spirits had risen over the course of the day, bid us a cheerful good night and then retired into his own suite. Beaumarchais, Franklin and I closed our own door thankfully behind us. The old doctor, his Crabtree stick in hand, crossed immediately to the wine carafe and poured from it an ample helping of Madeira.

"This has been a delightfully leisurely day," Franklin said to no one in particular.

"Tomorrow bodes more serious business," Beaumarchais remarked. He held up a sealed envelope, which had been placed beneath our door. "It bears the seal of the Foreign Ministry."

"Give it to Henri, so that he may read it...as it is undoubtedly in French."

Beaumarchais did so, and I broke the envelope's seal and drew from it a single sheet of perfumed paper.

"My dear Dr. Franklin," I read. "I wish to express to you, on behalf of his most Royal Majesty, King Louis XVI, our most sincere welcome to France, and to Paris. I have received your communiqué, passed onto me via your agent, Dr. Bancroft, and would be most honored if you would agree to meet with me at the Ministry of Foreign Affairs tomorrow, the 22nd of December, at the hour of three in the afternoon. It would be my pleasure to dispatch one of my drivers to collect you. Please notify me as to your availability. Your most earnest and humble servant, Charles Gravier, Comte de Vergennes."

I looked up from the letter. "You have your meeting, Ben!" I exclaimed.

"I never doubted it for a moment," Beaumarchais remarked.

Franklin grinned, his blue eyes sparkling from behind his spectacles. "I shall need you to pen a reply immediately, Henri. Please inform the comte that I shall be unable to attend on the 22nd, due to a prior commitment, but that I would be most happy to meet with him on the 23rd, and at any time that is consistent with his convenience. Write that up for me, will you? And bring it to me to sign. I shall need to have Edward send it out by messenger before we retire for the night."

"You're postponing the appointment?" I asked, aghast. "An appointment with the foreign minister?"

I glanced, horror-stricken, at Beaumarchais, who merely smiled.

"My dear Henri," Franklin said. "This is politics. And in politics, it is never well to allow your...opponent...to easily control your actions. I have often said in my writings that one should never put off until tomorrow what one can do today. But, in this instance, I should think it more apt to say: one should not put off until tomorrow what one can do as well the day after!"

"I don't understand," I said.

"Keep close watch, my boy," he replied, slowly lowering himself gratefully onto a settee. "In time, you shall."

Chapter Thirteen

"No nation was ever ruined by trade." - Benjamin Franklin

We did not take the official coach to the Ministry of Foreign Affairs, as the Comte de Vergennes had so generously offered in his letter. Instead, on the morning of the 23rd of December, we rode through the open gates of the ministry in the same hotel carriage that had conducted us upon our tour of Paris. There was only Franklin and myself, the old man having miraculously convinced Beaumarchais to remain behind, if only to better assure the appointment's required secrecy.

"It is important, Henri, for you to say little," Dr. Franklin instructed as our carriage drew to a stop before the Ministry's gilded entrance. "It is more important still for you to remain carefully aware of your facial expressions. Such things are easily read by experienced politicians, and one can reveal more with a poorly-chosen expression than by any misspoken word. Keep your face as though it were a mask, as unchanging as the façade of any statue. Do you think you can do that, my boy?"

"I think so, Ben," I said. To be completely truthful, I had no real notion of what he desired of me, other than for me to sit in my chair at this meeting and conduct myself as if I were a porcelain doll. "I'll do my best."

"I never doubted that you would. Come, our escort awaits."

A tall man in gray attire approached our carriage.

The face beneath his smooth baldpate appeared stern, and a small, dark moustache hung below his sharp nose. "Dr. Franklin?" he inquired in a thin, reedy voice.

"I am he." Franklin replied in his poor French.

"Very good, sir. I am Conrad Gérard, Secretary to the Foreign Minister. It will be my pleasure to escort you to the office of the Comte de Vergennes." He eyes registered my presence. "I was told to expect you alone."

I translated for Dr. Franklin.

"Were you?" Franklin replied. "How very odd. As you may have guessed, this is my translator, Monsieur Henri Gruel." I dutifully turned these words into French and, when Gérard did not respond, Dr. Franklin added. "I'm sure the comte would not object to my bringing a translator along with me. But if you are concerned, Monsieur, I suggest that we take the matter up with him."

"Of course," Gérard said after a moment's rumination. "Please come this way, Messieurs."

The office of the foreign minister occupied fully a quarter of the building's street-level floor space. As Monsieur Gérard opened the door and stepped politely aside to allow us to enter, I was rendered dumbstruck by the sheer size of this single chamber. So tremendous was the cavern in which this man made his office that, with the high windows heavily draped, it was quite difficult to discern details of one wall while standing with your back to its opposite. This spaciousness was made all the more poignant by the lack of furnishings: merely a large, ornate desk of polished wood and brass, a few bookcases, and a small sitting area arranged near one of the chamber's three fireplaces.

As Dr. Franklin and I advanced across the polished floor, a finely attired gentleman rose from behind that great desk. How small he looked, given the great space that surrounded him. Though not striking in appearance, the man was possessed of a strong and confident manner. He was wigged and dressed in an elaborately embroidered light blue waistcoat over a lacy, white shirt, silver-trimmed almond-colored hose and a coat of fine, dark blue linen adorned with silver thread and buttons. These last glistened in the firelight as he came around to meet us, smiling broadly, his hand outstretched in greeting.

"Dr. Franklin! It can be no other! How good it is to finally meet you!" His English was passable, and I looked to Franklin to see if he would require a translation. If he did, he gave no sign, but instead went right up and met that welcoming hand with his own.

"My dear comte! Your lordship, this is indeed a privilege. I have heard so many flattering things about you from Messieurs. Deane and Bancroft." Then he turned toward me. "May I present Henri Gruel? This is the young man who has agreed to serve as my translator during my stay in France."

"Gruel? Are you not the son of Bathelemy-Jacques Gruel?" Vergennes asked me in French.

"I am, Your Lordship."

"A fine man of business and an excellent friend of the crown. You are welcome, young man." Then, to Franklin in English: "Now, please, doctor. I have taken the liberty of having tea made ready."

He addressed Gérard, who remained at the open door. "Thank you, Conrad. That will be all." The secretary bowed and departed. The closing of the great door echoed like a thunderclap.

"Come. Come. Sit!" Vergennes implored.

We took places in the sitting area near the hearth, an assembly of fine furniture that might have been pleasantly cozy were it not for all the discomforting space around it. As we settled ourselves, Vergennes fixed upon me a curiously expectant look. Somewhat befuddled, I turned toward Dr. Franklin, who smiled mischievously and nodded his head in the direction of a convenient tea set. "Oh!" I exclaimed, feeling suddenly foolish. Then I set myself to the task of clumsily pouring cups of hot tea.

"Before we talk, Dr. Franklin," Vergennes said conversationally. "I should like to present you with an invitation."

"Really, sir?" Franklin said brightly. "I'm most delighted to hear it. I'm actually quite fond of invitations and am often known to accept them."

Vergennes seemed slightly taken aback. "You jest with me, sir," he said after a moment.

"Yes," Franklin replied. "Never fear. You'll grow used to it."

Vergennes offered a dry smile that lasted barely a moment. "Of course. As I was saying, doctor. I should like to invite you to a Christmas Eve ball being presented by His Most Royal Majesty, King Louis XVI, at his palace in Versailles. It would give you an opportunity to acquaint yourself with the very cream of French society, as well as to ease your homesick heart. I know how difficult it must be to travel during Yuletide."

"Most kind of you," Franklin said. "Henri and I will be happy to attend."

He glanced quickly in my direction. "Well, Dr. Franklin. Naturally, you will find that most sophisticated Frenchmen are at least moderately skilled in the English tongue. I'm sure that you will not need…"

"You misunderstand, my dear comte," Franklin said. "I do not require Henri's company merely as a translator. His father charged me with his continued education while he is in my service. What sort of a guardian would I be to deny him the rare experience of mingling with the very pinnacle of French society?"

"Still, sir," Vergennes said. "Given his social status…"

"I am an *American*, sir," Franklin interjected gently. "I have been taught all my life to pay little mind to the manner of a person's birth. I am myself of lowly parentage. Far lower, I should think, than is Henri. Would you *ban* me from this affair based upon that confession?"

Vergennes appeared suddenly flustered. "Absolutely not, Dr. Franklin! And, of course, we would be delighted if your…ward…might attend."

"Very gracious of you, I'm sure," Franklin said, accepting a cup of tea that I had poured for him. Vergennes also took a cup, and seemed rather put out when I poured one for myself as well.

"Now then, Dr. Franklin," he said. "I, of course, received word of your impending visit some weeks ago through friends that I have in the British colonies..."

"United States of America," Franklin interjected.

Vergennes smiled indulgently. "Well, sir...that remains to be seen."

"United States of America," Franklin repeated, more slowly this time.

"Yes," Vergennes said with a nod of acquiescence.

"Let us be frank, your lordship," Franklin said. "We both know why I'm here. I have traveled six thousand rather uncomfortable miles to sit in this chair and broach a subject with you regarding..."

Vergennes put up a hand. "Dr. Franklin. I must tell you that I am not in a position to discuss any…"

Franklin continued as if he had not heard him. "...a formal treaty of friendship and trade between our two nations."

"Trade?" Vergennes asked, surprised.

"Naturally, sir. As a fledgling nation, America desires to establish trade agreements with all the powerful European countries. France, for reasons I should think obvious, was the first to draw our interest. We have much to offer your people, my dear comte. Timber. Tobacco. Citrus fruits. Various dry goods. We seek a treaty promising a routine exchange of such wares."

"Wares," Vergennes repeated, as if he hadn't heard properly.

"Yes, sir. We would be most interested in a number of French exports. Your most excellent wine comes to mind, though that may be my own personal affection for it talking." Franklin chuckled and took a sip of tea. "More seriously, we find ourselves in need of certain luxury items which can be difficult to obtain in the United States these days. I have a list, of course, but I can name, from memory, such things as sewing needles, certain dyes, various spices and fragrances, etcetera."

"Spices?" Vergennes said, visibly confused. "Dyes?"

"Of course, sir. We are not barbarians, but we find ourselves unable to easily obtain these items."

"But...*this* is why you have come to France?" Vergennes asked. "To negotiate a treaty over dyes and spices?"

"And other things," Franklin said. "As I indicated, I have a list. It is my hope to barter for these items with your noble king."

"I...see," the comte said. He looked at Franklin and then at me. I remembered the American doctor's words, and kept my face carefully neutral. I let my jaw fall slack, and willed my eyes to glaze over. I did not meet his gaze, but rather looked past him, as if I had settled into a sleepy fog.

Vergennes gaped at me for a moment, glanced curiously over his shoulder, and then back to me one more time. "Dr. Franklin, is your boy all right?"

Franklin raised both his eyebrows. "He is not 'my boy', sir. He is rather a friend and a companion, and...yes...he's quite all right. Aren't you, Henri?"

"Yes, Ben," I said, but I never let my expression change.

"As you say," Vergennes remarked with a shrug. "Well, sir. Naturally, I would have to confer with His Majesty in such a matter. You say you have a list of requested items?"

"I do. They are quite benign, ordinary things, as you will see. If it would be convenient, I should be happy to bring the list along to the ball tomorrow night."

Vergennes nodded slowly. "Yes...I believe that would be satisfactory."

"I assume His Majesty will be there," Franklin said.

"Of course, along with the queen."

"Excellent. It will be a tremendous honor to meet them both."

The king and queen, I thought, still keeping my face as rigid as a statue's. I was actually going to meet the sovereign rulers of France! Twin knots of apprehension and excitement formed in the pit of my belly. I had nothing to wear, of course. Nothing at all! Worse still, I was not at all sure what I would be *expected* to wear!

"Tell me, comte," Franklin said. "Has Monsieur Deane or Dr. Bancroft provided you with a copy of the Declaration of American Independence?"

"I do believe so...yes, sir."

"And have you found the time to read it?"

"I have," Vergennes said, seeming suddenly more comfortable. This, at least, was expected territory. "Or, more precisely, I have had it read to me. I do not read English very well, I'm afraid."

"Quite understandable, sir," Franklin said. "I, myself, am not student of French. But, tell me then if you would, my dear comte...what did you think of it?"

Franklin leaned forward them, the very picture of rapt attention. "Sir," Vergennes said, "I must confess that I was rather put off by it. *Really* now, sir, all that business about a king governing with the consent of the governed!"

Franklin simply replied: "Yes."

"How are we to take that?" Vergennes continued. "Surely you do not mean to elicit our sympathy by assaulting the core of our very existence!"

Franklin rested his chin upon his walking stick. It was a gesture with which I would grow very familiar in the times ahead. "My dear comte," he said gently. "America is not France. Our declaration is not and has never been intended to provoke anyone, save Great Britain. Its purpose is to describe, as plainly as possible, the injustices and ill use that have driven us to the necessity of fighting for our independence. Read not more into it than what is there, your lordship."

"How can I not?" Vergennes pressed. "How can the king not, when you make such outrageous conjectures?"

"Then allow me to consult with King Louis myself, so that I may put his mind at rest," Franklin suggested.

"You *may* see him, doctor...tomorrow night at the ball, though I cannot say with certainty that he will find the time to meet with you for any real purpose. There shall be many guests."

"Indeed?" said Franklin. "Will Lord Stormont be

there?"

Vergennes smiled slyly. "He will."

"And Monsieur Leray de Chaumont?"

"Certainly," Vergennes replied.

"Then, with the interest of such personages to indulge my patriotic fervor, I'm sure I shall find myself given ample opportunity to make my case," Franklin said sardonically. "In any event, Your Lordship, I fail to see how a few phrases in a declaration may intercede in a simple trade of timber for pins between civilized nations!"

Vergennes fixed Franklin with a hard, appraising look, running his gaze across the American's wizened, sincere visage. Finally, with a thoughtful shake of his head, he said: "Neither can I, doctor. If timber for pins truly is the business of the day, then I see little reason for the king to object to such a benign and mutually beneficial transaction. I shall broach the subject with him at our regular daily audience this afternoon."

"Very kind of you," Franklin said, smiling. "Henri, I do believe that we have taken up more than enough of the minister's valuable time." He concluded his cup of tea with a single, healthy swallow, and then rose from his chair. I rose with him, my face still as immobile as a statue's visage.

"Is there nothing else you feel compelled to discuss with me, Dr. Franklin?" asked the comte.

Franklin seemed to consider this long and well. "No, I don't believe so," he replied thoughtfully. Then, just as he bade me to accompany him from the foreign minister's presence, he snapped his fingers and turned upon his heel "Ah yes! Comte, forgive me! I don't know what I was thinking!"

Vergennes, who had gone to his desk, looked up with interest. He smiled. "Yes, doctor? There was something else?"

"There certainly was. A most important matter. I truly cannot believe it slipped my mind."

Vergennes seemed a bit relieved. "To be honest, Dr. Franklin, I found the omission rather confusing myself.

Would you care to sit down again?"

"That won't be necessary, though I'm impressed that you seem to know beforehand the topic of my concern. It is this: on our way from Le Mans, myself, Henri and Monsieur Pierre Beaumarchais...with whom we were traveling...were set upon by a highwayman, who had apparently arranged the ambush with the help of our duplicitous driver. With Henri's brave assistance, Pierre was able to dispatch the rogues. However, it concerns me that the ambush may have been orchestrated by certain...foreign interests...located here in France, who might benefit from my untimely departure from this mortal coil."

Vergennes' smile faded. Genuine concern replaced it. "This I did not know, doctor. How dreadful! But surely you don't suspect conspiracy behind it!"

"I'm afraid that I do. I cannot name the culprit with certainty, but I felt that you should be made aware of the incident, given the grave ramifications implied by my death while on French soil."

"Of course, sir," Vergennes said. "Quite appropriate that you should. I shall look into the matter."

"My thanks to you. I bid you good day, my dear comte." Franklin made as if to depart.

"But Dr. Franklin!" Vergennes called aloud, taking a step after us.

"Yes, comte?

"What of the shipment of arms France had promised the American colonies for their fight against the British?" Vergennes asked in bewildered astonishment.

Franklin paused and treated the man to an expression of sincere surprise. "Arms? Arms, sir? What a generous offer! I shall give it serious consideration and avail you of my response at the earliest possible time. Again, good day."

Then, after having bade me open the door, Dr. Franklin strolled happily out into the vast hallway, where Monsieur Gérard awaited us. As we were escorted to our waiting carriage, I listened to the old man's pleasant whistling. I did not know the tune.

Chapter Fourteen

"Plough deep while sluggards sleep." - Benjamin Franklin

"Ben, I confess I'm a bit perplexed," I said as our carriage maneuvered the Paris streets, en route to the comfort of our hotel.

Dr. Franklin chuckled. "I should think the poor comte finds himself in similar straits."

"You mentioned nothing of the four French ships that have been delayed at port, loaded with arms for America."

"So I did not," Franklin admitted. "Though, you will notice, Henri, that eventually *he* did so."

"I fail to understand what was gained by his mentioning of the matter and not your own," I said.

Franklin nodded slowly. "What was gained was to present our friend Vergennes with questions, my boy! Right now, as we speak of him, he sits in his office, puzzling over our most peculiar exchange. He must surely know of my desire to see those stalled armaments sent promptly on their way. Why then did I not protest their delay? Why did I not beseech the American cause? Why did I not refute Stormont's claims that the Americans are near to beaten in the war?"

"All right, then," I said, perhaps a little impatiently. "Why *did* you not?"

"Because, Henri, to do so would have been to force a

confrontation. The first rule of international diplomacy is this, my boy: Never contradict anybody! My purpose in this meeting was to meet Vergennes, to learn...insofar as I could...his measure and mettle. It was also to push this French official slightly off center, to confuse him and pique his interest." Then, after a pause, he added: "There was also a third reason."

"And that was?"

"I wished to ascertain whether or not the foreign minister had foreknowledge of the attempt on our lives."

I was horrified. "You believe that the comte may have been behind the highwayman's ambush?"

"It was unlikely, but possible," Franklin said. "I did not yet know the man. People can be quite adept at concealing their true loyalties." The words bit deep into my conscience.

"Besides," Franklin continued. "Stormont has agents everywhere."

"But...surely not the foreign minister?"

"Why not? Men can be bought, Henri. Remember that always. But the question is irrelevant. I watched Vergennes closely as I revealed to him the nature of our dire adventure. He was quite genuinely surprised. I would confidently wager my fur hat on this. Whatever other motivations he may have, the comte did not orchestrate the attack on us."

I nodded, feeling quite relieved. The Comte de Vergennes did not strike me as a man to wisely call one's enemy.

"What will happen now?" I asked.

"Now?" Franklin asked. "Now we shall shop, my dear boy. We must buy you clothes suitable for tomorrow night's Yuletide celebration."

The notion appealed to me mightily. "And you, Ben? Will you not be shopping for a garment more befitting a royal audience?"

Franklin grinned mischievously. "I shall wear that which you see me in now," he announced. "Or something not dissimilar."

I studied his unembroidered overcoat and fur cap. "To meet the king? Ben!"

"My reputation has preceded me to Paris, Henri. Unfortunately, as is sometimes the case, that reputation has developed a life all its own, somewhat removed from the true nature of the subject. In France, I have been designated a 'noble peasant", a scientist and...Lord spare me...a philosopher, from a land of pioneers and explorers. As such, I am not expected to exhibit the same airs and attention to fashion normally attributed to Europeans of high social status. This reputation is extremely valuable to me, as it provides me with the most singular opportunity to garner both attention and respect. I must do nothing to diminish this impression."

"I should think that they would refuse you entrance at the palace door," I said sourly.

He laughed. "Me? Never! You, perhaps. That is why we must make for the tailor shops."

"May I have a wig?" I asked eagerly.

Franklin scowled. "A macaroni? I think not! Don't you ever adopt such a silly and ostentatious vanity, Henri, or I should strike you soundly upon the head with my cane! Powdered wigs are for fops and fools, not for a young man of intelligence and insight...especially not if he is to spend his days in *my* company."

Something in my crestfallen demeanor must have amused him, for he suddenly patted me on my back and chuckled. "Don't look so sullen, Henri. I promise that you will not be disappointed with your new wardrobe. First we must find a color that suits you. What do you think of vermilion?"

"Isn't that a bit...bright?"

Our driver deposited us upon the Rue St. Germain, and here we browsed the exclusive garment shops and haberdasheries. The air was crisp, but there was thankfully little wind, allowing Franklin and myself to stroll from one shop to the next in reasonable comfort. The streets were crowded, but no one recognized Franklin by sight, and so we enjoyed a morning uninterrupted by the doctor's usual flock of well-wishers and admirers.

Franklin shopped with an experienced and cynical eye, rubbing each garment carefully between thumb and forefinger, testing, as he put it, "the fabric's pedigree." When he judged something as potentially suitable, he notified the shopkeeper of his interest, introduced me as his grandson, and then commenced to conspire with the man regarding how best to fit and clothe me.

I admit that I found the entire experience in equal measures exhilarating and discomfiting. Franklin's careful consideration of each purchase flattered me, as did the enjoyment that he so obviously took from the task. By the same token, however, I came quickly to feel akin to a tailor's mannequin, obliged to don hat and hose, breeches and shirt, vest, cravat and coat, all while being permitted little or no opinion of my own as to their fit, color or suitability.

By the time the morning had turned into afternoon, I was the owner of an auspicious garment. The coat was of a soft puce, with mother-of-pearl buttons and elegant gold thread embroidery along the seams. Franklin further selected a band-collared silk shirt with lace cuffs, bone-colored vest and breeches, and white hose—with tall-heeled, black, silver-buckled shoes to support me. Upon my head he placed a three-cornered hat-uncommon in France at the time. "It is important not too conform too completely to the fashion of the day," he explained. "One must fit, and yet rise just slightly above simply 'fitting'. A statement must be made."

I examined myself in the mirror. My earlier enthusiasm at the thought of such attire had since waned. My reflection displayed a boy enveloped in unfamiliar finery—like a dog wrapped in a silken cape—out of place and unhappy to be so.

"I look like a fop," I said sourly.

"Precisely!" Franklin replied brightly. "And so you shall have little trouble finding your way into the community surrounding the French court."

"Why can I not be plain, as you shall be?" I asked

The Franklin Affair

him plaintively.

"I explained this, Henri."

"But this is uncomfortable. The shoes hurt my feet!"

Franklin chuckled. "Such a fuss! Only a fop would fret thus over so simple a thing as clothing."

I glowered at him.

It was nearly three in the afternoon by the time our carriage turned onto the Rue de l'Université. I was quite exhausted, and craved a warm pillow and a glass of port. Franklin was kneading his foot, his face twisted into a pained grimace. The day's excursion had evidently aggravated his gout. "You should rest yourself for the remainder of the afternoon," I suggested.

"I shall do just that," he said. "Today has been well spent, wouldn't you say?"

"Indeed," I told him. "Do you *really* believe the new attire appropriate for tomorrow's regalia?"

"I do. Stop fretting! Honestly, Henri, I sometimes forget which of us is the cantankerous old man!"

I smiled. "Ben, you may have collected the necessary years...but you are the least cantankerous gentleman that I have ever known."

"Very gracious of you," he said, rubbing at his swollen foot. "If this poor big toe grows any worse, however, you may well find yourself recanting that opinion."

As our carriage approached the Hôtel d'Entragues, I heard Dr. Franklin utter a weary sigh. We were both keenly aware that the lobby would be well occupied by those who admired him and sought his company. Ordinarily, Franklin favored such insistent souls with encouragement and friendly deference, but I could see today that his pain and exhaustion were gaining the better of him.

"Driver," I called, knocking upon the underside of the bench. "Take us around to the servant's entrance. To Franklin, I said: "We'll make our way through to the kitchen. Perhaps Madame Devereux can spirit us upstairs without our being noticed."

"An excellent notion, Henri," he replied. "I thank you."

I kept an eye out the carriage window as our driver took us past the hotel's lighted threshold. There were a number of people occupying the steps and sidewalk. Their eyes scanned the street expectantly; eagerly anticipating Franklin's return. When their collective gaze settled upon our own coach, I sat back in the shadows and hoped that Franklin would not be readily identified.

The ruse worked on all but one of them. There stood among them a woman of tender years, perhaps only slightly older than myself. As our carriage passed, she seemed to follow it with her eyes far longer than the rest of them. As I watched, chagrined, she took to walking after us, following us toward the corner, her pace increasing. The expression on her youthful, yet heavily painted face, changed from curiosity to recognition to desperation.

As our driver took us around the corner she followed us, moving at a most undignified pace. The servant's entrance of the hotel stood upon a narrow side street, little more than an alley, which terminated within yards of the river's edge. As our carriage halted, I unhappily resigned myself to having avoided all of Franklin's many admirers—save one.

"Excuse me! Excuse me, sirs!" the young woman called, her tone breathless and most urgent.

With a sigh, I threw open the shutters. "I'm sorry, mademoiselle," I said. "But Dr. Franklin is in ill health. Whatever you feel you must say, it will have to wait until tomorrow."

"No, that mustn't be!" she cried, and the measure of panic that I perceived in her voice gave me pause. "Dr. Franklin!" she exclaimed in broken but understandable English, slapping the side of the coach with one hand. "Dr Franklin! *Please!*"

The old man came to the carriage window, wincing as he leaned upon his aching foot. Still, he regarded this interloper with gentle, patient eyes. "I'm here, dear girl.

The Franklin Affair

Do calm yourself. What can possibly be so terrible?"

At the sight of him, I saw the young woman pale slightly. She started to speak, and then, quite abruptly, the door to the servants entrance opened. She spun around, gasping aloud.

Madame Devereux and her cook stood at the threshold, looking curiously at us. The girl stared at them for a long, harrowing moment. Then, as if seeing something that filled her with the most awful dread, she turned back to us and spoke in a whisper. "I'm sorry! I've...made a mistake! Forgive me, gentlemen."

Then, in a most inappropriate gesture, this inexplicable creature came forward, took Dr. Franklin's hands in her own and placed upon his weathered cheek a lingering kiss. I could do naught but bear astonished witness. Franklin, too, seemed speechless with surprise. But then, as she withdrew, he smiled and patted her cheek. "You are a charming child," he said. "Off with you now, lest you miss your mother's supper!"

With a weak smile that never reached her eyes, the girl turned and made her way back up the side street with all the unseemly urgency that she had previously demonstrated. Franklin and I gauged her progress until she had gone from our sight.

"How extraordinary," I muttered.

"A curious young lady," Franklin said. "Imagine! All that fuss and bother merely to thank me. Apparently a lightning rod saved her mother's house last month."

The driver came down and opened the carriage door. Franklin stepped out first, wincing upon his treacherous foot. As he did so, Madame Devereux hurried forward to take his arm. Together with the cook, the three of them stepped within the servants entrance doorway.

I stayed behind to gather the fruits of our day in the shops and to thank our driver. As I neared the hotel's threshold, my arms filled with packages, a figure abruptly emerged from a shadowy recess in the wall beside the doorway. I uttered a startled gasp before I saw that it was Father Hilliard. He placed a finger to his lips.

"What was that business?"

I regarded him warily, not wishing to see him, not wishing to be reminded of the task that he and Chaumont had set upon me. "If you have been standing there like a thief the whole time, then you saw what I saw, and know as much as I do," I said crossly.

He reached out and took hold of my collar, dragging me toward him. "Take not that tone with me, Mouse!" he growled. "You are not so important as all that. I will need a report from you, boy. Do you understand me?"

"I have...not the...time," I stammered.

"Then meet me here tonight, at nine o'clock, and be ready to tell me everything that has transpired since Franklin came to Paris. Is that clear?"

"It's clear," I said.

He released me. "Off with you, then. I shall expect you in a few hours time. Do not fail me."

I left him without looking back, my heart drumming.

Chapter Fifteen

"A little neglect may breed mischief...for want of a nail, the shoe was lost; for want of a shoe the horse was lost; and for want of a horse, the rider was lost." - Benjamin Franklin

By the time I returned to our rooms on the hotel's second floor, Dr. Franklin's comfort had already been accommodated, and the elderly doctor was enjoying the lavish attentions of Madame Devereux, who moved about him like a sick-nurse. When I came upon them in the sitting room, she was casting about for another pillow to place under Franklin's swollen foot, and was actively berating a valet for not producing Franklin's glass of Madeira with sufficient alacrity. Franklin, nestled upon the settee, made of himself quite a suffering patient, moaning theatrically each time his foot was elevated and more cushions added beneath it.

In the doorway to his bedchamber stood Beaumarchais, smiling with amusement.

"Oh, Henri!" Franklin called when at last he saw me. "I shall have to spend the night upon this settee, I fear. My foot simply shall not bear the walk to my bed! Be a good lad and fetch me my sleeping clothes? I shall need blankets and pillows, as well."

"Poor man!" Madame Devereux cooed. "Poor, dear man!"

"Of course. Ben." I said.

"I shall need some supper," Franklin said, sounding quite miserable. His blue eyes looked upon our hostess most beseechingly.

"You shall have anything that you desire, dear man," the lady replied. "Charles! Fetch bread and cheese! Off with you now!" Then she turned and spoke again to Dr. Franklin, her tone most gentle: "Will this content you while you decide on whatever else you may wish to eat?"

"Most assuredly, madame," Franklin said. "Your kindness endeavors to surpass your beauty. Alas, I fear it can never do so!"

Madame Devereux flushed prettily. "Dear man," she muttered.

The next several hours were spent attending to Dr. Franklin's copious needs. I served him wine, gathered empty plates of food, replaced them with fresh platters, and more than once was obliged to aid the old man in reaching the nearest privy. Beaumarchais was little help in these matters, seemingly content to share conversation and spirits with Deane and Bancroft, who arrived to consult with Franklin as to the particulars of his meeting with Vergennes. While the three men found the American doctor's suffering laments a bit tiresome, they also took no small amusement from witnessing my frenetic efforts to attend him, as well as Franklin's apparent determination to summon me anew the very moment that I had managed to enjoy a instant's rest.

In this flurry of activity, I had little time to reflect upon the business to which I had committed myself with Father Hilliard. As the evening wore on, however, and the hour of nine grew close, I found myself ruminating more and more upon what course of action to choose. Had I not promised myself—and my father—that, in Paris, I should set about deciding, for good and all, with which faction I would finally and unequivocally ally myself? I had put off the matter for some days, but now the question had forced itself.

The hour grew late. Beaumarchais retired to his bedchamber, and Franklin bade me put out the lamps and blanket him well upon the sitting room's settee. As I complied, I regarded the old man thoughtfully and settled upon my course. To call Dr. Franklin remarkable was to do him a disservice. He was much more than that, capable of extreme generosity and virtue, and yet not above such self-indulgence as would allow him to exaggerate his own injury in order to take full advantage of my service and that of Madame Devereux. My respect for him, great though it was, had begun to develop into a deep affection.

"No more," I murmured to myself. This arrangement with Hilliard and Chaumont would end tonight. Let the priest, if that was indeed his calling, rant and threaten. Let him strike me dead in the street. I would no longer betray this kind and brilliant gentleman.

How can I describe the sense of relief that swept over me upon making this resolution? It was as if the vise that gripped my heart had been abruptly loosened— as if the cloud that had settled above me had surrendered to the sun. After the evening meal, I went into my room to prepare myself for my appointment with Hilliard, fearful, but content that I had finally placed myself unwaveringly upon the right road.

Then something occurred to shake my resolve, and cast me once more upon the turbulent waters of confusion.

As I stepped from my bedchamber and into the darkened sitting room, with the mantel clock only minutes from nine bells, I saw immediately that the settee stood empty. Dr. Franklin, who had wondered only hours before how he should ever manage to walk again, had gone. His Crabtree stick, which had been resting upon the floor by the hearth, pointing faithfully westward, was missing also.

I went at once to his bedchamber, the door to which stood open, and peered warily within. The bed, just visible in the gloom, stood unused.

I was about to call for Beaumarchais, but then I noticed that, upon the bed, garments had been carefully folded. I advanced into the empty room and looked down in bewilderment at the very sleeping clothes that I had, myself, provided to Franklin earlier that evening. Confounded, I went to the dressing cabinet and, upon opening it, discovered that a set of Franklin's day clothes was missing, along with his coat and fur hat.

With growing alarm, I hurried once more out into the sitting room and crossed to the main door. This I opened carefully.

Dr. Franklin was just visible upon the stairs, making his way cautiously down toward the lobby. Had I taken to opening that door only moments later, I should have missed him completely!

But where was he going? And why had he not mentioned an appointment? Surely this was more than a recreational walk, given the severity of his gout and the lateness of the hour.

Frowning, I once again thought to wake Beaumarchais, but decided against it as, in the time it would take to do so, Franklin would likely be on the street and gone from sight.

So, without a look back, I set out after him, dogging his footsteps as carefully and quietly as a child advancing upon a jar of sweets. As he descended the long staircase, I could see that at least some of his complaints of gout had not been false. He was obviously in considerable discomfort, but quite resolute in his determination to go somewhere, and to go as quickly and quietly as he may.

The lobby, though thankfully free of admirers, was not altogether empty. Madame Devereux was not in attendance, but a few of her valets were. At the sight of Dr. Franklin, they advanced to his aid, only to be impatiently waved away. As I followed, some two dozen feet behind him, they took sight of me and made as though to address me. I quickly smiled and held up my hand, trying to convey that all was well and prayed that they would not betray me to Dr. Franklin by speaking. Blessedly, they did not.

Out upon the Rue l'Universite, the night air was still and cold. Franklin stood for a moment upon the curb, looking left and right. I watched from the doorway, peering carefully down the carpeted steps, as Franklin drew the attention of a *fiacre*, or public carriage, and spoke in earnest to the driver, struggling to make his destination known using his poor French. Eventually, some understanding was reached, and Franklin was aided into the coach by its driver, who then resumed his place and made ready to depart.

Once I felt certain than neither man would see me, I threw open the hotel's door and took after them at a full run, advancing upon the departing carriage before its horse could gather speed. With a great leap I dropped down upon the retreating coach's baggage bench. I perched there most precariously, clutching one of the rear rails for purchase and trying to ignore the chill in the air.

We rode deeper into the nighttime city. Our journey seemed to take a long while. When, at last, the carriage came to a halt, I found that my hindquarters had gone quite to sleep—so much so that it was an effort to stand. The region in which we found ourselves, somewhere in the city's Latin Quarter, seemed of low social standing. The street was narrow, the houses small and pressed tightly together. There were few lights.

I kept my place as I heard the driver come down from his bench and speak to Franklin through the coach's open door. Their conversation was lengthy, given the obstacle of language, but the gist of it was this: that Franklin wished the coachman to remain until he had completed his business, while the coachman had no wish to linger in so sordid a neighborhood. It was finally agreed that the driver would bring his *fiacre* around the long block every few minutes, until Franklin should reappear. If he did not do so within an hour's time, the driver would abandon him.

With this business settled, I listened as Franklin's

distinct footsteps receded upon the street. As the carriage began to move beneath me, I took my leave from it, hurrying to the shadows of a nearby doorway. From this place of concealment, I watched Franklin approach the unlit doorway of a particular abode, his walking stick in one hand and a small slip of yellow paper in the other.

He rapped tentatively upon the door. It opened at once. The dwelling within was lit and, though Franklin moved quickly across the threshold and the door shut behind him, I did manage to glimpse the face of his host.

It was the young woman who, earlier that day, had accosted our carriage in such an inexplicable manner.

Had Franklin known the young woman before today? How else could he have gleaned her place of residence? Then I recalled the small slip of paper he held, and also the way the girl had clutched Dr. Franklin's hand while placing a long kiss upon his cheek. Had her small, gloved fingers contained a note? Had there been brief words behind her lengthy kiss?

What *was* this dark business, which brought such a man as Benjamin Franklin out into the night as if he was a thief?

Thrice, from my place of hiding, I watched the public carriage clatter by. Thrice, the driver paused outside the door in question, before setting off to begin another circuit. I estimated ten minutes between each new visitation. So, by that reckoning, Franklin spent approximately thirty minutes in the young woman's company.

Then, as the coach passed for the fourth time, the door to the modest abode opened, and Franklin emerged. As his face passed briefly through a patch of light, I read the anxiety that played upon his features. Whatever mysterious purpose had brought him here, its completion had done nothing to ease the seriousness of his disposition.

At the sight of him, the coach abruptly stopped, and the driver leapt down to open the door for the visibly weary old man. Franklin climbed up into the carriage without a word and, as the coach moved away, I followed after it, resuming my precarious perch upon the baggage board.

So it was that Franklin returned to the lighted, welcoming façade of the Hôtel d'Entragues, with myself as his careful shadow. Once more, I followed him through the nearly vacant lobby, past valets who did not bother to approach us this time, and up to our room.

I watched from around the corner of the hall as he let himself into our chambers. His face wore a terrible frown, and his hands shook badly as he worked the key into the lock. Once he had gone inside, I waited for a count of two hundred before I followed.

The sitting room was dark when I entered. The door to Franklin's bedchamber stood closed. Apparently, the old man had chosen his warm bed over the settee.

I went into my own room, my weary mind busily reviewing the night's queer events.

It did not occur to me until I had, at last, pulled the quilt up around my chilled and aching body, that Father Hilliard had undoubtedly waited for me in the alley outside the hotel's servants entrance—in vain.

He would be none too pleased, I knew.

Chapter Sixteen

"The great secret of succeeding in conversation is to admire little, to hear much; always to distrust our own reason, and sometimes that of our friends; never to pretend to wit, but to make that of others appear as much as possible we can; to harken to what is said and to answer to the purpose." - Benjamin Franklin

"Your Majesty," the royal butler announced, reading from his list as Dr. Franklin and I finally reached the end of the king and queen's receiving line. "We here present Dr. Benjamin Franklin and his ward, Henri Gruel."

Though I would never have said so aloud, my first close inspection of King Louis XVI did not impress me. The error rested not necessarily with him, as he was a reasonable-looking fellow, but rather with me, and my boyish, romantic fancy regarding how a monarch should appear. Louis was neither tall nor strong-featured, but rather a bit short and thick about the middle. He wore a grand powdered wig, heavily curled, a lavishly embroidered waistcoat fashioned of the finest linen, and a coat of soft lavender, with pearls and silver thread sewn throughout it. Yet, none of these accessories could overcome his bland expression, nor the soft, doughy characteristics of his face. He bore, in fact, so little resemblance to his image upon coinage and statuary, that I briefly entertained the notion that he was not the king, but in fact a buffoon, hired by Louis as a joke to be played upon his guests.

The Franklin Affair

"Your Majesty," Franklin said, bowing very low. "I thank you, on behalf of the American government, for your kind invitation."

"Yes," Louis said in English. "America. Yes. Doctor, may I present my foreign minister, the Comte de Vergennes?"

Vergennes, dressed in lavender and black hose, appeared beside his liege. His eyes met Franklin's, the communication between the two men swift, but unmistakable.

"An honor, comte," Franklin said.

"Your servant, Dr. Franklin," Vergennes replied with a bow.

The king smiled broadly, as if he found this exchange most satisfactory. "May I assure you, the honor is ours, Dr. Franklin. All of Paris sings to us of your praises. Printer. Author. Statesman. The inventor of the stove and the lightning rod. A truly remarkable development that! We really should have one at the palace. Tell me Vergennes...do we have a lightning rod at Versailles?"

"Several, Your Majesty," the comte replied.

"Excellent!" Louis said, sounding quite sincere. "I shall sleep all the better knowing that. May I have the honor of presenting my wife, Her Royal Majesty, Queen Marie Antoinette?"

The lady who stood beside her king turned at the sound of her name. She appeared slightly taller than her husband—not beautiful, precisely, but with handsome features and large, intelligent eyes. Those eyes seemed to collect mine, to draw them in, as a flame might draw a moth. I glanced at Franklin, and found him predictably captivated. The queen offered her hand, which Franklin took and bowed over, but did not have the temerity to kiss.

"Your Majesty's beauty has rendered me mute," he whispered softly. The queen looked to me, and I hastily translated.

"I hardly think so," the bejeweled woman replied with a smile. "Pray, find your tongue, good doctor, lest we suffer for want of your famous wit."

"I shall endeavor not to disappoint you, Your Majesty," Franklin said after I'd turned the royal words to English. "Sadly, wit is a thing that, when come upon honestly, brings pleasure to all; but should a man choose to force it, he may find a fool's cap placed quickly upon his head."

Upon hearing my translation, the queen uttered a gentle laugh. It was a deep, sultry thing. "Well said, sir! But I have found that men of good humor rise above their fellows, as though illuminated within by the fire of their own charm. I've little doubt that, if pressed, you would find that light within yourself, Dr. Franklin. Don't you agree, my husband?"

"Indeed," Louis said dubiously, as though he were still trying to work out what the American and his wife, the queen, had said to one another.

"Your Majesty is indeed gracious," Franklin said to Marie Antoinette. "Beauty is a rose, milady, but it is not the *only* rose. Intellect also flowers, and its blooms are often the most delicate and wondrous of all. If you will forgive an old man's innocent observation, Your Majesty...you seem in possession of a most splendid bouquet."

A genuine smile illuminated the queen's face. For a moment, I thought she might blush like a young girl. But instead, she bowed her head in a most regal manner. "Thank you, sir," she said, her tone and manner most sincere.

"Yes," the king added abruptly. "Well. Please excuse us now, doctor. Your company is most entertaining. However...sadly...we have other guests to greet. We hope to have time to enjoy further your honest humor before the night is done."

"I would be honored, Your Majesty," Franklin said.

Then Franklin and I left the royal couple to their duties, and stepped deeper into the exquisite Galarie des Glaces—the Hall of Mirrors.

A hundred men, standing with their arms outstretched and their fingers barely touching, could not have spanned the chamber's length. One entire wall was devoted to windows, great panels of glass that exceeded three times my height and offered a splendid view of the court of the Chateau de Versailles. Literally thousands of lanterns cast their light upon the stone and marble, until the whole of the vast palace seemed to glow from within. Upon the gallery's opposite wall, great mirrors hung like tapestries, interspersed with wall panels inlaid with gold and silver, and great bronze busts and other statuary mounted atop gilded pedestals. Magnificent, crystal chandeliers hung from the vaulted ceiling, and the tile floor had been polished to such a shine that these lighted accoutrements were thereupon readily reflected.

Still, for all its volume of space, the gallery could make no claim to emptiness—for men and women abounded! Dressed in fanciful and extravagant Yuletide costume, they ate of the finest food, drank of the most precious wine, talked and laughed and danced prettily to the music of a twenty-piece orchestra.

These sights and sounds bedazzled me, nearly besting the great tremors of unease and confusion, which had gripped my heart since last night's adventure.

I'd awakened that morning half-believing the previous night's foray to be naught but an ill dream. This illusion seemed supported by Dr. Franklin, who was in pleasant, if not especially exuberant spirits, having ordered breakfast by the time I found the strength to stagger out amongst the men who shared my quarters.

Franklin's gout had apparently eased itself. There was no mention of his jaunt into the Paris night. So persuasive was this omission that I was quite unable to broach the subject myself. I sat down at the breakfast table, despite a scant appetite, feeling confounded and more than a bit frightened. This dogged anxiety pursued me throughout the day, as we planned for the evening's gala in Versailles. Despite my objections, Franklin bade me model my new attire for the benefit of Beaumarchais, Deane and Bancroft, all of who seemed to find great sport in this merchant's son who dressed as a foppish aristocrat.

"It suits me," Franklin had said to them, "that Henri should dress so, as a means to lend credibility to myself and...more importantly...my words. These are people of luxury, who value fashion as you and I value virtue. While, upon the one hand, I must keep my own simple attire so as to maintain my reputation amongst them, I must also bear with me a ward so well adorned as to demand their serious notice."

So upon the afternoon, the five of us acquired from Madame Devereux a splendid carriage, and set out for the Royal Palace at Versailles. My American companions all wore respectable, though unimpressive clothing. Only Beaumarchais was dressed as I—trussed up in a blue suit of uncut velvet, with gray linen vest and breeches, matching white hose and cravat, and even a macaroni wig upon his head, despite Franklin's vocalized distaste of that particular vanity.

On the way, Franklin spoke much to me of what I would see and how I should behave. "Let nothing startle you. If something is said which confuses or angers you, you must remain silent. Speak only when directly addressed, and never, come what may, allow your true opinion of anyone to make itself known."

And now, dressed as a nobleman's son and surrounded by the trappings of aristocracy, I followed closely as Dr. Franklin made his way through the energetic crowd.

"The comte pretended not to know you," I remarked quietly.

"And well that he did so," Franklin replied. "Our meeting, as you will recall, was to be a circumspect matter."

"Still, he offered to send us an official carriage! Surely that implies some measure of public recognition!"

Franklin chuckled. "That was a test, my boy. He wished to see if I would accept such an offer. The fact that I did not assured him that I was a man of some subtlety. Without that assurance, I doubt that he would have seen us at all."

"Is the king aware of your meeting?" I asked.

"Without a doubt. The foreign minister's subterfuge at the receiving line was meant not for His Majesty, but rather for those others within earshot. It is important, for the time being, that our brief encounter be kept most confidential. Toward this end, I've little doubt but that Vergennes wisely advised the king not to mention it. I suggest you and I do the same for the remainder of the evening."

"Then when will you present the comte with your list of items for the treaty?" I asked.

"I have no list, Henri."

"No list? But isn't the foreign minister expecting one?"

Franklin paused and took my arm. Around us, finely attired men and women flowed by as if carried upon a river's current. Some took notice of us. Gradually, recognition of Franklin—if not by his features, then certainly by his simplicity of dress—began to spread throughout the gallery. The American seemed to recognize this, for he spoke to me in an urgent whisper. "While I admire your questions, my boy, and would like nothing better than to complete this lesson in diplomacy, I regret that now is not the time. Soon we will find ourselves drawn into difficult conversation. You must carry yourself well, and mind your every word and gesture. For now, I will say this...in answer to your last question: the comte no longer believes that I am here for the purpose I stated at our meeting. He is too canny a fellow for that. By now, he has worked out my true intentions and no longer expects me to deliver to him a list that we both know does not exist."

I shook my head in befuddlement. "The closer the look, the thicker the soup," I said.

"It will be stew before we're done, make no mistake!" Franklin said with a smile. "Look there. I do believe I see Silas and Edward speaking with an elderly woman of obvious means. Come."

"Ah, Benjamin! There you are!" Deane said as we approached, though I thought I detected a certain wary agitation in his eyes. "But where is Pierre?"

"Henri and I were waylaid by a group of well-wishers as we exited our carriage," Franklin said, coming to stand beside his fellow commissioner. "They engaged me in a brief discussion of fire fighting methods. Beaumarchais was impatient to escape the cold, and so I sent him on ahead."

"More likely he was impatient to sample the king's spirits," Bancroft remarked.

"Nevertheless," said Franklin with a grin. "I trust that our paths will cross before this evening ends. As for Henri and myself, we have just been paying our regards to the king and queen. Still, had I known that you would be monopolizing the attentions of so lovely and gracious a lady as this, I should have disengaged myself more quickly from the royal presence."

"Yes," Deane said, looking rather unsettled. Hesitantly, he gestured toward the elderly noblewoman. "Umm...May I present the Marquise du Deffand? My dear marquise this is Dr. Benjamin Franklin."

The woman turned toward Franklin, fixing upon him eyes that had gone milky in their centers. She was obviously nearly blind, but nevertheless regarded the American with critical interest. "Dr. Franklin, is it? Yes, I've heard of you. You invented that...pole...which pulls lightning from the sky." Her English was heavily accented, but passable.

"You are too gracious, madame."

"You shall address me as 'marquise' or as 'milady'," the woman said, as though lecturing to an idiot. "And I am never 'too gracious', doctor, nor do I find myself at all impressed with pretentious colonial peasants."

Franklin's smile faded. He blinked once, and then twice, regarding the venerable French aristocrat as if she had just reached up and struck him. The marquise seemed to take this as some minor victory, for a grim smile touched her thin lips.

"If Milady is not entertained by my presence," Franklin said dryly. "I shall be obliged to remove myself at once."

"Do so," the marquise replied, waggling her fingers at him. "Remove yourself. From my presence, from this palace, from France, if at all possible. You have no place here."

A silence, as cold and unyielding as a slab of marble, fell upon our small circle. Finally, Dr. Bancroft cleared his throat noisily and said: "Dr. Franklin, there is a matter which I must discuss with you. May I take you aside, sir?"

"Yes," Deane said beseechingly. "It is a matter of import, Benjamin. Go now, and discuss it with Edward."

"I shall," Franklin said, his eyes still on the old woman. "But, presently. I must now address myself to the marquise's concerns."

"I have no concerns, sir," the woman remarked haughtily.

"Milady considers me a peasant," Franklin said. "I should like to know why."

"You come here in such attire and dare to ask that impertinent question?" she replied. "You are a peasant from a land populated by peasants. You have no place at an affair such as this." She turned her head and regarded Bancroft and Deane. "*Any* of you," she added coldly.

The two commissioners and their secretary stood together, wrapped in an embarrassed silence. Bancroft's face had become quite flushed, whereas Deane's chose instead to turn as pale as the snow that blanketed the palace grounds. Franklin's features moved swiftly through myriad expressions, while his hands worked nervously upon the knob of his Crabtree stick.

I, who had never before experienced such a gala as this, who had never imagined that such blatant rudeness could ever manifest itself in such a setting, was the first to find his tongue. The words left my mouth before I had time to snatch them back: "Her Majesty the Queen seemed rather taken with Dr. Franklin, milady."

She turned and fixed upon me a gaze fit to chill my blood blue. "This? Who is this?" she demanded, speaking as if I were not even present.

Deane and Brancroft regarded me with abject horror,

as though I had just placed my head in a tiger's mouth. Dr. Franklin peered at me from behind his spectacles, his expression carefully neutral.

"I am Henri Gruel, Marquise," I said, mustering my courage and standing just as straight as I could manage. "I am the son of Bathelemy-Jacques Gruel of Nogent-le-Rotrou."

"Who?" For a moment the old woman's caustic demeanor became agitated, perhaps even confused. "I don't know that name. Is he titled?"

With reluctance I said: "No, milady, he is not. He is a merchant of some wealth and..."

"A *merchant!*" she cried, throwing up her bejeweled hands. "First foreigners and now tradesmen' sons! Is this what has become of courtly tradition? Out with you...you...vagabond! Out, I say! What are we to have next? *Englishmen?*"

A voice said: "Surely one Englishman would not prove too distasteful, Marquise."

It was a voice that I knew, and the very sound of it sent a great shiver along my spine. I turned about with the others as two men approached. One was of medium build and dressed in green finery. The other was stout, wigged, and wrapped in gilded linen. The first man was a stranger to me, but I could see from his manner and bearing that he was a figure of note. His companion, however, I recognized at once, and that recognition carried with it a shock of unease that filled me from shoes to scalp.

"Monsieur Leray de Chaumont," the marquise said dryly. Then, she turned and fixed her failing eyes upon the other man. For a moment, she frowned in confusion, and then a most remarkable thing transpired. The old woman's demeanor abruptly changed. Her face brightened, and a genuine smile placed itself upon her lips. "Lord Stormont!" she declared, clasping her hands together before her bosom. "'Tis you! How marvelous it is to see you again, Milord!"

The man in green stepped forward, bowed low and then took the marquise's hand and kissed it gently. "My dear Marquise," the Englishman said in flawless French. "How lovely you look this evening. Would that I were a bachelor, milady."

The caustic aristocrat actually giggled.

"Oh, Milord," she crooned. "Forgive my earlier statement. Such Englishmen as yourself are always welcome in my company. But rescue me, I beg you. Lead me away from these peasants who disgrace our king's palace with their gauche, New World manners!"

Stormont regarded the commissioners, paying no attention whatsoever to me. The smile upon his face seemed genuine enough, but it never even approached his small, gray, unblinking eyes. These fixed themselves upon Dr. Franklin with a predatory intensity—so full of fierce disdain that I felt obliged to step protectively closer to the old doctor.

"Rescue you, milady?" Stormont said to the marquise, this time in English, never taking his eyes from Franklin. "You say more than you think, Marquise. Before you, stands the most dangerous man in Europe."

"Indeed?" Franklin replied, raising his eyebrows. "Lord Stormont, I must confess to have heard the very thing said of you on more than one occasion."

Stormont laughed, a cold and bitter thing. "Would that were so, doctor," he said. "Sadly, the facts do not bear you out. You see...if I were indeed so dangerous as that, I doubt very much if you would have dared come to France at all."

"Lord Stormont..." Deane began, but Franklin interceded.

"I am a very old man, sir," Franklin replied flatly. "I have little life left to lose, and so am less easily frightened than a younger fellow might be."

Another heavy silence closed around our gradually increasing circle. It was finally broken by Chaumont, who came suddenly forward and placed a heavy hand upon my shoulder. "Master Henri!" he exclaimed. "How delightful it is to see you, and in such a setting! How your social standing must have improved since our last encounter!"

I stared up at him, reading something in his eyes that I could not identify. "I've fallen into fortunate company," I said, feeling my throat grow suddenly dry.

"So I see! Dr. Franklin, your reputation precedes you, sir!" Chaumont said, bowing to the American doctor.

"Does it?" Franklin replied, returning the bow. "And after all my brave efforts to stay ahead of it."

Chaumont laughed. Stormont did not.

"What intrigue is this?" the Marquise de Deffand asked with interest in her strange eyes. "Dr. Franklin...frightened?"

"Dr. Franklin speaks unwisely," Stormont replied dryly.

"Come, come, Milord," Franklin replied. "What purpose is there in being so inscrutable? Milady, there was...an unfortunate incident on the road to Paris. A highwayman."

"Indeed?" the old lady pressed, looking upon Franklin with renewed curiosity. Still, I could see that her interest was in no way kind. "A frightening experience, certainly...but what is the connection to Lord Stormont? Why do you address him as you do?"

Both Stormont and Dr. Franklin looked about to answer. Neither man was given the opportunity, for yet another voice joined in loudly: "Because the blackheart was behind it, Marquise!"

I saw Franklin close his eyes and sigh mightily as Monsieur Beaumarchais joined us, followed closely by the Comte de Vergennes, who trailed the playwright with urgent intent. Beaumarchais had evidently avoided the receiving line, preferring instead to find himself a wine butler, as Dr. Bancroft had suggested. Though by no means inebriated, I could see from the flush in his cheeks that the spirits had already taken some toll.

Vergennes looked from Franklin to Stormont and back again, wringing his hands. In the meantime, Beaumarchais' voice had carried a bit in the crowded gallery. A small collection of scandal-seekers had formed around us.

The Franklin Affair

"Monsieur," Vergennes said to Beaumarchais, as the two men joined our widening circle. "Surely you jest! A distinguished man such as the ambassador would never involve himself in..."

"The devil he wouldn't!" Beaumarchais replied loudly. He turned upon Stormont, whom he outmatched in height by nearly half-a-foot. "Admit it, Englishman! You arranged for our driver to lead us into an ambush on the road outside of Le Mans!"

Beaumarchais' eyes were afire, and his manner filled with accusation and menace. Yet Lord Stormont seemed to regard him as one might regard the bark of a toothless dog. "I admit nothing of the kind. comte, please do something to control this clown. He is making a scene!"

"Clown!" Beaumarchais declared. "How *dare* you, sir!"

"Pierre," Franklin said quietly. "Calm yourself."

"Such accusations are dangerous to make, Monsieur," said Chaumont. "Lest one have proof of them."

"Scandalous ravings," the marquise remarked. She glared at Beaumarchais as though he were something she had spotted scuttling out from beneath a chamber pot. "Monsieur, your rants are as spurious as the plots of the so-called plays that you write."

Beaumarchais turned toward the old woman, a sharp reply readily upon his tongue. Before he could utter it, however, Franklin abruptly stepped forward and placed a hand upon his arm. "That will do, Pierre. There is no quarter to be gained by such a display."

"Indeed," said Vergennes eagerly. "And, as it happens, I see that a new cask of wine is being opened. Come, let me escort you..."

"Tell me, Gravier," Stormont said abruptly. All eyes turned toward him. He smiled. "Have you met Dr. Franklin?"

Even Beaumarchais seemed upset by the question. Vergennes looked up, his expression carefully blank.

So, I recall thinking, that's how to do that face!

"Briefly, Ambassador," Vergennes replied. "While he was being received by His Majesty."

"Not before?" Stormont asked. "Not yesterday morning?"

"Yesterday morning?" Franklin asked, the picture of innocence.

Stormont nodded sagely. "I have it on good authority that Dr. Franklin and his young translator paid you a call at your office...early, around nine...before your clerks had come in."

"Quite impossible, sir," Vergennes said. "I was not in my office until well past ten o'clock. Perhaps my secretary made some sort of error. Conrad is quite dependable, but no one is perfect. Tell me, doctor...did you come to the ministry seeking me and go away empty handed."

"No," Franklin said with a small smile. "I did not."

"Then my information must be flawed," Stormont said, though it was obvious to everyone that he did not believe it. "My apologies."

"There is nothing to apologize for, sir," Vergennes said graciously. "Come, Pierre. Let us see if we can find someone to refill your goblet. Dr. Franklin, can I convince you to join us?"

"Milord flatters me," Franklin replied formally. "I would be honored to share a drink with you. However, at present, Lord Stormont and I are discussing certain matters of relevance to us both. May I humbly suggest that we rendezvous later this evening?"

Vergennes appeared quite unhappy with this, but staying to witness what transpired meant allowing Beaumarchais to do the same—a prospect that appealed to him even less. "As you wish, doctor," he said. He offered the members of our circle a single, curt bow. "Messieurs. Madames."

Then he and a reluctant Beaumarchais departed, leaving myself, Stormont, Chaumont, the Marquise and the Americans together once more, with a growing audience of curious gossipmongers looking on.

"Lord Stormont," Franklin said. "May I apologize for my friend's behavior? Pierre tends to over-indulge, and often forgets himself at such times."

"I am aware of Monsieur Beaumarchais' shortcomings, doctor," Stormont said dryly. "Then you agree that there is no truth in his outrageous accusation?"

"There is no *proof* in it, sir," Franklin replied. "*Truth is for God, alone.*"

Brancroft smiled a little at that. Deane merely looked uncomfortable.

"Quite so," said Chaumont. "For myself, I must say that it is an honor to finally meet you, Dr. Franklin. My wife speaks highly of you."

At this, Franklin smiled. "A lovely woman, and wed to a fortunate man, Monsieur. Tell me, is the fair Thérèse about?"

"She is," Chaumont said. "Away with her friends, no doubt. Madame Leray de Chaumont is conspicuous at court."

This was a shocking revelation, given that, to me, Thérèse had always held a servant's role. I had never seen her when she was not at work at my family's country home. I reminded myself that, despite her humble beginnings, she had married a man of wealth and influence. By that reckoning, why should she not be well known is such affluent circles? How also, must she be treated by the likes of the Marquise, who clearly despised everyone not born to noble parentage? It occurred to me that Thérèse must possess strength of character with which I had never before credited her.

I recalled, suddenly, the day of our departure from La Barbarie, and my inspiration regarding the caretaker's daughter. Upon this point, I turned to Chaumont, who met me with a look of thoughtful interest. "Tell me, Monsieur," I said boldly. "Is Madame Chaumont's command of English as strong as your own?"

Chaumont's face darkened for a moment. Then he offered me a stiff smile. "Young master," he said. "Whatever would make you ask such a thing? My wife has no head for languages."

He was lying. I saw that immediately, and what was even more striking was that he seemed fully aware that everyone in our circle recognized his lie. *So this is poli-*

tics, I thought. *Deception upon deception, wherein it matters not if a lie is believed, only that it cannot be safely gainsaid.* It was a lesson that I would do well to remember.

"Poor Pierre," Franklin mused. "He's going to have an ill head in the morning. I really must have a word with him about his drinking." He smiled at Stormont and the Marquise. "He has offered himself up as my bodyguard. Did you know that?"

"I had heard," Stormont said. "I recall that one from his days in Britain. Monsieur Beaumarchais tries quite hard to be clever, but simply lacks the subtlety."

"One cannot fault him his sword arm, however," Franklin said.

"Perhaps," conceded Stormont. "But his blade is no match for a pistol ball. Firearms are the new order, Dr. Franklin. The day will come when swordsmanship will be a lost and useless art."

"It may be so," said Franklin. "But I am, as I've said, an old man; I doubt very much if I shall see that day. In the meantime, it is a comfort to have a capable protector by one's side."

"He's a buffoon," the marquise remarked sharply.

"Confusing passion with stupidity, milady," Franklin told her, "is a monarch's most bitter folly. Pierre may be temperamental, but he is no buffoon."

The Marquise scowled at the old man, as if affronted by the very notion of being contradicted by an American "peasant". Franklin simply smiled.

"I shall confess what it is *I* would like to know," said Chaumont suddenly. All heads turned toward him. He continued in a hushed, conspiratorial tone: "I have heard it said, Dr. Franklin, that *you* are not without the very subtleties that Lord Stormont finds lacking in Monsieur Beaumarchais. My wife describes you as a man of singular intellect."

Franklin regarded Chaumont, his manner suddenly wary. "Does she? That's most kind of her, sir."

"Not at all. The rumors in Paris submit that the famous Dr. Franklin is a man of considerable proficiency and expertise, and not merely in the scientific arts."

Franklin did not reply. Beside him, I saw Deane stiffen, a warning in his eyes. Bancroft appeared suddenly apprehensive. We all looked upon Chaumont, who smiled at the rapt attention he now commanded.

"I'm afraid you have the best of me, sir," Franklin said. "I don't know what it is you mean."

Stormont was regarding his companion with curious interest.

"What I mean is simply this, Dr. Franklin," Chaumont replied. "That you have come to Paris to do more than simply take in the sights and enjoy the local wines."

Franklin chuckled, but I could hear little humor in it. "Quite so. I should think this no great secret. I have come on behalf of my country..." Stormont frowned, but didn't object. "...to negotiate with the French government for a treaty of amity and commerce."

"Commerce!" the marquise said sharply, as though the word were a curse.

"America has much to offer France," Deane said.

"Not as much as the reverse, I think," said Stormont quietly.

"No more than this?" Chaumont remarked with feigned disappointment. "Just simple trade and innocent friendship?"

"Nothing more," said Franklin, and once again I could read the rare character of a lie that is never meant to be believed.

"Yet you have taken pains to conceal the identities of some of your French acquaintances," Chaumont pressed. "Is that not so? Who knew beforehand that you have enjoyed a friendship with our temperamental Monsieur Beaumarchais, for example?"

"My associations are my own," Franklin said. "I neither promote nor hide them."

"Yet," continued Chaumont, "I have heard tell that you have a 'special friend' in France...in Paris, to be precise."

At this, Franklin uttered a genuine laugh. "I assure

you, Monsieur, that I have not enjoyed the attentions of a 'special friend', since the death of my dear wife some years ago."

"No. No," said Chaumont, smiling and shaking his wigged head. "You misunderstand me, sir. I speak not of a romantic liaison, but rather of a *political* one. The rumors are that you have maintained, for some years now, a correspondence with a Frenchman of most singular rank and influence...that this 'special friend' has done much to prepare the way for your mission to France, and that you, in return, do much to preserve that person's...anonymity."

"What an interesting tale," Stormont remarked. Both men studied Franklin carefully. "Is there any truth to this, doctor?"

"There you go again," Franklin said, still smiling, "speaking of 'truth'. Politics and truth are two sides of the same coin, gentlemen. While examining one side, you can never see the other...but a wise man knows it's there, nonetheless."

Again, Chaumont laughed while Stormont did not. "Very amusing, Dr. Franklin," the Frenchman said. "But not, I think, an answer to his lordship's question."

Franklin looked thoughtful. "I do not recall promising his lordship an answer to his question," he said after a moment. Then, abruptly, his demeanor brightened. "But, look here! Madame Chaumont approaches!"

Chapter Seventeen

"Like a man traveling in foggy weather, those at some distance before him on the road he sees wrapped up in the fog, as well as those behind him, and also the people in fields on each side, but near him, all appears clear, though in truth he is as much in the fog as any of them."
- Benjamin Franklin.

At the sight of Madame Thérèse Leray de Chaumont advancing toward us across the shining tile floor of the Galarie des Glaces, I found myself rendered quite mute with shock.

This both was and was not the woman whom I had known since childhood. Though her face and figure remained unchanged, all else about her had undergone a most singular transformation. Gone was the simple cotton dress and gentle white bow to hold her long, ebony hair. These had been replaced by a layered gown of red linen and gold lace—with pearls at the cuffs and collar, and a magnificently styled white wig, its hair mounted high upon its wearer's head in a most cosmopolitan fashion.

So lovely was this creature that, as she moved amongst the other revelers, they turned to regard her with appreciative or envious eyes. Many called to her, and she smiled in return, but never did she slow her pace toward us, nor take eyes from the man fortunate enough to call himself her husband.

"My dear, I have found you at last," she said in French. Her speech and manner were as much of a surprise to me as was her dress. This was no washwoman. This was a lady of means and breeding, in every respect the model of French nobility, though her husband, for all his wealth and influence, was not of noble birth. Nevertheless, his success had earned him the right to mingle with the cream of French aristocracy and, as such, he required a wife capable of conducting herself appropriately within that demanding and unforgiving realm. Thérèse was obviously more than a match for this challenge.

"Madame," Chaumont said, and his expression caused me to regard him with a less critical eye. No man could gaze upon his wife with such obvious devotion and be otherwise truly wicked. "Would that you had not left my side at all. Come and stand with me. We have here a gentlemen with whom you are acquainted."

"Indeed!" she said, smiling graciously at the enraptured men around her. Only the bitter Marquise de Deffand seemed less than captivated. I began to understand that she looked upon everyone assembled around her as, at best, well beneath her and, at worst, well beneath contempt. She stayed with our circle only because the British Ambassador remained—Lord Stormont who, like she, had been born an aristocrat.

"Dr. Franklin," said Thérèse. "How wonderful to see you again. I'm so glad to have the opportunity to renew our acquaintance."

Dr. Franklin bore all the appearances of a man bewitched. Without waiting for me to translate, he stepped forward, took the lady's offered hand in his own, and bowed. "Madame Chaumont," he said, his voice laced with unfettered admiration. "You have amazed me beyond words!"

After I had obediently turned his words to French, Madame Chaumont smiled upon the old man with what looked to be genuine affection. I found myself quite unable to believe that *this* exquisite creature could be the same woman who had made my breakfast on the day of our departure from La Barbarie!

There comes a time in the life of every young man, when the world as he knows it is cast suddenly upon its ear—when all of his former convictions regarding society and its members are irrevocably shaken. It is at this moment that he both comprehends and regrets the flawed and narrow perspective that has dogged him all his life, and he finds himself open to new possibilities. I believe this to be a most singular milestone upon the road to adulthood, and that no boy can truly become a man until this epiphany—both wonderful and terrible—is realized.

If Thérèse could be so different from she whom I had always known, then how well could I trust my other conceptions. I suddenly recalled the strange events of the night before, and found myself gazing upon Franklin, another person I thought I knew. What secret side did this kind, brilliant old gentleman keep concealed?

Then there was a fair, pale face before me, smiling with kindness and recognition, and all such musings were banished from my mind, cast aside like demons before the holy symbol that is a woman's beauty.

"Master Henri," Thérèse said, offering me her hand. "How well you look!"

I took the hand, the gesture feeling strange to me. "Madame Chaumont," I said, my voice hoarse. "How...lovely...uh..."

"Madame Chaumont, is it?" she asked, feigning offense. "Well, I like that! Sir, you shall address me as you always have. It that understood?"

"I shall try...Thérèse, though it is difficult," I replied, trying my best to smile and behave charmingly. "In return, you must agree to remove 'Master' from the forefront of my name. I shall be merely 'Henri'."

She laughed. "Indeed? I shall need time to grow accustomed to that change. Shall I do so henceforth, or only for tonight?"

"You should do so," I said, "for however long you

wear that wig!"

Those around us who understood French laughed appreciatively, all but the Marquise de Deffand, whom I supposed refused to smile for fear that her cheeks might crack. The rest, including Dr. Franklin, read enough of what had transpired in the flush of my cheeks, and readily lent their own laughter to that of the rest.

"I take it, madame," the old woman said stonily, "that you and Dr. Franklin are acquainted."

It was Chaumont who answered: "My wife played hostess to the good doctor during his stay in Nantes." This wasn't strictly true but, for Thérèse's sake, I did not object.

"It was Henri who played host," the splendid woman explained, smiling at her husband's chagrin. "I merely...assisted...as required."

"I take it, therefore, madame," Lord Stormont said, "that Dr. Franklin acquainted you with the particulars of his purpose here in France?"

"I am not politically minded," Thérèse replied gently.

As this exchange continued, I came to stand beside Dr. Franklin, hastily translating for him, struggling to keep up with what was being said.

"Politics is the affair of men," Chaumont added.

"I wonder if Catherine of Russia would agree with you, Monsieur," Franklin remarked wryly after I had turned this last statement to French.

Thérèse laughed prettily. Chaumont frowned, but did not respond.

"And you, young fellow," Lord Stormont said, speaking, for the first time, directly to me. This time, he employed his native tongue. "You are obviously quite attached to Dr. Franklin. Does he ever discuss his politics with you?"

"Frequently," I said.

"And what is your opinion of the rebel uprising in the British Colonies?" Stormont asked. To my right, I saw Deane stiffen, and Bancroft's face turn to a worried frown.

"United States of America," I corrected quietly.

"What was that, young Monsieur?" Stormont asked, his brow furrowing. "What did you say?"

I looked directly upon Franklin, who met my eyes with gratitude and—something else—pride?

"United States of America," I said, more loudly this time.

"Bah!" Chaumont said, turning away. The Marquise de Deffand scowled but offered no rebuke.

Stormont's face reddened. "How easily you say those words, boy. You speak as if saying them made them so. Is my king to so readily abandon his own property on the say so of traitors and rebels?"

"His own property, sir?" Franklin asked. "How so?"

Stormont turned on him. "By divine right, sir!" he declared. "George III is sovereign of all the British lands in the New World! You and your...fellows..." he nodded dismissively at Bancroft and Deane. "have no business standing against that sovereignty! To do so is worse than treason. It's blasphemy!"

"Well said!" added the marquise.

The force of the ambassador's voice had drawn the attention of still more scandal-seekers. They closed about us now like vultures around a dying animal. "Your lordship," Franklin said, his voice gentle but his tone quite firm. "George III rules, by divine right, over all British lands. However, I submit to you that the souls who inhabit the thirteen states are no longer British, and have not been so for quite some time."

"Why, doctor?" Stormont demanded. "Simply by virtue of their say-so?"

"No, sir," Franklin replied. "By virtue of the rights which have been denied them...rights that, by law, every *Briton* enjoys."

"Rights?" Stormont asked, smiling bitterly. "Yes, it has been necessary to curtail certain privileges for the sake of maintaining the peace. But in these times of strife..."

"He who gives up some of his liberty in order to obtain a little temporary safety, deserves neither liberty nor safety," Franklin said.

"That's a good one," Deane remarked.

"Thank you, Silas. I rather like it, myself."

"So, tell me, Dr. Franklin," Stormont said. "All of your clever axioms aside. If the Townsend Act were repealed...if free trade were restored and trial by jury reinstituted, would your fellow colonials miraculously transform themselves back into Britons once more?"

"No, sir," Franklin said. "It matters not what concessions Britain makes. It matters not what restitutions you may offer. We are no longer a part of Britain. We are no longer subject to its laws. We are a new race, your lordship. We have our own, highly unique identity. We are pioneers and backwoodsmen. We lack your education and refinement, whilst being more adventurous and more prone to violence. We must have the freedom...the *autonomy*...to explore this identity and to see where it will take us. We will fight to secure that freedom, sir. We will fight to the death, if necessary!"

Around us, dozens of French men and women raised their hands in applause. Lord Stormont glowered at them, and then focused his attention once more upon Franklin, who stood, smiling gently, in the midst of this vortex of attention and admiration.

"Look to Kips Bay, doctor," Stormont said, just loudly enough to be heard by those closest to him. "It may well be necessary for you to do just that. *All* of you."

Then, with the marquise upon his arm, he turned and shouldered his way through the rows of applauding onlookers.

"Well now," Franklin said with a sigh, as the jubilation around us gradually subsided. "I did not think that the sour fellow would ever leave! And you, Monsieur Chaumont, are you not going to follow after him?"

"You and I share few common opinions, Dr. Franklin," Chaumont replied in a most serious tone. "Yet I would not wish harm upon you. For your own sake, please mark well his lordship's words." He turned to his wife and offered his hand. "Madame? May I escort you onto the dance floor?" he said in French.

Thérèse, whose manner had stiffened somewhat, now smiled anew. "Thank you, my husband...but I would prefer to stay and share a dance with this noble gentleman." She nodded toward Franklin.

Chaumont looked from one to the other of them, his expression one of consternation. "Indeed, madame? Well then, if you wish to share music with this...colonial...I shall not forbid it." Then, in English: "Dr. Franklin, would you be so kind as to escort my wife out upon the dance floor?"

Franklin stepped immediately forward, meeting Chaumont's somewhat disgruntled gaze with a look of innocent humor. "Monsieur, I would be honored by such an opportunity. I ask only that madame be patient with an old man, whose feet often betray him."

Chaumont reluctantly translated.

"Sir," Thérèse replied. "The honor is mine."

With that, they departed, Franklin and Madame Chaumont. Every head turned to follow them, as though drawn by a common string.

It was not until they had taken themselves upon the dance floor, moving to the flutes and violins that issued forth from the orchestra, that I realized—with some horror—my new position. Deane and Bancroft were gone, I knew not where. The scandal-seekers around us had dispersed, no doubt to seek greener fields upon which to graze. I stood alone now, save for Monsieur Chaumont, who had placed himself directly beside me.

"So, Henri," he said softly. "You handled yourself quite well, if I may say so."

My chest suddenly felt tight. "Monsieur is too kind," I replied, trying to dispel the nervousness from my voice.

"Not at all. Obviously, Dr. Franklin holds you in high regard. This is most well...most well...considering your mission for the king." He looked down upon me, fixing me with his eyes. "I trust you have not *forgotten* that obligation, young master."

"I have not," I said.

"I spoke today with Father Hilliard," Chaumont said. "He is quite beside himself. Apparently, he had instructed you to meet with him, yet you chose to disregard that instruction."

"There were reasons," I said, thinking once again of the previous night and its strange happenings.

"Whatever the reasons, such a lapse is unwise," warned Chaumont. "Hilliard is a committed man. Such men can be...dangerous...if taken lightly."

"Circumstances prevented my keeping our rendezvous," I said. "I meant no offense to the father...if he *is* a priest."

Chaumont regarded me with suspicion. "Do you have concerns that you would care to share with me, Henri?"

Mustering my courage, I said: "I do. You, yourself, heard of the attack upon Dr. Franklin, Monsieur Beaumarchais and myself while on the road between Le Mans and Paris?"

Chaumont's face lost all expression. "Most unsettling, that," he said quietly.

"Dr. Franklin is of the belief that the robbery attempt was, in fact, a thinly-veiled attempt on his life."

"He is a dramatist," Chaumont said dismissively. "So is Beaumarchais. One cannot take some men too seriously."

"Dr. Franklin made a convincing argument at the time," I continued. "And with the vague threat that Lord Stormont has just made against him..."

"You have a point, young master?" Chaumont asked coldly.

"I do, and it is this..." I fixed my eyes hard upon him, endeavoring to convey earnest intent. "When first I was brought into this business, it was with the firm assurance that no harm would come to Dr. Franklin. Is that not so, Monsieur?"

"It is," Chaumont said. "And, as you can see, Dr. Franklin remains unharmed as he continues to dance with my wife."

"Still, his life *was* in jeopardy," I persisted.

"There is nothing to be gained by pursuing this," insisted Chaumont. "The American doctor is unharmed and will remain so, if I am to have any say in the matter. To that, I swear upon the life of my beloved Thérèse."

This seemed a sincere pledge, and I was not unmoved by it. Still, I forced myself to remain firm in my purpose to confront this man and to obtain from him the answers I required. "Then my next concern is this, Monsieur," I said. "You and Father Hilliard assured me at the beginning that my recruitment into your service came by the king's order?"

"Through his foreign minister, the Comte de Vergennes," Chaumont replied with a nod.

"I should like to see that order," I said.

He laughed. "Such things are never committed to paper, Henri," he said, his manner that of a schoolmaster addressing an addled pupil. "The word was given to Vergennes, and Vergennes then passed it to me."

"I see," I said, and my father's warning to me of Chaumont's possible duplicity suddenly filled my memory. "Then, on yet another subject, I must observe that you and Lord Stormont appear to get along quite well."

"Yes. That bonhomie required quite some time to cultivate." Chaumont's tone was even, but his face betrayed a certain annoyance. He clearly perceived the direction of my inquiries.

"A more suspicious man than I might draw some...disquieting inferences...from the closeness of your association with the British ambassador."

"A *man* might," Chaumont replied icily. "But then, you are not a *man*, are you, Henri? You're a boy, and a loyal French subject. I came to you at your father's home in Nantes as a representative to the king. How dare you question that?"

Such force of personality! I was nearly cowed. I must admit that. I nearly bowed my head in subjugation and offered an apology. But then, for some unfathomable reason, Dr. Franklin's Declaration filled my memory. One line, in particular, made its way into the forefront of my thoughts.

All men are created equal.

"Sir," I said, meeting Chaumont's offended gaze. "You seem surprised by my concerns. You shouldn't be, given that you have already lied to me once tonight."

"Now see here, boy..."

"You assured me that your wife, Madame Chaumont, does not speak English...indeed, that she possesses no 'head for languages'."

"As indeed she does not!" Chaumont replied sharply.

"Yet," I said, "only minutes ago, when Dr. Franklin uttered his quip regarding the Empress of Russia, I do believe I heard Thérèse laugh. Now, how might she do that, sir, if she had not understood what was said?"

Chaumont's mouth fell open slightly. He made as though to reply, but I denied him the opportunity. "Monsieur, I regret that I can no longer serve you or Father Hilliard without written proof of the source of your purpose."

"Damn you, boy!" Chaumont exclaimed. Then, glancing uncomfortably at the people around us, he continued in a harsh whisper. "This matter has gone too far for you to suddenly question me now! Would you have me reveal your duplicity to Dr. Franklin, whom you seem to hold in such high regard? Do you believe he would forgive you? Or would he cast you from his presence as a spy and a deceiver?"

This thought had not occurred to me, and it filled me with dread. I could not bear it if Franklin should come to learn of my betrayal—to say nothing of Beaumarchais' threats against me, should I prove untrustworthy.

Nevertheless, I stood my ground. "Say what you will. Do what you will. But please inform Father Hilliard that I shall no longer heed his demands."

The Franklin Affair

I expected Chaumont's rage to boil over like an unwatched pot of porridge. Strangely, this did not happen. Instead, he regarded me with a reappraising smile. "You are more than I took you for, Monsieur Gruel," he said quietly. "I will trouble you no longer."

Then, he abruptly left me to stand alone in the midst of the great crowd of people. I felt both fearful and elated—part knight-errant and part court jester—and more like a man than I had ever believed I could.

"What were you and that pompous fool discussing in so conspiratorial a fashion?" a voice demanded.

My heart leapt into my throat. I turned and found myself met by Beaumarchais. He was alone now. Apparently, the Comte de Vergennes had abandoned the fiery playwright to his own fate. There was a goblet in Beaumarchais' hand, and he smelled of rum. He looked upon me with dark distrust—the same manner in which he had regarded me at the beginning of our association. Apparently, my vindication with the highwayman had been forgotten, at least for the moment.

"I asked you a question," he said darkly.

"We were...discussing...Dr. Franklin," I stammered.

He uttered a half-drunken laugh. "I don't doubt it. But to what end? Chaumont has always made his opinions concerning Americans quite clear. I cannot believe the two of you were conspiring to treat the old man to a Christmas present."

"I..." But my words failed me. Evidently, whatever remained of my nightsworth of manly bravado had followed Monsieur Chaumont across the gallery. I looked up at Beaumarchais. He stared back at me, his eyes blurred by strong drink, but also hardened with suspicion.

"What's that?" he demanded crossly. "What were you going to say?"

"Nothing," I replied.

"Nothing! Nothing! What were you going to say?"

I lowered my eyes. "Pierre," I asked quietly. "Are you and I...*friends*?"

The query seemed to confound him for a moment. "What? Well...yes. Damn it, yes, I suppose we are."

"Then why do you find it so hard to trust me?"

He seemed to struggle with this for several moments. Then he sighed loudly, as if in surrender, and took yet another long draught of rum. "Oh, Henri, I do apologize. The fact is that I'm never quite sure *whom* to trust. I am continually surrounded by men who seem to make an art out of saying one thing and meaning another. I spent years trying to win my acceptance within this social circle, and now that I am here, I find it sometimes...straining."

"Surely you trust *Ben*," I said.

"I do," Beaumarchais replied with conviction. "He is the best and most virtuous man I have ever known." Then, with some trepidation: "Yet I fear there may be things that even *he* keeps from me. Not that I can truly blame him. My tongue loosens when I drink, and I drink too much." Another draught passed his lips. "I will tell you something, Henri. I have done no small share of acting in my life. I thought that my thespian experiences would prepare me for the theatre of politics. But the longer I play upon this stage, I feel ever less the hero and more the fool. Can you understand that?"

"Well enough," I said with a laugh. "Since taking you two as companions, I sometimes doubt whether I understand even half of what transpires around me!"

"Well said, Henri," Beaumarchais replied, slapping my back "Very well said. And look, here is our Dr. Franklin now, and with such a *creature* upon his arm!"

"Henri! Pierre!" The old man sounded winded, and his face shone red. Yet his spirits were high, and light danced in his blue eyes. Beside him, her gloved hand upon his arm, Thérèse smiled at the two of us. To Beaumarchais, she said in French: "Monsieur, how good it is to see you again. You are well, I trust?"

Beaumarchais' practiced bow was only slightly hampered by his inebriation. "Madame," he said, without a trace of slur. "I do not believe I have made your acquaintance."

Franklin, despite the barrier of language, seemed to discern Beaumarchais' confusion. He laughed heartily and said in English: "Never fear, my good fellow. I should not have recognized the lady any better than you have. Therefore, may I then present Madame Thérèse Leray de Chaumont?"

"Madame Chau..." the words faded from Beaumarchais' lips. "This is...I cannot..." To the lady, he said in French: "Forgive me, madame. I...that is...you..."

"Charming as always," Thérèse remarked with a smile. "Gentlemen, I am afraid that I must take my leave of you. My husband beckons me."

I translated for Franklin. "Madame," he said. "I thank you for the dance and for the opportunity to sample your company once more. I look forward most eagerly to our next meeting."

Again I translated. For the first time, I was finding this duty somewhat tiresome, owing to my firm conviction that Chaumont's wife understood every word spoken.

"I hope it will be soon," she replied, smiling graciously. "Henri. Monsieur Beaumarchais. Good night and a Happy Christmas to you both."

She left us then. The three of us watched her depart, moving like a swan across a summer's pond, leaving ripples of admiration and attention as her wake. "A splendid lady," Franklin said, more to himself than to either of us. "Really quite miraculous."

"I cannot agree more," I said.

"Ben," Beaumarchais remarked, a bit uncertainly. "Would you please tell me again who that lady was?"

We both laughed as Franklin faced his friend and protector. "Never mind, Pierre. Tomorrow is Christmas and, unless I have misjudged your condition, you shall likely be spending it in a darkened room with a damp cloth upon your forehead and a tonic in your hand. Henri, would you please be kind enough to call for our coach?"

"Our coach?" I asked with some surprise. "Are we leaving, then?"

"Not I," he said gently. "But I would ask that you escort our friend here back to our rooms. Once you are there, ask Madame Devereux to send the driver back for Silas, Edward and myself."

I found the suggestion disheartening. Franklin seemed to recognize this, for he came forward suddenly and placed a grandfatherly hand upon my shoulder. "Do not mistake me, Henri," he explained in earnest. "I find your language skills, to say nothing of your companionship, of increasing importance to me. However, I believe my public role at this affair has been satisfied. It has been communicated to me...by means I do not wish to explain...that the Comte de Vergennes wishes to meet with me in one of the private chambers that are adjacent to this fine gallery. As the foreign minister's command of English is strong, I believe that Pierre's need for an escort outweighs my need for a translator, at least in this instance. Can you appreciate that, my boy?"

"Yes, I can," I said.

He smiled brightly. "Excellent. You're a splendid fellow. Return to the hotel and send back the carriage. Goodnight and a Happy Christmas to you both. Oh...and Henri? Don't wait for me before retiring. The comte and I are, I believe, ready to speak more plainly of matters that warrant considerable discussion. I expect to be quite late."

Chapter Eighteen

"I wish it (Christianity) were more productive of good works...I mean real good works...not holy-day keeping, sermon-hearing...or making long prayers, filled with flatteries and compliments despised by wise men, and much less capable of pleasing the Deity." - Benjamin Franklin

Christmas morning brought with it a winter's snowfall that filled the windows and blanketed the streets of Paris. By the time I awakened, dressed and emerged from my room, one of Madame Devereux's valets had already set out a fine holiday breakfast, which Dr. Franklin had done his best to decimate with his usual passion. Beaumarchais was, as anticipated, exiled to his bedchamber, meeting the price of his Yuletide's overindulgence.

"Ah! There you are my boy. Come join me," Franklin said. He seemed possessed of quite a garrulous demeanor.

"What time did the three of you finally get in?" I asked him, stifling a yawn.

"Oh rather late I'm afraid. After midnight. Imagine, I rang in Christmas with Silas and Edward and the Comte deVergennes." He seemed to find this quite amusing.

I crossed the room and settled myself down at the table. "I suffered a terrible dream last night," I muttered.

"Did you? Tell me all about it. I rather enjoy my

dreams most of the time."

"I dreamt that I was running, quite panicked, through the streets of Paris...and that in pursuit of me was a most hideous Cerberus. Only, in my case, the creature had *three* heads."

Franklin remarked through a mouthful of food: "Cerberus *had* three heads, hadn't he?"

"Did he?" I asked. "Well, in this case one of the heads was Stormont's, except that his teeth were fangs and his tongue was forked...like a viper's."

"Who would notice?" Franklin mused, chuckling.

"The second head belonged to the Marquise de Deffand," I continued. "She seemed unchanged."

"Awful enough as she is, I suppose," Franklin suggested. "What of the third head...whose was that?"

"Monsieur Chaumont's," I replied, shuddering as I recalled the vision. "And his head was perhaps the least agreeable of all. He had *two* faces. The one seemed normal enough, but the other...oh, the *other*, Ben! It was a twisted and misshapen affair, his eye out of place and his hair like jagged spikes. Most terrible!"

"I can imagine," Franklin said, more thoughtfully this time. "Tell me, my poor boy, did this nightmare creature overtake you?"

"No," I said earnestly. "You came and held it at bay with your Crabtree stick."

A gentle smile spread across his features. "Did I? How courageous of me. But enough of this unpleasant imagery. Tell me, did Pierre give you any trouble last night?"

"None," I said, reaching over and serving myself a slice of ham. "He fell asleep in the carriage. When we reached the hotel, I summoned a pair of valets to assist him up the stairs. They were most accommodating. They even readied him for bed."

"Yes, Madame Devereux manages this fine establishment with an artist's hand. In any case, I think that we shall see little of Pierre this morning," Franklin said. "Before you awoke, I visited his bedchamber and found him ill in both head and temper. He is in there claiming that even the fall of the snowflakes is more than his tender ears may bear." He chuckled. "Never fear, however. The fair Madame Devereux is seeing to his every need. Already three valets have come in answer to his bell rope, one with a tonic, one with an extra pillow and the last with a basin of cool water and a cloth for his head."

"He indulges himself a bit too much," I remarked.

"That he does."

"Does he often behave at social functions at he did last night at the palace?" I inquired. "I should think him rather a burden in such circumstances."

"No, in most such settings Pierre makes of himself the very model of charm and aplomb. Last night's behavior was born out of his concern for me and his dislike of Ambassador Stormont. Our friend pretends at being politically astute. However, I fear he lacks the subtle hand, and when he feels overwhelmed by events he tends to turn toward strong drink and quick temper by way of a defense. But now...let us leave Pierre to his own lamentations. There are matters that you and I must discuss."

"Such as how we are to spend our Christmas," I supposed.

He smiled. "In what manner does your own family celebrate the birth of Our Lord?"

"In church," I said. "Christmas Mass. The church in Nogent-le-Rotrou is modest. I have never visited Notre Dame." I said this with some eagerness, for the grand Paris cathedral was renowned throughout France.

Franklin frowned with distaste. "I'm afraid that Catholic ritual holds little appeal for me."

"Then what *are* your plans, Ben?" I asked, not without some disappointment.

"I expect to spend my time here, counting snowflakes and, more productively, reviewing with Silas and Edward the business of our proposed treaty with your king." Franklin replied. "However, if you wish to pursue your own spiritual well-being, I shall certainly not gainsay you."

"Yes? Thank you!" I replied, my exuberance returning. "I shall have to discover the times for Mass. I doubt that I shall hear the bells from this far off."

"No doubt such times are posted. We shall ask Madame Devereux." Franklin touched a linen napkin to his mouth. "However, this is not what I wished to discuss."

There was a sudden seriousness to his bearing, which inspired within me a certain unease. "Ben, is something wrong?"

"No," he said. "Not 'wrong'. Merely unfortunate. But...first things first." He rose from the table and bade me stay while he retrieved something from his bedchamber. He returned within moments and placed before me a small, white box, upon which he had tied a simple bow. I looked down at the package, and then up at the old man. "It's a present for you," he said with a small, slightly sad smile. "Don't look so surprised. It's not much, simply a small token of my esteem."

"Ben," I said, taking up the parcel. "This is...truly generous! I...I have nothing for you!"

"You have much for me, Henri," Franklin said sincerely. "If you do not know that, then you should. Go on. Open it."

I did so, lifting the lid as gently as if its contents were of the most fragile crystal. Within lay a quizzing glass, an accessory commonly worn by aristocrats and men of note and means. It consisted of a single, oval ground lens, which magnified anything viewed beneath it. The glass was smooth and clear, obviously of the highest quality. This was framed within a circlet of gleaming gold and fastened to one end of a silver chain, some ten inches long.

"I have never seen such a thing as this," I said with genuine appreciation. "I thank you, Ben...most deeply."

"You are as deeply welcome, Henri," he said. "Yet now I'm afraid that I must dampen your spirits." He took his chair once more and faced me from across the table, his manner most grave.

The Franklin Affair

Slowly, expectantly, I regarded him.

"Henri," he said, gently. "I am sorry to say that the time has come for you to go home."

"Home?" I asked, more perplexed than shocked. "I don't understand."

"It is my wish for you to leave Paris and return to your father's estates at Nogent-le-Rotrou."

"When?"

"I would prefer it if you could leave today. But, as it is Christmas, I shall settle for first thing tomorrow morning."

This pronouncement, unexpected as it was, left me in a most unsettled state, still clutching the gifted quizzing glass. Franklin looked upon me with deep regret. The sight of him made me feel suddenly strangely empty. "Why must I leave?" I asked in a small voice—a child's voice.

"The reasons are..." Franklin swallowed, as though he were tasting something sour. "...not for you to know at the present time."

"Ben!" I declared, rising to my feet. "You cannot *do* this!"

From behind the closed door to Beaumarchais' bedchamber, a voice wailed: "For the love of He whose birthday we all celebrate, do be quiet!" Then, overwhelmed by his own volume, the suffering playwright wailed piteously.

"Poor fellow. Most other men would know better than to raise their voice while in such a condition. But, here now, sit back down, my boy," Franklin beseeched. "We must part, but I do not wish us to do so in anger."

I stood my ground. "Have I offended you, sir?"

"No, Henri," he said. "You have done nothing to offend me. Quite the opposite. I have found you an excellent friend and companion in all circumstances."

"Then why must you send me away?" I pleaded.

At that moment, there came a rap upon the door. At Franklin's bidding, Monsieur Deane entered, with Dr. Bancroft close behind him. "Good morning, gentlemen,"

Deane said. "And a Happy Christmas to you both." Then he evidently read something in our faces, for his smile faltered. "Is something amiss?"

"Edward," Franklin said, his manner most circumspect. "Please consult Madame Devereux as to her knowledge regarding the scheduled times of Holy Mass to be held today at Notre Dame Cathedral."

"Certainly, Dr. Franklin," Bancroft replied.

"Planning a morning at church, Ben?" Deane asked with a hesitant smile.

"Not myself—Henri," Franklin explained. "And Edward...please inform our hostess that Henri will be leaving for home in the morning. See that his belongings are prepared accordingly."

"Leaving us?" Deane asked, turning toward me. He tried, as usual, to keep his tone light, but I could read the puzzlement and unease in his eyes. "What's this, Henri?"

"I've decided..." I stammered. "That is...Ben has decided..."

"Henri is lonely for home," Franklin interjected. "You know how such things can be, Silas...especially at this time of year. Edward, I would also ask you to accompany our young friend during his trip into the city. Ordinarily, I should ask Pierre, but I doubt that our friend is in any condition to serve as an escort."

"I need no escort," I said.

"I say that you do," Franklin replied, in a tone both gentle and commanding. "Paris is a dangerous place, even at Yuletide. I should never forgive myself if ill fortune befell you on the very eve of your return to your father."

"How is Beaumarchais?" Deane asked.

"His head suffers," Franklin replied.

"We all suffered his tongue last night," Bancroft remarked, rather bitterly.

Franklin sighed heavily. "Strong drink does little for Pierre's already dubious discretion. I'll not deny it. He and I shall have to have a talk about that in the near future. Not today, however. Today, Silas, I feel obliged that we two should sit and review certain articles and papers, which I have brought with me from America. The business with the comte last night went quite well, I thought."

"I am optimistic," Deane replied. "Though he stopped short of promising us open French support."

"Still, we did secure further monies for Pierre's venture, the Roderigue Hortalez et Cie, as well as his personal vow to further our cause as best he may," said Franklin.

"It's not enough," Bancroft remarked.

"I did not expect it would be," Franklin said. "It is a beginning, nothing more. It does, however, prepare the way for further, more public negotiations. In that spirit, gentlemen, I believe the time has come to consider the finer points of our mission."

"The articles of the proposed treaty," Deane said.

"Yes. Exactly."

"Should we not wait for Arthur Lee to arrive from England?" asked Deane.

Franklin frowned. "Our fellow commissioner will come when he comes, Silas. His presence and manner will be disruptive enough at that time. I see little reason to allow it to trouble us now. Let us set ourselves to this task, and complete as much of it as we may, before the storm blows in from London."

Deane smiled thinly. "As you say, Ben."

Franklin turned to me. "Henri, may I suggest that you change for Mass while Edward speaks with Madame Devereux on your behalf. Dress warmly, my boy, as I expect it shall be difficult to arrange for a carriage this day, and the walk to the Île de la Cité shall be a long, cold one. I would offer you my fur cap, but I fear that it has gone missing."

I looked hard upon this old man who had become so quickly my friend and mentor. How strange and ironic it was to be sent away the very morning after finally resolving to deliver unto him my undivided loyalty. "As you say, Ben," I mumbled, making for my bedchamber door. At the threshold, I turned once more toward the table where the American doctor had sat himself. He was regarding me with sadness in his blue eyes, his regret so evident that I felt compelled to address it.

"What is that I have done, Ben?" I asked—rather piteously, I'm afraid. "Why must you send me away?"

Dr. Franklin spoke not a word for several moments, while Bancroft left our rooms to seek Madame Devereux, and Deane stood near the hearth, shuffling his feet uncomfortably. "Done, Henri?" Franklin asked me finally, his tone sardonic, but without a trace of either anger or humor. "Why, you have done the inexcusable. You have made me love you."

That morning, two hours before the noonday bells, I attended Catholic Mass with both Dr. Bancroft and Madame Devereux as escorts. The snowfall had ceased, and the morning sky had cleared to a brilliant blue.

We went in the lady's personal carriage, a finely appointed affair of red velvet against dark wood. She was dressed in elegant black cashmere, with a long cloak to warm her and protect her head. Bancroft wore what he always wore, a costume of respectable fashion, but by no means exceptional with its gray coat and white hose. I, myself, was dressed simply—as the son of a wealthy, provincial family should dress—having no further interest in the finery that Franklin had purchased on my behalf in the Rue St. Germain. Paris was soon to be behind me, I thought bitterly, and I vowed to take as little of it with me as I could. It was, I admit, a churlish and pointless gesture.

The bishop spoke at length of the birthday of Our Lord. He recited the scriptures in careful Latin, and bade us repeat the words. I knew the litany, of course—so much so that I found my mind wandering from matters spiritual, and away into the vast darkness of the surrounding cathedral.

It was my first experience in Notre Dame, and the church did not disappoint. It was a great, cavernous

The Franklin Affair

place, filled with light and shadow, with huge, ornate stained glass windows to catch the winter's sun, and a floor that repelled the barest footfalls, sending them echoing along both transepts. The pews were all filled, and candles had been lit everywhere, casting upon the faces of the faithful a strange, almost deathly pallor that I found somewhat unsettling. It was like taking Mass amongst an army of corpses.

As the service concluded and we prepared to depart, Madame Devereux took me aside, leaving Bancroft to deposit coins into the poor box in the nave. "Master Henri," the lady inquired. "I have been told that you shall be leaving us in the morning."

"That's so," I said.

"What is the cause of this? I thought that you were Dr. Franklin's translator."

I looked into her lovely face. "Madame," I said. "Dr. Franklin evidently has no further use for me in that capacity."

"I have spoken to the doctor regarding you several times during these past days," she said. "And I can fairly say that his affection for you is boundless."

"Not so boundless as to compel him to give me a reason for my dismissal," I said unhappily.

"That is wrong of him," she said, her tone resolute. "He is a careful man, and careful men are often circumspect when they have no reason to be. In truth, I did not know that he had decided to send you away. But, now that I do, I can say with certainty what I believe his reason to be. It is because he fears for you."

"Fears for me?"

"Indeed. He fears the dangers inherent in his position, and he wishes to distance you from him, lest you suffer harm for his sake."

"We have been in danger before, madame," I protested. I recalled the highwayman, and then further remembered the way Ben had ordered me to remain safely in the coach. He had been so uncharacteristically commanding—almost parental. Then there was the way he had embraced me with such fevered relief once the crisis had passed.

"There is trouble coming, Master Henri," Madame Devereux said to me quietly. "Dr. Franklin, who sees more clearly than any hundred men, recognizes this as surely as he would recognize an approaching storm."

"What trouble? From Stormont?"

"I cannot say," she replied. "I am not privy to the details of Dr. Franklin's affairs. I am, however, the keeper of a hotel that is not unknown in political circles. I have learned to read certain signs, and to recognize certain patterns of behavior. Dr. Franklin's arrival in Paris has been deemed most dangerous by certain parties, and those parties are preparing, right now, to move against him. He desires to have you safely out of harm's way."

"What should I do, then?"

"You should *go*, Henri," Madame Devereux beseeched. "You should return to your home so that you shall not become a distraction to him."

"Do you think he will send for me again when the crisis has passed?"

"I cannot say. But, for his sake as well as your own, you must go. I shall have a coach ready first thing in the morning. My valets will pack your belongings."

"You both seem so eager to see the back of me," I muttered.

"I respect Dr. Franklin's desire to remove you from the tide of events," she said.

"What are you two conspiring about?" Dr. Bancroft asked, approaching us from the nave. "Let us go from here, before the bishop discovers that I am not of the Catholic faith!"

Madame Devereux fixed him with an expression of shock. "But, sir! You took the Sacrament."

"How could I have done otherwise, madame?" Bancroft said dismissively. "Failure to do so would have been to reveal a Protestant in a cathedral filled with Roman Catholics. It simply would not *do*." With that he led us from the church and out into the Yuletide chill.

As we rode back to the hotel in Madame Devereux's fine carriage, I suffered feelings of regret and discomfiture. The last time I had seen Dr. Franklin, he had admonished me for earning his grandfatherly regard. Upon dressing for Mass, I had emerged from my bedchamber to find him already departed. He and Monsieur Deane had retired to the latter's rooms to begin their discussions. In his stead, I was left with Dr. Bancroft and Madame Devereux.

I knew that Franklin intended to spend his entire day with his fellow commissioner, busily reviewing the points of the treaty that they would offer to King Louis after the New Year. I wondered what opportunity I would have to speak with Dr. Franklin before my departure in the morning. I simply could not return to Nogent-le-Rotrou without having conveyed to the grand old gentleman that, most whole-heartedly, his love for me was returned.

As it happened, I needn't have worried.

Chapter Nineteen

"He that blows coals in quarrels that he has nothing to do with, has no right to complain if the sparks fly in his face." - Benjamin Franklin

I did not see Dr. Franklin at all that afternoon. Upon our return from Notre Dame, Bancroft joined the two commissioners, while Madame Devereux pleaded of duties that required her attention. So I was left to my own devices, and spent the next few hours sampling the rather uninteresting library offered by our suite, and tinkering with Dr. Franklin's Yuletide gift to me—the golden quizzing glass.

It truly was a marvelous accessory, and I occupied considerable time in youthful experimentation with it. Through it, I examined the magnified image of my own palm, the letters of one of Dr. Franklin's books, even the detailed weave of the rug that adorned our hearth. Upon further inspection of the quizzing glass, I came upon a weighted bob, which occupied the end of the silver chain. Upon this bob, which appeared fashioned of brass and gold, there were words etched into the metal. So small was this pronouncement that I required the power of the quizzing glass itself, to discern what it said. I'd hoped to find some meaningful inscription, but instead discovered only the importer's label. To my surprise, I recognized the name: Chaumont Shipping and Import, with an address here in Paris. Had Franklin purchased the device from Chaumont, himself? That seemed unlikely.

Also, it struck me that I could not fathom when the old man had found the time to make such a purchase. I had been his nearly constant companion since we had come to the city. The only separation of any length had come last night, when I'd left him at the palace. Surely there had been no opportunity to arrange any sort of purchase under those circumstances! I promised myself to explore this riddle when I was once more reunited with Dr. Franklin. It was a promise that I would not keep.

In the evening, when Beaumarchais finally managed to pull himself from his sickbed and join me for supper in our rooms, there remained no sign of the American doctor. He was still in closed conference with Messieurs Deane and Bancroft. The wait left me feeling anxious and disconcerted.

Shortly after the evening meal, Madame Devereux's valets arrived to begin packing my belongings. Beaumarchais watched them from the sofa, with a pipe in one hand and a glass of port in the other. "What's this?" he asked quizzically.

Beaumarchais had said little to me during our meal, perhaps remembering and regretting his poor performance during the Christmas Eve gala. For myself, I felt less than gregarious, as my concern over my impending departure weighed heavily upon me. I had not yet bothered to inform my friend of the change that Dr. Franklin had made in my plans. I did so now.

"There is some wisdom in it," he conceded. "There is The Fox to consider."

"And Stormont," I admitted. "He quite openly threatened Ben last night, after you had left our circle."

"The Fox and Stormont," Beaumarchais remarked with disdain. "Stormont commands The Fox, and so their ends amount to the same. Ben is right. While I'm sorry to see you go, boy, you'll be far safer in your father's house."

"Perhaps I've no wish to be safe, Pierre," I said petulantly. "Perhaps all I want to remain here, and to be a part of these events...a part of *him*."

"Mayhap when this business is settled, Ben will recall you."

"Yes, and mayhap he won't." With a disgusted sigh I rose to my feet. "The hour grows late. I was hoping to wait for Ben to return from his long conference, but I fear my exhaustion is earning the better of me."

"To bed with you," Beaumarchais commanded. "Ben will be here to see you off in the morning. And don't fret so, Henri. It truly is for the best."

So I took to my chamber, feeling none the better despite my friend's assurances. My sleep proved fitful, and the first rays of dawn found me very much awake, and ruminating unhappily upon my impending exile. Sometime during the night my fire had gone out. The room felt cold and, in the bitterness of my mood, strangely foreign.

Today I would leave for home. I was being sent away, discarded, for the crime of earning an old man's grandfatherly regard. He feared for me, and so he was removing me from harm's way. It was, in its fashion, quite touching. But that sentiment did nothing to alleviate my sense of loss. Danger or not, I had no wish to go. The very notion filled me with a bitter and, I admit, somewhat childish anger.

Lying there, in that chilled bedchamber, I was suddenly gripped by a selfish folly. I would leave *now*, before my companions awakened. I would abandon them as they were abandoning me, without so much as a proper good-bye. I would find Madame Devereux, or one of her valets, and arrange for a coach to carry me back to Nogent-le-Rotrou. My father would see to the expense.

Resolved to this petty task, I set myself to packing. It took little time, as the hotel valets had accomplished much of it during the previous evening. Within scant minutes, I had dressed and stood ready to exit the bed-

The Franklin Affair

chamber for what I assumed would be the last time, my bags in my hand and bitterness in my heart.

The sitting room was quiet, its draperies closed against the early morning sun. Slowly, I crossed to the main door and stood there, alone in the dim light, the only sound the tick of the mantel clock and my own slow breathing. More than a minute passed in this way, with me poised on the brink of departure as though frozen within a single moment of time while, inwardly, conflicting emotions warred against one another.

Finally, acting on an impulse beyond true awareness, I lowered my bags and took from my pocket a small object. This I examined, turning it over and over in my hands. It was the quizzing glass, my Christmas gift from Dr. Franklin. Slowly, I turned back toward his closed bedchamber door, my resolution faltering.

Leaving my bags where they were, I walked carefully across the sitting room to that door and found it unlocked. Cautiously, I opened it, fearing at any moment to hear the shrill protest of an un-oiled hinge. But Madame Devereux kept too fine a house for that, and the portal presented itself to me in blessed silence. The room within proved even darker than the sitting room. Only the barest sliver of gold peeking around the rim of the closed window treatments betrayed the sun's presence in the sky.

Possessed of an uncertain spirit, I crossed to the bedside and looked down for a time upon the figure of the old man in repose. Dr. Franklin's face appeared relaxed and blissful. Despite his tribulations, a gentle smile played upon his lips. His walking stick lay beside the bed, facing ever westward, while his spectacles sat atop the table, near the washbasin.

Slowly, I placed my quizzing glass-his quizzing glass-down upon that bedside table.

"Good-bye, Ben," I whispered. "I shan't forget you, sir."

Then I turned and left the room.

Sadly, all this high drama met with a foul and unbefitting end. For, as I neared the main door, there came suddenly upon it a most urgent knocking. The sound was so abrupt and so unexpected that I gasped aloud, nearly jumping from my shoes. The hard drumming of fist upon wood reverberated in the silence, falling upon me like a lantern light upon a midnight thief.

For a moment, I was quite paralyzed.

Elsewhere in our suite, I heard Beaumarchais groan and mutter unintelligible words of protest. From Franklin's bedchamber there was still no sound. But surely the old man could not fail to register such a cacophony! Within moments, the empty sitting room would be bustling with activity.

Gripped by a child's panic, I rushed forward and collected my bags, trying to ignore the incessant rapping upon our door. Gathering them clumsily up into my arms, I hurried into my bedchamber with my burden, finally depositing the lot of them sloppily upon the bed. As I did so, I heard both Franklin's and Beaumarchais' doors open at the same time. A moment later, the playwright's booming voice filled the sitting room!

"What is this? Don't they know the time?"

"The sun is up, Pierre," Franklin replied with a yawn. "For some people, that's enough."

"We'll soon see about that!"

I turned toward my open bedchamber threshold, wondering if I dared to close it and try to change once again into my sleeping clothes, lest my cowardly intentions be discovered. Sadly, I saw that there was no time for this. Already, my companions had come into view. Beaumarchais turned and looked blearily upon me as he advanced toward the exterior door.

"I'll see to it!" I said, coming suddenly forward-ever the obedient servant.

Franklin regarded me with curiosity as I hurried from my chamber, across the sitting room and then came to stand before both men as they neared the door. Beyond it, the knocking had finally ceased.

"I can open a door for myself, Henri," Beaumarchais

The Franklin Affair

snapped.

"How's your head, Pierre?" I asked innocently.

"My head is fine enough. Don't be insolent with me, boy!"

"Pierre, do calm yourself," said Franklin. "Henri obviously wishes to make a good impression for our guests. After all, did *you* take the time to dress before coming out here?"

"What?" Beaumarchais said, frowning. "Ah," he said, looking at me with fresh eyes. "Very well then. Play the manservant."

I opened the door, feeling sweat upon my palms as I did so.

Three men filled our threshold. All were strangers. Two were dressed in the uniforms of French soldiers. The last wore a dark coat, a black three-pointed hat, and orange hose. He was smaller than his companions, but in obvious command. His smooth, delicately featured face fixed me with fierce regard.

"I am looking for Dr. Benjamin Franklin of America."

So completely did the fellow's manner distract me, that I quite lost my tongue.

"I am Franklin," the old man said, coming to stand beside me. Apparently, he had recognized the use of his name, despite the language barrier.

The visitor's eyes narrowed. "Dr. Franklin," he said. "I am Inspector Marat of the Ministry of Justice. Sir, I have orders to bring you to the ministry for questioning."

I dutifully translated, though the words filled me with a most horrible dread. Franklin seemed to consider this news for several moments. Then he stepped aside and bade me allow our visitors to enter. They did so, Marat's two soldiers dominating the room with their uniformed presence.

"What is this?" Beaumarchais demanded.

Marat treated him with a look of such suspicion that even the blustery playwright was rendered momentarily mute. "And *you* are, monsieur?"

"Me? Why I am Pierre-Augustin Beaumarchais!"

"I do not know you," the man from the Ministry of Justice said after some reflection. "Please stand aside. Dr. Franklin, you will dress and accompany us immediately."

Again I translated. The American doctor looked aghast. "The hour is quite inappropriate for this sort of thing, Inspector Marat. May I suggest we share breakfast?"

I turned his words to French.

"My orders are to bring you to the ministry at once, sir. No delays."

"This is appalling!" Beaumarchais cried. "I shall speak to the king!"

"Do as pleases you, sir. I have my orders. Dr. Franklin, I am within my rights to collect you regardless of your attire. But, in deference to your age and position, I shall allow you the courtesy to dress...if you avail yourself of that courtesy at once."

Upon hearing my translation, Dr. Franklin's usually jovial expression grew dark with consternation. "Am I under arrest, Monsieur?" he asked.

"That is yet to be determined."

"I would like my translator to accompany me."

"We will provide you with someone to turn our words to English," Marat said dismissively.

Franklin stepped up to the man, leaning heavily upon his Crabtree stick. "Sir," Franklin said, his eyes hard. "I am not a common street villain that you can threaten and order about. I am a representative of the United States of America. I *will* dress and I *will* bring my translator. The only way that you shall otherwise earn my company is to order your men to strike me senseless and drag me from this room. Despite your bravado, I'm quite confident that your 'orders' do not extend to such dire business as that."

I turned his words to French and watched Marat's face twist in anger. "As you wish, doctor," he said, a knife's edge in his voice. "Dress yourself. Your boy may accompany us. But the loud fellow remains here."

"Loud fellow!" Beaumarchais raged.

"Steady, Pierre. Heed me. Wake Silas and Edward. Tell them what has happened. Have them seek out the Comte de Vergennes."

"Stormont's behind this, Ben," Beaumarchais declared. "I don't know how, but..."

"There will be more time..." He glanced in Marat's direction. "...and more privacy...to discuss that possibility. Henri, find one of Madame Devereux's valets and ask him to supply breakfast cakes for us to eat along the way. Then try to find my fur hat. It seems to have gone missing over this past day or two."

"It is not missing, doctor," Marat said. Suddenly, a cold smile touched his thin, bloodless lips. "I know precisely where it is."

Chapter Twenty

"Where sense is wanting, everything is wanting. - Benjamin Franklin

We were not taken to the Palais de Justice, as it had suffered a recent fire and was currently unused. Instead, Inspector Marat conducted us to the Foreign Ministry where, he rather curtly informed us, we would be detained until the time of our interrogation.

"I am a busy man," Franklin said with undisguised effrontery as he sat between the two soldiers in the belly of Marat's large, shuttered carriage. The inspector and I occupied the opposite bench. "How long shall this business take?"

"I, too, am a man most occupied," was Marat's cold reply, upon hearing my translation. "I shall endeavor to detain you for no more than a day or two."

"A day or two!" Franklin exclaimed, once I had turned Marat's words to English. "That is unspeakable!"

"Calm yourself, doctor," Marat told him haughtily. "French justice is swift enough, as you shall see."

As it happened, blessed fortune intervened. Upon our arrival at the threshold of the ministry building, we were met by a small contingent of soldiers, the appearance of which seemed to cause Inspector Marat no small unease. As we exited the carriage, Monsieur Conrad Gérard, Vergennes' faithful secretary, advanced from amidst these soldiers and delivered into the hand of an astonished Marat a sealed letter. The investigator read

The Franklin Affair

the message, and I could see from his expression that its contents did nothing to relieve his displeasure.

"I am ordered to bring you both to the office of the Foreign Minister," Marat declared with clear distaste. "Apparently, you have friends in high places, doctor."

I translated for Franklin, who grinned with relief. "You'll forgive me, inspector," he said, not without some superciliousness, "if I feel obliged to decline the offer of your 'hospitality'."

"Have a care, doctor," Marat warned. "This business is far from over."

Within minutes, we were seated in the foreign minister's cavernous office. The drapes had been drawn. Only the firelight from the hearth kept the shadows at bay. In attendance were Dr. Franklin, myself, the comte, two soldiers of the Ministry of Justice, and the sour-faced Marat, who sat alone upon a velvet settee, his arms folded across his chest.

"Please understand, Dr. Franklin," said the Comte de Vergennes, his manner respectful. "We mean no harm to you in this matter."

His words, reminiscent as they were of Chaumont's, uttered back at the beginning of this relentless confusion, filled me with bitter irony. Beside me, Dr. Franklin met Vergennes' assurances with carefully controlled anger.

"To be frank, sir, I take little comfort in that. You have this day dragged me from my abode, bodily and quite openly. I find this conduct not all conducive to customary diplomatic protocol."

"This is a terrible business," Vergennes remarked. "A most unhappy affair. Dr. Franklin, I cannot fully express my sorrow and regret at your having been treated thus. However, painful though it may be, the matter at hand is of such import that we...His Majesty's government...could hardly do otherwise."

"I shall withhold my opinion on that subject," Franklin remarked, "until you avail me of the nature of this 'unhappy affair'."

Vergennes turned toward Marat. "You have not told

him?" he asked in French.

"It was not required that I should do so. The law stipulates that the accused may be interrogated, and the full nature of the charge against him withheld until it can be used during that interrogation to the most effect."

Vergennes' face darkened. "This is not a common cutpurse or tavern bully, Marat!" He motioned to Franklin, who, though he could not understand what was being said, straightened in his chair, and managed to muster a wealth of pride into his bearing. "This is Dr. Benjamin Franklin, commissioner from America."

"I am aware of his identity, your lordship," Marat replied stiffly. "I am also aware of the facts of this case. My duty is to justice and to France."

"As is mine, Marat." Vergennes returned his attention to Dr. Franklin and his language to English. "Doctor," he said gently. "I am not, as you may imagine, typically involved in those matters that most usually interest Inspector Marat. However, given the nature of your position and purpose here in France, I felt obliged to intervene on your behalf."

"I do appreciate that, my dear comte," Franklin said. "Otherwise, Henri and I should have found ourselves enjoying the less gentle hospitalities of this queer little man."

Marat looked to me, expecting a translation. I did not even meet his eyes.

"The fact remains," Vergennes continued, "that I must assume an uncomfortable role if I am to settle this unpleasant business. Toward that end, I must ask you, sir: where were you two nights ago, on the evening of the 23rd of December?"

Franklin was startled by the question—perhaps even alarmed. He did his best to conceal this reaction, but it demonstrated itself in a certain widening of the blue eyes behind his spectacles. I, myself, was left in no less discomfiture, as I knew exactly where the doctor had been on the night in question.

"I was in my rooms," Franklin said.

"The entire evening?" Vergennes asked carefully.

The Franklin Affair

"Quite so."

"I see." He translated for Marat, whose only response was a derisive grunt.

"Dr. Franklin," Vergennes said. "Do you know a woman by the name of Marie Truneux?"

"I do not believe I do," said Franklin.

"Indeed?" asked Vergennes. "Inspector Marat has spoken to both the manager and head chef of the Hôtel d'Entragues. The manager, one Madame Devereux, was loath to speak of you. Her cook, however, proved more forthcoming. He reported and, after some cajoling, Madame Devereux confirmed, witnessing you in the company of this young woman."

"Did they?" Franklin asked.

"Yes. It was in a street that addresses the servant's entrance of the hotel. By all accounts, your ward here was with you."

"Ah yes!" Franklin exclaimed. "Of course! The young woman who approached our carriage. Henri, you remember, don't you?"

"I do, Ben," I said, trying to conceal my distress.

"Is that what all this fuss is about?" Franklin asked, sounding quite relieved. "I never knew the poor creature's name." Then he described our return from the shopping trip to the Rue St. Germain, and our attempt to avoid the usual crowd of well-wishers. "Henri bade the driver take us down the alley, with the intent that we should use the servants entrance to procure safer ingress. The young woman in question, however, proved more observant than her fellows clustered at the hotel's main entrance. She followed our carriage into the alley, running in a most unseemly manner. She seemed intent to speak with me."

"And did she?" Vergennes asked.

"Yes...though, in truth, she said precious little. The poor thing was so skittish that, when Madame Devereux and her cook suddenly appeared, she departed in great haste."

"And she said nothing to you?"

"Only that her mother's home had been rescued by a

lightning rod, and that she wished to thank me," Franklin said. "It was a child's gesture, though one I gladly accepted. But that was as far as the matter went."

"And you did not see her again?" Vergennes asked.

"I did not," said Franklin.

"And she took nothing from you? No personal effects?"

Franklin seemed to consider this for several moments. "I do not believe so," he said.

Vergennes conferred with Marat in French, relaying Franklin's words. Marat's dark eyes gleamed wickedly as he leaned forward. "Show him!" he demanded of the comte. "You must show him now!"

"As you say, inspector," Vergennes replied with obvious reluctance. "Do you have the article?"

Marat nodded to one of his two soldiers, who advanced and presented him with a small package, wrapped in linen. He unbound this bundle and, with a predatory sneer, lifted its contents for all of us to see.

It was a fur cap—one that I recognized at once.

"Is this yours, Dr. Franklin?" Marat asked. This time, it was Vergennes who provided the translation.

I almost shouted out that it was, but something in Franklin's demeanor gave me pause. He appeared circumspect, and strangely reserved. He leaned forward and rested his chin upon the knob of his cane. "It may be so," he said noncommittally. "There are many fur hats."

I turned his words to French. Marat's sneer deepened. "There are initials within," he said, with clear triumph. "They have been scratched into the hide. Two letters. 'B' and 'F'. Are these not your initials, sir?"

Franklin did not immediately react to my translation. This confused me, as I could see little reason in his reticence to acknowledge ownership of so familiar a possession. Still, his circumspection inspired the same from me, and so I held my expression in careful check.

"May I ask where this hat was found?" Franklin inquired.

"In the Latin Quarter," Vergennes reported in English. "In the room of a young woman of questionable

The Franklin Affair

morality. Her name, as I have stated, was Mademoiselle Marie Truneux. She was well known to the Ministry of Justice, having been often in trouble with the law."

"I see," said Franklin. "I take it, by your careful use of the past tense, that the young lady in question is no longer with us."

"She was found murdered yesterday evening, when friends came to escort her to a Christmas meal," Vergennes said.

Franklin's face paled very slightly. The hands upon the Crabtree stick trembled. "A tragedy," he said in a whisper.

"Indeed," said Vergennes, "and one that leaves behind unanswered questions. Tell me plain, sir...did you know Mademoiselle Truneux beyond the brief exchange you have already recounted?"

For half a minute, Dr. Franklin sat in silence. Vergennes waited most patiently. Marat sat stiffly, his sneer faded but still apparent, his dark eyes fixed upon the American doctor. I felt myself seized by dread. Of course, Franklin had been there that night. I had followed him to the woman's very door. But to think that this fine, old gentleman could be somehow involved in so grim and dreadful a task as murder—

"I have no recollection of any further meeting with Mademoiselle Truneux," Franklin finally said.

Vergennes nodded slowly, as if he had expected this, though did not, for a moment, believe it. He turned to Marat and quickly translated. Marat scoffed and declared: "Then have him explain how his hat...this very hat...happened to be found with the young woman's body!"

"I have no explanation," Dr. Franklin replied after I'd turned these words to English. "It is true that my hat has gone missing of late, but I cannot say with certainty that the one you hold in your hand is the same as my own."

Vergennes said: "But it bears your initials."

"It does. Yet 'B' and 'F' are not so uncommon a pairing of letters, are they? Surely there could be simple coincidence at work here, my dear comte."

Lie upon lie. With each new word the doctor uttered, a knot tightened further around my heart. Why should he dissemble so, if he were not involved in the young woman's demise?

"How was she killed?" I asked suddenly.

For a moment, my two countrymen regarded me as though I were a tailor's mannequin that had just demonstrated a moment's sentience. Franklin's face remained passive, but his eyes found mine and held them. He tried to convey something to me, but in my agitation, I proved an ineffectual recipient.

"Mademoiselle Truneux was bludgeoned to death, Monsieur Gruel," Vergennes explained in French.

Beside him, Marat said: "...with a weapon not dissimilar from the cane that Dr. Franklin carries."

"Henri, what did he say?" Franklin asked me. Haltingly, I translated. "I see. And why should I possibly wish harm upon this poor child?"

Vergennes translated for Marat, who took from his inside coat pocket a folded sheet of inexpensive writing paper. This he offered to Franklin who, upon seeing the French words, passed the paper on to me.

I read it aloud: "My Dear Doctor Franklin: How distressed I am that you have refused to treat with me! I have come to you in earnest, and have shown you my mother's letters, so that there should be little doubt in your mind, but that I am, indeed, your daughter by her. Yet, still, you refuse to acknowledge me in even private correspondence. Please know that, if you do not change your attitude towards me, I shall be forced to reveal publicly the irrefutable facts of our relationship. This would sadden me greatly, Father, as I have no wish to make of you an enemy. But, for my mother's honor and my own, you are leaving me little choice. I beseech you, do not mistake my earnestness, nor unwisely force my hand, lest we both be the sorrier for it." It was signed simply "M".

When I'd finished reading my throat felt dry. Marat was grinning now, apparently in expectation of a full

The Franklin Affair

confession. Vergennes appeared uncomfortable, almost to the point of distraction. Only Franklin remained stoic, his manner controlled, his expression thoughtful.

"I must now ask you, sir," Vergennes said. "Was Mademoiselle Truneux your bastard child?"

Franklin's expression did not change as he spoke: "Your lordship, I am aware that my reputation preceded me to Paris, and also that said reputation included a certain familiarity with the fairer sex. However, sir, I wish to make it plain that my actual adventures in this area are somewhat less than the rumors would imply. I do not have any bastard children in France."

"Yet you have been to Paris before, doctor," Marat remarked slyly, once I had turned Franklin's words to French.

"I have," Franklin admitted. "However, as my first visit was in 1767, less than a decade ago, I could scarcely be the father of a child of Mademoiselle Truneux's age."

"Still, you might have met the murdered woman's mother whilst you were both in England for some purpose." Marat pressed. "It is done often enough...a romantic subterfuge perhaps?"

Again I translated. "That subterfuge is at work here can be of little doubt," Franklin replied. "I submit that this letter is a forgery, intended to discredit me. If you desire a villain in this business, inspector, I suggest you look to the British agent who calls himself The Fox."

Vergennes' expression became one of complete dismay. Upon hearing my translation, Marat uttered a condescending laugh and remarked to Vergennes: "What did I tell you, My Lord? Did I not predict this reaction?"

"You did," Vergennes reluctantly replied.

"Arrest him," Marat demanded. It was very nearly a command.

"When I deem it appropriate to do so, Monsieur," Vergennes said.

"His talk of conspiracies is mere shadow," the inspector insisted. "Arrest him, sir. The evidence demands it!"

Vergennes turned upon him, his manner suddenly sharp: "Do not press your point! Keep your place!"

"I know my place, comte," said Marat. "And I know yours as well. Mayhap our two places are not so different as you would care to imagine."

At this, Vergennes fixed angry eyes upon the other man. "With a word I can have you and your uniformed brigands ejected from my office. I care not who your uncle is, nor what authority you presume yourself to hold, based upon that relationship. I will *not* be spoken to in such a manner! I am an aristocrat as well as the Foreign Minister of France, Marat! You are a sullen, bitter little policeman who lacks the imagination and subtlety for a more important post. *I* will decide when...and *if*...this man shall face a French court."

"Decide then," Marat said, looking little affected by Vergennes' fierce denouncement. "For if this man flees before you take action against him, I fear for your position...and your title."

Dr. Franklin leaned sharply in my direction and whispered: "What is happening, Henri? What are they talking about?"

I regarded the old man, whom I had come to hold in such high esteem, with a mixture of sorrow and deep distress. Nevertheless, I answered him, speaking softly: "Marat wishes to have you jailed. Vergennes is not prepared to go that far. Apparently the inspector's uncle holds some authority in the government, so much so that Marat is rendered secure enough to dare address the Foreign Minister with disrespect."

Franklin actually smiled at this, and returned to his formal posture as though I had merely availed him of the current weather.

"Dr. Franklin," Vergennes said. He seemed flustered and angry over his confrontation with Marat. "Please understand, sir, that I hold you...all of France holds you...in the very highest regard."

"Comforting," Dr. Franklin replied.

"Nevertheless, I cannot deny that Marat possesses sufficient evidence to warrant further investigation into

The Franklin Affair

this matter. You understand that, surely."

"Of course, my dear comte," the old man replied genially. "Do not worry yourself on my account. Conduct any investigation you wish. When you find poor Mademoiselle Truneux's murderer, I am completely confident that you will discover him wearing a face quite other than mine. However, as this investigation is liable to prove lengthy, may I humbly ask that Henri and I be permitted to return to our hotel?"

Marat began to protest after I had turned these words into French, but Vergennes silenced him with a sharp, impatient motion of his hand. To Franklin, the comte said: "You and your ward are free to leave. I must ask, however, that you remain in Paris until this business has been satisfactorily concluded."

"Let me assure you, sir," Franklin said. "I have no intention of leaving Paris in the near future...certainly not before I meet formally with the king."

"Yes," Vergennes said. "Well...I regret to say, doctor that, until this matter has been resolved, you will be denied access to any and all government buildings or officials. No correspondence from you will be accepted, nor messengers of any character."

"Comte!" Franklin said with alarm. "That's quite unreasonable, sir! I have a mission! My treaty..."

"...will, by necessity, have to wait. I am truly sorry, doctor."

"It's The Fox, Vergennes," Franklin remarked urgently. "You know it as surely as I. Stormont is trying to remove me from the tide of events."

"I shall not gainsay you, doctor. Unfortunately, no firm evidence suggests that this assassin even exists, less still that he may have set himself against you and your mission. Without proof of this phantom English agent, how can I even broach the subject with Marat's superiors?"

"Or his uncle?" Franklin asked.

Vergennes hesitated, and then nodded. "He is the Deputy Minister of Justice," the comte explained, "and an even more disagreeable person than his loathsome nephew. Dr. Franklin, I suggest that you return to your hotel and remain there. I shall do everything possible to keep this matter confidential, lest it soil your reputation in France. I shall also endeavor to shield you from the worst of Marat's tenacity." Then he turned and addressed the infuriated Marat in French: "I am releasing Dr. Franklin to his own devices."

"Your lordship!" the inspector declared, his face reddened.

"You may conduct your inquiries, Marat," Vergennes told him coldly. "When you have someone who can place Dr. Franklin at the scene...not merely a hat which *might* be his, or a note which *might* have been penned by the murdered whore...but an actual witness, then I will consider more drastic measures."

I translated for Franklin.

"Come, Henri," the American said. "I do believe these gentlemen are done with us. Comte, the closed carriage in which we were transported is conspicuous by virtue of its Justice Ministry insignia. Might I request the temporary use of an unmarked coach and driver from your office's livery?"

"Of course, Dr. Franklin," Vergennes replied at once. Then he rang a small butler's bell. When Monsieur Gérard responded, the comte availed him of our request. "Conrad will see to the arrangements, himself. Thank you for your cooperation in this matter, Dr. Franklin."

"Under the circumstances, sir," Franklin replied gravely. "I could scarcely have done otherwise."

I followed him as he rose from his chair and accompanied the solicitous Monsieur Gérard toward the waiting office door. The old man's gait seemed uncharacteristically sluggish—his manner weary. Dr. Franklin appeared, for the first time since I had made his acquaintance, to truly wear his years.

Chapter Twenty-One

"Dost thou love life, then do not squander time, for that's the stuff life is made of." - Benjamin Franklin

A weighty silence occupied much of the carriage ride back to the Hôtel d'Entragues. Dr. Franklin sat lost in silent rumination, gazing vacantly out through the window at the snow-covered streets of Paris. For myself, I wallowed in uncomfortable remembrances of two nights past, when I had followed Franklin on his strange nocturnal sojourn. I recalled his urgent character as he'd knocked upon the door to Mademoiselle Truneux's rooms. How clearly I could see the young woman's pale, anxious face, briefly glimpsed, as she offered the American doctor ingress. I could not, however, compel my reticent memory to recall the moment of Franklin's departure from the company of the murdered lady.

Had he been wearing his familiar fur hat? I could not be sure.

Yet, as I now regarded this fine old man, neither could I convince myself that a foul murderer lay hidden beneath that simple, unembroidered brown coat. This was a gentle soul, a man of peace and good humor. Surely he could not harbor so dark a secret nature!

Yet, had not Thérèse Leray de Chaumont similarly surprised me, demonstrating her own dual nature?

"Ben..." I asked tentatively.

Several long moments passed. Finally, he looked

upon me with weary eyes. "My boy, I did *not* murder that child."

"But you *were* there," I said.

He regarded me thoughtfully. "As were you, it seems."

"I followed you from the hotel," I said, the words coming out in a guilty rush, "and stowed away upon the rear of your *fiacre*."

The barest of smiles touched his lips. "Clever fellow," he said. "I fear that everyone in this business has underestimated you, my dear Henri...myself most shamefully of all. You possess an uncanny talent for observation and good timing. Given your youth and inexperience, you actually miss very little of what occurs around you. It's a valuable gift, my boy." Then, in a more serious manner: "Yes, I *was* there, though I saw little good purpose in availing Inspector Marat of that fact. But, I swear on the soul of my departed wife, that young girl was alive when I left her."

"Why did you go there?" I asked. "Did she not communicate to you in some way when she took your hand at the carriage that afternoon?"

"Well done. Yes, indeed she did. She tucked into my fist a slip of paper and, in the guise of a kiss, whispered to me a brief message."

"What message?" I asked eagerly.

"'Come to me,' she said. 'I know the face of The Fox.'" Franklin replied. "The slip of paper held upon it a time and place for the rendezvous."

"The Fox!" I exclaimed. "She knew that assassin's name? How?"

"Sadly, when I went to her, she told me precious little. Instead, she demanded an audience with certain...parties...within the French government, to secure her safety once she revealed what she knew. She wished me to champion her cause to the king. That was starry-eyed of her, given that I have not, myself, secured access to His Majesty as yet. But she was young and frightened, and she believed herself to be clever. Despite my most patient urgings, she refused to reveal the name of The Fox until she was safely protected by word of King Louis, himself."

"So what did you do?" I asked.

Franklin frowned and offered a slight shrug of his shoulders. "What *could* I do, Henri? I begged her to let me share her secret. I vowed to secure her safety, and to keep her confidence until the proper time. She would have none of it. The only aid from me that this poor, naïve thing desired was a royal introduction."

"Then why come to you at all?" I asked. "Why not present herself to Vergennes, or someone in the Ministry of Justice?"

"I doubt Mademoiselle Truneux even knew of the Comte de Vergennes and, as a known criminal, she would scarcely have been inclined to take her tale to the likes of Inspector Marat. She chose me for my reputation in Paris, and for the esteem that she assumed was held for me throughout the society of the French elite." Franklin spread his arms in a gesture of helplessness. "In the end, I was forced to leave her empty-handed."

"When you did so," I said. "Could you have left your hat behind?"

"Most certainly, I did not, Henri," Franklin replied with conviction. "I am a man of some years, but my faculties are still quite strong. I placed my hat upon my head and my walking stick in my hand and made my apologies. I told her that I would do what I could, but that it would take time and that, in the interim, she must tell her story to no one else. She so agreed."

"Then who killed her?" I asked.

"The Fox," Franklin replied. "Or one of his agents."

"What makes you so certain? If Mademoiselle Truneux was, as Inspector Marat suggests, a woman of...dubious virtue, might she not have been struck down by some random villain? The streets in that area of Paris are quite dangerous, I'm told."

"*Quite* dangerous," Franklin affirmed. "But, no. This poor child's life was taken for two very specific reasons.

The first was, of course, to silence her. The second was to implicate me in her death. This is evident by the falsified paternity letter and by the discovery of my hat upon the scene. I can only assume that it was somehow stolen from our suite and deposited there at the time of the murder."

"Fortunately, this falsified evidence seems insufficient to warrant your arrest," I said.

"My status as a foreign dignitary shields me," Franklin replied. "However, the evidence *is* enough to besmirch my reputation and to cost me any hope of a worthwhile audience with the king. In short, to effectively undermine my mission to France."

"Then it must be Stormont," I said.

"I'm certain that he knew of the plan and gave it his blessing. But its true author is undoubtedly The Fox," Franklin replied firmly. "Recall our adventure with the highwayman. I told you then that such an obvious ruse was beneath The Fox's subtle expertise. But this... *this*...is exactly the sort of machination that has earned him his appellation."

Then the old man regarded me with a plea in his eyes. "Tell me, Henri. Ease an old man's troubled spirit. You do believe me, do you not? It is really *most* important to me. Please tell me you cannot imagine that I would actually do harm to this young creature."

I looked into his earnest face, the question already decided in my mind. "Dr. Franklin," I said. "I believe you absolutely, sir."

He grinned—truly grinned—for the first time that day. It was a relief to see it.

"Then we must return to our hotel and make our report to our colleagues," Franklin said. "While I am denied access to the French government, surely Silas and Edward are not. We can reasonably assume that Pierre has already informed them of the situation. I can only imagine the reaction of my fellow Americans, when the *real* deviltry behind this business is made known to them."

"And Pierre's reaction," I added with a grim smile, "when he learns of this plot against you."

Franklin chuckled softly. "I do believe Pierre's reaction is...predictable."

And so it was.

"Scandalous! Libelous! You? You? *You!*"

"Calm yourself, Pierre," Franklin entreated. "It will do the matter little good to have you collapse into a fit of apoplexy. Henri, fetch some wine for our friend here, and a glass for myself, if you please."

I did so, placing refreshments before each of the four men seated around the small hearth in our sitting room. Beaumarchais, his face reddened by fury, took up his glass and drained it in a single, long draught.

"My God, Ben! You? Of all men, this fool Marat has the gall to accuse *you* of murdering some Latin Quarter whore?"

"Pierre!" Franklin said sharply. "Mind your language!"

"My *language*, is it? Dear God, Ben! You?"

"I'm surprised the Comte de Vergennes has done so much on your behalf in this matter," Deane remarked.

"True," added Dr. Bancroft. "Mayhap he is not the cowardly politician that we first took him to be."

"Bah!" cried Beaumarchais dismissively, waving his empty glass in my direction. With a sigh of irritation, I refilled it for him.

"Vergennes has his enemies at court," Franklin observed. "If it has become known that the two of us met in secret two days ago, then it must be clear to one and all that the Foreign Minister is leaning favorably toward the American cause in France."

"Still," Deane said, "the shipment of French armaments remains delayed."

"And now you, Ben, have been most viciously slandered," Beaumarchais added.

"Vergennes' enemies will use my scandal against him, if they can," said Franklin. "If Vergennes' faith in me proves unwise, it may cost him favor with the king...perhaps even his post as Foreign Minister. If that happens, our deportation, or even imprisonment, is assured...even if these charges against me are eventually dismissed."

"I shall draft a letter of formal protest to the French Foreign Ministry," Bancroft declared.

"No, Edward," said Franklin. "That is exactly what you must *not* do. We must draw as little attention to this business as possible. To act otherwise is to risk increasing general knowledge of the scandal."

"Stormont has his sources within the French press," Deane said. "It will not be difficult for him to attack your good name, now that he may cite this horrible murder."

"Perhaps, but it will take him time, time that we can use to our advantage." Franklin addressed Beaumarchais. "Pierre, would you be willing to travel immediately to the Latin Quarter? I will give you the exact address. Discover what you may regarding our poor Marie Truneux. If she *did* know the identity of The Fox, then she must have gleaned that knowledge from some source. Perhaps she had friends...a landlord."

Beaumarchais nodded. "A reasonable course of action, Ben. But aren't Marat's men likely to be about the same business?"

"The inspector has already convinced himself of my guilt," Franklin replied. "Whatever further investigation he is conducting should be minimal, at best."

"I'll go with you," said Bancroft. "We can cover more ground..."

"No," said Beaumarchais. "It must be a Frenchman or no one. I know the Latin Quarter. To the ignorant rabble who make their home there, Americans are no different from Englishmen, and Englishmen are despised. You'd be lucky to come away with your throat uncut. I'll take Henri."

"The devil you will!" Franklin declared, with surprising vigor. "Henri is bound for home. This business does nothing to change that."

"Ben..."

"No, Pierre! I'm quite resolute about this. Henri is homeward bound and I will brook no further discussion on the topic."

"No, Ben," I said. "I'm not going home."

He frowned upon me. "You'll do as I tell you, my boy," he said. "Otherwise, I shall by needs..."

"...discharge me?" I asked sardonically. "Is that not already your intention? No, Ben. Pierre is right. An American would accomplish nothing in the Latin Quarter. You need Frenchmen to aid you. Right now, that means Pierre and myself."

"Henri," Franklin said, his tone filled with touching concern. "I can forbid this."

The echo of my father's words tugged at my heart. "Yes, you can, Ben, but to no effect. At best, you have the right to dismiss me from your service, in which case I shall forsake my home, and venture forth instead to clear your good name. So you see, sir, you have little choice but to accept my help."

For most of a minute, no one spoke. Finally, in a weary voice, Franklin said: "Then, so be it. Pierre, take Henri with you into the Latin Quarter. But guard him well. I charge you with his safety. If that boy suffers so much as a bruise, you shall answer to me."

Beaumarchais laughed and rose to his feet. "And what shall you do to me, Ben? Strike me about the head with your cane?"

"Under the circumstances, Pierre," Franklin said seriously, "that is not remotely amusing. Henri, come here."

I did so, coming to sit beside him. He placed a hand upon my shoulder. "Do you have a weapon, my boy?"

"A dagger," I said. "My father made a gift of it to me before we left Nogent-le-Rotrou."

Franklin nodded grimly. "Very forward-thinking of him. Tell me, Henri, have you any training in the art of combat by dagger?"

"No, Ben," I admitted.

"I thought not. Then keep your dagger sheathed. Never draw a weapon, Henri, unless you mean to take a life with it. Look to Pierre for your defense. Do you understand me?"

I nodded my head.

"And you will heed me?" he pressed.

"I shall," I said.

"Then go, the both of you!" Franklin declared. "Discover what you may of this terrible business. But, make no point of being away too long. Dangerous things are afoot, my friends, and I greatly fear that matters shall grow worse more quickly than better."

Chapter Twenty-Two

"Energy and persistence conquer all things" - Benjamin Franklin

As Beaumarchais and I prepared to depart, Monsieur Deane summoned a valet and requested a public carriage. After a hasty farewell, my companion and I conducted ourselves downstairs and through the crowded lobby, hurriedly navigating Franklin's typical congregation of well-wishers. We emerged upon the street to find Madame Devereux in conversation with the driver of a *fiacre*. At the sight of us, the lady smiled and beckoned.

"Ah, at last," she said as we approached. "As you can see, everything is ready. But messieurs, why travel in these filthy beggar carts when my own coach is at your disposal?"

"Where we are going, madame," Beaumarchais replied with a grim smile. "We are safest riding in a filthy beggar cart."

The lady frowned at this, but did not press the point. "Then, before you both depart, may I be so bold as to inquire after Dr. Franklin's situation?"

"His situation is in hand, madame," Beaumarchais replied. "Why would you think otherwise?"

Our hostess grew suddenly circumspect. "I was not present when Dr. Franklin...departed from my hotel in the company of two soldiers of the Ministry of Justice. But I have heard the story from others' lips. Already, word has spread well beyond my lobby that the esteemed American doctor may have become involved in some terrible scandal."

"I cannot remark on that, madame. My apologies. Come, Henri." He made as though to step around her, but she took hold of him, closing her delicate, bejeweled fingers around his wrist.

"Please do not misunderstand my interest, Pierre," Madame Devereux beseeched. "I do not gossip. No one in my business ever does. My concern for the gentleman is quite genuine, as is this promise: if Dr. Franklin is ever in need of me, I am at his service. I am not without influence in certain Paris circles. I may be of use to him in that capacity."

Beaumarchais' attitude softened. He gently withdrew her hand and kissed it tenderly. "Madame, that is most kind and gracious of you."

As we departed, I looked back through the window to see Madame Devereux standing in the street, holding her kissed hand against a flushed, crimson cheek. To Beaumarchais, I said: "She seems taken with you. May I assume that you are so well received by all women?"

Beaumarchais uttered a sputtering, surprised laugh. "That's a boy's question, Henri," he declared. "No man may claim to be well received by all women, and I fare no better or worse than any other."

"Yet, she seemed so charmed by your displays of gallantry," I protested.

"It is a game we play. You would do well not to underestimate that creature, Henri. She is a singular woman, full of cunning and self-interest. She plays the genteel lady and I play the chivalrous gentlemen. Each of us understands the other's folly, and so we see little harm is continuing the pretense. But it is only street theatre."

"I see," I said, though I surely did not.

"If anyone has caught that lady's eye, it's Ben," Beaumarchais added.

"You jest!"

"Don't look so surprised. Have you forgotten my warning to him on the day we arrived in Paris? Madame Devereux has already attended three of her own weddings. This career has left her a woman of means and influence. Her hotel is one of the most well respected in Paris. All she lacks now is a certain measure of prestige...the sort of respect that one earns by marrying a socially desirable husband."

"But Ben must have thirty years on the lady?" I declared.

"Closer to twenty, I should think. Also, while I am not certain of this, I believe that there may be some history between the two of them."

"History? Between Ben and Madame Devereux?"

"Ben has visited Paris twice before, Henri," Beaumarchais explained. "This city is not so large, after all...and given the social circles they share, and Ben's eye for beauty, it is not inconceivable that he might have associated himself with Madame Devereux well before now."

"Do you believe they were intimate?" I asked, astonished.

"Another boy's question. In truth, I do not know. But I *do* know that Madame Devereux did *not* come to Bancroft to ask for a description of Ben before his arrival, as he told us she did. I spoke to Deane about it, and discovered that it was Deane who courteously presented himself to the lady and *offered* such a description."

"You believe that she already knew Ben's face," I said.

"I do."

Beaumarchais fell then into a thoughtful silence—one that I was only too willing to accommodate, as it gave me time to indulge my own ruminations. Dr. Franklin and Madame Devereux? How remarkable a thought was this!

The view through our window gradually degraded as our coachman delivered us ever deeper into Paris' poverty-laden Latin Quarter. Here, though the sun shone brightly overhead, the narrow streets and closeness of the structures cast upon our surroundings a gloomy twilight. Beggars filled every doorway. The buildings were mostly of drab wood and crumbling brick. There were no other carriages to be seen—nor even horses. Here, everyone walked.

"A terrible place," I said.

"A den of thieves," Beaumarchais replied. "Look, we near our address. I have instructed our driver to stop at the corner, in case there are soldiers guarding the murder scene. Now, remain close at my side. Say as little as possible."

I felt no inclination to argue.

We left the cab. Beaumarchais paid the driver and bade him remain and wait for us. At first he refused, but the playwright regarded him with such menace that the man fearfully acquiesced. "Come," my companion said to me. "I see no men at watch. Let us go see what we may learn of this matter."

With that he led me onward, away from the relative safety of the coach. We reached the correct house and scaled the steps to the apartment door, which Beaumarchais beat upon fiercely. His pounding went unanswered for some time. He did not appear impatient at this, however, but only continued his attack upon the stout door until, at last, a man answered his call.

He was a gaunt fellow of some sixty years. His head was quite bald and he wore a shabby slate-colored coat of patchwork linen. His small eyes squinted and his toothless mouth moved nervously as he regarded us. "What do you want?"

"Are you the landlord?" Beaumarchais asked.

The old man's expression grew cautious. "I might know him," he said after a moment. "What's your business with him?"

"We wish to speak with him regarding Mademoiselle Truneux," my companion replied in a tone meant to relay grim authority.

"You don't look like police. You're too foppish." He

nodded his head in my direction. "And that one's too young."

Beaumarchais reached out his fist. The old man recoiled a moment, as though from the head of a viper. Then, slowly, the playwright turned his hand and opened it, revealing a glint of silver. "Does it matter?" he asked quietly.

"I'm the landlord," the man affirmed at once, one wrinkled hand reaching greedily for the coin. Beaumarchais' great fist closed like the door of a safe.

"We have questions," he said.

The old man looked first one way up the street and then the other. Apparently confident that we were unobserved, he opened his door wide and bade us enter. The corridor within was filthy, and smelled of terrible things. Beaumarchais seemed to take this in stride, though I felt obliged to place a hand over my mouth to quell my protesting stomach.

"Give me the coin," the old man said.

Beaumarchais placed the precious silver into the waiting palm.

"I always knew that strumpet would come to a bad end," the landlord announced, his face twisting into a judgmental scowl. "Most of them do."

"Them?" Beaumarchais asked.

The old man grinned wolfishly. His toothless mouth made the gesture grotesque. "Whores," he elaborated. "Marie was young, but not as young as some."

"Did you tell this to the police?" Beaumarchais asked.

The landlord spat upon the ground. "Marat! We know him around here. I told him nothing...pretended I was deaf and senile."

"How clever of you."

"Ask your question, fop. I don't like being seen with the likes of you. Makes my neighbors nervous."

"Of course. Tell me then: did Mademoiselle Truneux seem afraid when you saw her last?"

"Marie was always afraid. She had the wrong temperament for this business. If anything, I would say she seemed better the day she died...rather than worse."

"How so?"

"She smiled when I passed her in the hall," the old man recalled. "The little strumpet hardly ever smiled at me." He winked rakishly. "Not even when she was short of rent and I took the rest from her in trade."

"Please spare us the details of your sordid life," Beaumarchais said scornfully. "Keep to the girl. Did she say why her manner had been so elevated?"

"No, Marie was never one for talking," the old man replied with a shrug. "Only that she hoped to finally get...how did she say it...'that leech from her back'."

"Leech?" Beaumarchais echoed thoughtfully. "Was there, in Mademoiselle Truneux's life, someone who conducted himself as her manager?"

"They all have managers, fop," said the old man. "Every strumpet has her master."

"Who was master to Mademoiselle Truneux?" Beaumarchais asked. There was no mistaking the urgency in his voice.

The old man offered a cunning smile. "Sadly, if I knew, I have no recollection it. I'm afraid your coin, generous though it was, proved insufficient to jog my aging memory."

"I've paid you enough. Answer my question."

"Would that I could, fop," the landlord replied, still grinning. "Perhaps another coin would spark some remembrance...that is, if you *really* care to know."

Beaumarchais stepped back and regarded the old man with disgust. After a moment, he said evenly. "You have made a mistake, sir. That was no coin I gave you."

Confusion showed upon the landlord's features. "No coin?"

"None at all. Rather, it was a carrot."

The old man felt for the silver in his pocket. Satisfied of its reality, he met Beaumarchais scornful gaze with one of his own. "What is this game?"

Suddenly, the playwright was upon him, moving

with such alacrity that I jumped back in alarm. The old man uttered a single, piteous cry as my companion seized him by his collar and bore him against the wall. Plaster rained down upon them from the cracked ceiling. "And this is the stick!" Beaumarchais declared, his deep voice like the roar of a lion. How well I knew the power of that voice. "No more coins, thief! Tell me what I want to know or I will surely break your neck!"

"Please..." the old man groaned. "I am injured. You have done harm to me! Help me!"

"Don't pretend with me, you sly old bastard. Answer! Who was Mademoiselle Truneux's manager?"

"I don't know! I swear it! I never saw him!"

"You *lie!*" One of Beaumarchais great hands took hold of the landlord's scrawny throat.

"Pierre..." I protested, but was ignored.

"Speak, damn you!"

The old man sputtered: "I know only what he is called...here in the Quarter!"

"Tell me that, then," Beaumarchais commanded through clenched teeth. "Quickly, now. My patience wears thin."

"Vos!" the old man declared, terror filling his small eyes. "His name is Vos. I know nothing more! Now, for the Holy Mother's sake, let me be!"

Beaumarchais stepped back, allowing the brutalized fellow to collapse back against the wall, kneading his bruised throat. He regarded my companion with bitter hatred.

"Where can I find Monsieur Vos?" Beaumarchais asked.

"I've no idea. Speak to some of the other strumpets in the neighborhood."

"How shall I find them?"

The landlord sneered. "Take yourself out and stroll up the boulevard. The virtue of your handsome face will draw them to you quickly enough, I'd wager."

"An excellent suggestion. Come, Henri. I believe we are done here."

I opened the door and two of us emerged once again upon the cramped and dreary street. Behind us, the portal to Marie Truneux's lodgings were firmly closed and barred against us. Beaumarchais uttered a brief laugh. "A sour fellow," he remarked. "Yet, we learned enough to begin. We have a name."

"Yes and no," I said.

He regarded me, frowning in confusion.

"Pierre," I said quietly. "'Vos' is Dutch for 'Fox'."

He seemed to require several moments to ruminate upon this revelation. As it happened, he was not provided the opportunity to do so.

Below us, occupying the base of the short flight of stone stairs between ourselves and the street, two men stood with menacing demeanor. Beaumarchais spotted them as quickly as I, and his hand went immediately for his sword.

The two brigands, whose faces remained carefully concealed beneath black scarves, did the same. The larger of them came forward. "Have at thee!" he challenged fiercely.

Chapter Twenty-Three

"Never confuse motion with action." - Benjamin Franklin

"Henri!" Beaumarchais commanded. "Stand well back. When I make a path for you, run for the carriage. Do not wait for me!"

"I'll not!" I declared, as bravely as I could manage. The first man had come up upon the lowest step, the blade of his weapon cutting small circles in the air before us. His companion's weapon was longer and more ornate, and he wielded it less with a brigand's street bravado than with the subtler, more lethal grace of a gentleman warrior.

"Do as I say, boy!" Beaumarchais demanded. Then, uttering a battle cry, he bounded down the stairs and pitted himself against the first attacker.

I was momentarily thankful that the space between the banisters was so narrow as to prevent the second assassin from making his way around the raging combat to reach me.

He must have seen the truth of this also, for he retreated and then advanced upon the left, clearly intending to mount the building's crumbling brick frontage and reach me from the flank. I took myself immediately in the opposite direction, slipping easily under the railing and making the five-foot leap down onto the cobblestones. The attacker saw this and altered his path at once, taking pursuit of me as I fled up the street toward the *fiacre*.

As I ran, I could hear the hard clash of metal upon metal as Beaumarchais and his own opponent continued to conduct themselves with deadly intent upon the steps of Marie Truneux's apartment house. More alarming were the hurried footfalls of my own assailant, and his ragged breath beneath his scarf as he pursued me along the cobblestones.

Then, with the utmost horror, I witnessed the driver of our coach regard our predicament with sudden alarm and, with a great crack of his whip, drive his team off in a clatter of hooves.

We had been abandoned!

Behind me, the distance between us inexorably closing, I heard my pursuer utter a cry of triumph.

Still fleeing, I suddenly recalled my father's dagger, hidden in a pocket beneath my coat. Instantly discounting Franklin's directive, I worked at my buttons with trembling hands, ever mindful of the sharpened death that dogged me. Clumsily, I reached within my coat and felt for the hilt of the sheathed weapon, only to have it become entangled as I struggled to draw it forth. Desperate, I peered awkwardly within my coat, seeking to free the blade from its shoulder sheath.

So embroiled was I upon my task and my terror, that I took no notice of the washwoman until I was nearly upon her. She emerged from a nearby doorway, a toothless creature of indeterminate years, wrapped in rags and carrying a wooden tub of foul-smelling fluid. Despite my panic, I recognized this fetid brew for what it must be: the refuse from a privy or common outhouse, being cast upon the gutter to wash away into the sewers.

Without thinking, I abandoned my frantic search for the uncooperative dagger. Instead, I seized the old woman's tub—causing her to shriek in alarm—and launched its contents directly into the face of my disguised attacker. The swordsman cried out in disgust. Then, with an animal's growl, I spun upon my heel and swung the full weight of the empty tub against his temple. Caught completely off guard, the man stumbled and collapsed to the cobblestones. The saber fell from his grasp, clattering away down the street. Behind me, the washwoman continued to scream.

"Damn you, Mouse!" the assassin exclaimed as he lay writhing upon the ground.

I hurried to locate and recover the villain's blade. The long sword proved dreadfully heavy. I thought angrily of striking down my assassin, but then dismissed this notion when I regarded Beaumarchais, who remained in combat with the second brigand upon the apartment house stairs, now some distance from me.

As I watched, the playwright parried a thrust, pivoted, and attempted to drive his rapier into his opponent's chest. The other man proved his match, however, and neatly sidestepped his thrust, stabbing my companion in the shoulder. I heard Beaumarchais exclaim his injury before staggering back, clutching at his wounded arm. Seizing his opportunity, the assassin advanced, his blade poised for the fatal strike.

Demonstrating more courage than I surely felt, I charged forward, ignoring my own fallen opponent, hurrying instead back up the street, toward where my friend stood in mortal jeopardy. As I did so, I took to swinging the heavy sword back and forth in a manner that I hoped would prove most intimidating.

Beaumarchais' opponent started when he heard my adolescent battle cry, and hesitated, his masked face turning up toward me.

The playwright recognized his chance. Pivoting, he brought his blade down upon the man's sword wrist, cutting deeply into the flesh and earning a cry of pain and outrage. The weapon fell from his attacker's grasp. Beaumarchais, his face maddened with fury, then crashed his full weight into the injured villain, driving him down upon the steps of Marie Truneux's apartment house. The man collapsed under the blow, still clutching his wounded hand.

"Don't kill him!" I cried to Beaumarchais who, red-faced, now loomed over the fallen assassin, his blade scant inches from the man's throat.

"I shan't," the playwright muttered as I reached his side. He turned to me. "Are you injured, Henri?"

"No," I said, suddenly remembering my own assailant. A hasty look up the street confirmed that the second swordsman had fled. All that remained of my imaginative defense was an empty washtub and a wide puddle of seeping sewerage upon the cobblestones. "But, Pierre... you!" I exclaimed, turning back. "You're wounded!"

"It's not deep," Beaumarchais muttered, his eyes fixed murderously upon the fallen man, who writhed upon the steps, staining them crimson with his blood.

"The other villain has fled," I said. "So has our driver. We're stranded here."

"We still have our feet. You there! Listen to me, I say, or I'll finish you now!" Then he reached down and drew away the man's scarf, revealing a youthful face, framed by long dark hair.

The brigand regarded us through a haze of agony.

"Whom do you serve?" Beaumarchais asked him. "Speak or die."

"I was...hired by the other," he stammered.

"Then whom did this other man serve?" Beaumarchais snapped, brandishing his sword. "Quickly now, my blade itches to test your flesh again!"

The man recoiled. "He mentioned an American to me," he said through quivering lips. "Someone called...The Fox!"

Beaumarchais started. I felt my heart leap suddenly into my throat. The Fox...an American!

"If you're lying to me..." the playwright warned.

"On my mother's eyes!" the man cried. "Please! My hand!"

"I should kill you and call it justice," growled Beaumarchais.

"Please, sir. I have no quarrel with you. I was paid

The Franklin Affair

for what I did and I deeply regret it."

"You mean that you regret failing at it. Be off, then, you worthless fiend. You'll never handle a sword with *that* hand again. Go quickly, lest I change my mind!"

Without another word, the unsuccessful assassin struggled clumsily to his feet and made off along the cobblestones, trailing blood with every step. "He'll bleed to death," I said.

"Regrettably, no," Beaumarchais replied. "The cut is not so deep as he thinks, though his fingers shall likely never again obey him. He'll meet his end as a beggar, mark my words."

I looked up at my companion, and the unease upon his face must surely have mirrored my own. "The Fox," I said, incredulous. "Can he truly be an American?"

"It may be so. We must make our way back to the hotel and inform Ben of this as quickly as possible."

As we moved off along the street, with the eyes of beggars and thieves and women of pleasure to disdainfully regard our retreating backs, I suddenly recalled the only words spoken by my own attacker. They had been uttered while in the grip of disgust, wastewater filling his nose and stinging his eyes.

"Damn you, Mouse!"

It occurred to me, with terrible certainty, that only one man in my life had ever addressed me using that particular condescension.

As we moved through the Latin Quarter in the direction of the river, I found myself becoming ever more thankful for having Pierre-Augustin Beaumarchais as my friend and companion. For, though we passed through truly perilous circumstances, the sight of Beaumarchais, with blood flowing from his shoulder and his sword gripped tightly in his massive fist, was enough to dissuade the most pernicious of predators. We reached the east bank of the Seine without incident.

From here we undertook in vain to attract the attentions of a passing coach. Those few that took sufficient notice of us to slow, quickly reversed their generous inclinations upon sight of Beaumarchais' bloodied and bedraggled countenance.

Finally, after hearing my companion curse one failed Samaritan after another, I bade him to conduct himself into a nearby doorway. I then took from my pocket a silver coin, stepped cautiously out upon the road, and lifted the token in such a way as would catch upon it the afternoon sun. Its glint attracted attention from those around me—many of whom appeared to be of ill financial circumstance. But the risk of robbery was one that I had, in our desperation, readily accepted. As it happened, however, fortune eventually shone. A *fiacre* driver expressed his interest by drawing his team alongside the curb and tipping his cap.

"Good afternoon, my fine young sir! Are you in need of transportation?" he asked, eyeing the coin with clear avarice.

"Myself, and my friend," I said quickly, opening the carriage door. A moment later, Beaumarchais emerged from the shadows.

The driver, though less than pleased by the sight of my injured companion, nevertheless found it in his generous heart to accept the silver and take us across the river, paying the toll from within the value of that single coin. Within a short time, we returned to the comforting frontage of the Hôtel d'Entragues.

Beaumarchais bounded from the carriage. Blood now saturated his shirt, but this did not deter him from mounting the staircase with all the stamina of a wild beast. I followed after him, marveling at the man's strength and fortitude. And to think, I had once wondered why Franklin kept this fellow around!

We returned to find both suites in a state of dire pandemonium. Two valets were stationed at the corridor entrance, to prevent well-wishers or curious guests from intruding upon the situation. Others conducted themselves hither and yon with great urgency. From within our own suite, I could readily discern the concerned voice of Madame Devereux, issuing urgent orders with

The Franklin Affair

militaristic command presence. There could be no mistaking her distress.

Beaumarchais and I reached the door together. Our hostess occupied a chair in the sitting area, one which had been drawn quite near the settee. A figure lay upon this latter, unmoving. I could see dark, moist stains upon the rug beneath it.

"Ben!" my companion cried, anguish resonating in his tone. He rushed into the room, knocking a valet aside. The poor fellow toppled to the floor. "Ben! Dear God! What has happened?" Beaumarchais reached the foot of the settee. There he paused, gazing down upon the figure lain thereupon. After a moment, the playwright's tone changed from grief to one of relieved annoyance. "Deane! What is this? Madame Devereux, where is Dr. Franklin? Deane...why does your head bleed?"

"It bleeds because he was struck down!" Madame Devereux declared impatiently.

"Struck down? By whom...and where is Dr. Franklin?"

"Gone," said Silas Deane in a voice edged with pain and sorrow. "They've taken him."

Chapter Twenty-Four

"Hide not your talents. They for use were made. What's a sundial in the shade?" - Benjamin Franklin

"I came to ask after Dr. Franklin's supper," Madame Devereux said. The lady's voice and hands trembled, but she did not weep. Her manner remained resolute. "I happened upon the open door, and discovered Monsieur Deane upon the floor of the sitting room. His head rested in a pool of...blood."

"Yes? Yes?" Beaumarchais exclaimed. He paced the room in a most disconcerting manner, his face twisted with worry. His wound, which had indeed proved slight, had been attended to by one of Madame's valets, who had then cajoled the impatient playwright into a clean shirt and waistcoat. "But what of Ben? Who took him?"

Deane took up a wine glass in both hands and drank from it greedily. As I saw that he would drain the vessel, I rose from my chair to ferry him another. The lump upon the side of his head, beneath Madame's bandage, looked as large as a robin's egg. "I never saw the villain!" he cried piteously. "I visited for the purpose of discussing some treaty point with Benjamin. I found the door open and the sitting room within unoccupied."

"Why didn't you call immediately for the valets?" Beaumarchais demanded.

"I was not aware that anything was truly amiss!" Deane replied irritably. "For all I knew, the fellow had stepped out for a moment and forgotten to shut his door. So, I entered and called for him. His bedchamber door was closed, though I could hear movement within. I approached it, still calling. It opened suddenly. A figure stood before me...a tall man...but the curtains behind him had been parted, and the sunlight at his back made of him only a darkened silhouette. Then he struck me down..." Deane touched his wounded temple with tentative fingers. "When I awoke, I lay upon this settee, with Madame Devereux and her valets attending to me."

"Where is Dr. Bancroft?" I asked.

Deane glanced unhappily around the room. "He left some hours ago."

"Left?" said Beaumarchais. "Left for where?"

"He has..." Another uncomfortable look about the room. "...a friend whom he sees quite regularly."

"A woman?" Beaumarchais pressed.

Deane nodded. "Naturally, it would be indiscreet of me to say more."

"I'm afraid that you will have to say more, sir," the playwright said sharply. "Dr. Franklin is missing. You have been assaulted. And Henri and I have reason to believe that The Fox may be an American!"

"The Fox?" Madame Devereux asked, looked perplexed.

"That's blatantly absurd!" Deane exclaimed. The vehemence of his protests must have upset his head, for he fell back upon the settee, uttering anguished moans.

I recited the events in the Latin Quarter, including our discovery of the Fox's role as a manager of fallen women, the attack made upon us on the steps outside Mademoiselle Truneux's apartment house, and the one assassin's description of the man who had bought his sword.

"Beaumarchais," Deane protested, "surely you cannot suspect Edward of..."

"I returned here this afternoon suspecting both of you. Your injury, however, seems to lend itself to your own innocence. That leaves Bancroft. You must tell me where this 'friend' of his might be found."

"What will you do?" I asked him.

"Go there and discover the truth. Also, I hope to learn where Ben has been taken. Have you a better notion, Henri?"

I slowly shook my head.

"I should like to know how this villain came to be here at all!" Beaumarchais demanded. He faced Madame Devereux. "How could this have happened? Where were your precious valets?"

"Monsieur," the lady said, her words edged with ice. "This is a hotel, not a fortress. My servants do their best to keep intruders away from the American Commission. But mistakes can be made. I assure you..."

"And I assure *you*, madame...that should anything harmful befall that great man...anything at all..."

"Pierre!" I cried, and the force of my voice startled even me. When Beaumarchais turned, I could read the worried anger in his eyes. He wanted, perhaps needed, to lash out at someone. "This serves us nothing," I said to him. "Surely this horrible misfortune is not due to any error of Madame Devereux's. If you must find fault in someone, find it in *me*."

"You?" Beaumarchais advanced. "How can this be your doing?"

"Because I know who attacked us today."

The room fell silent. All eyes settled upon me. Beaumarchais stiffened, and the old suspicion filled his face. "Tell me," he said, his voice a harsh whisper.

So, with a heart filled with shame, terror and relief, I did. I began with the night at La Barbarie, when Chaumont and Hilliard came to see me. I described their proposal, and the winsome, naïve confidence with which I joined their cause. Then I recounted my subsequent association with Dr. Franklin, and the conflict that had so confounded me. I described meeting Father Hilliard in the Nantes stableyard, and then again in the alley outside the hotel's servants entrance. "I denied them, for good and all, at the Christmas Eve ball," I said finally, keeping my eyes lowered. "I told Chaumont that I should have no more to do with him."

"But you are certain it was this priest who attacked you today?" Madame Devereux asked.

"I am," I said. "He addressed me as 'Mouse', and only Father Hilliard ever labeled me thus."

"Oh, my boy," Silas said, with sympathy. Somewhat heartened, I looked to find him gazing up at me, his injury momentarily forgotten. "Oh, Henri. What a position in which to find yourself...and at your age."

At this moment, I dared to face Beaumarchais, who stood some feet away. He wore an expression of outraged betrayal. His eyes burned like twin coals. I tried to find even the smallest scrap of forgiveness there, but none was evident.

"You treacherous pup!" he finally exclaimed. In two quick steps, he crossed the space between us and cuffed me mightily about the head. I cried out and crashed to the floor, upending a serving table and spilling its contents. One side of my face burned as though branded. Despite my best efforts to withhold them, tears filled my eyes.

Beaumarchais towered above me, his great hands balled into murderous fists. Beside him, Deane was rising unsteadily to his feet, reaching out a feeble hand to restrain the playwright. It would be like endeavoring to restrain a team of horses with a hat ribbon.

"He *trusted* you!" the playwright bellowed. "I trusted you! And you've been a spy all along! You've been working for The Fox from the very beginning!"

"I did not *know!*" I cried piteously. "I was...I was...misled."

"Misled? Misled! Ben offered you friendship and you repaid him with deceit! If you had revealed Hilliard to me at the beginning, I might have forestalled this disaster!"

"Beaumarchais, don't," Deane begged, pulling uselessly at the playwright's coat sleeve. "He's just a boy. A child."

"Yes, Pierre," Madame Devereux said gently. "Please, calm yourself."

"Calm myself," Beaumarchais echoed. His glared down at me, contempt written into every line of his face. He turned suddenly, shaking away Deane's poor restraint. "Tell me where I may find this 'friend' of Bancroft's," he demanded of the American.

Deane recoiled before the force of the playwright's glare. Meekly, he recited an address. Nodding, Beaumarchais moved around him and crossed toward the open door. "I will find Bancroft and learn the truth," he said. Then, at the last moment, he turned and faced me with eyes as hard as marble. "When I return," he said coldly. "You will be gone from here. If you are not, I shall surely kill you."

Then he left us, slamming the door behind him.

For several moments, the three of us looked after him, wrapped in a silence born of shock and misery. Then I felt sobs rise up in my throat. I let them come— let them fill me until my entire body trembled. Madame Devereux knelt and put her arms around me. "It's not your fault, Henri," she whispered.

"Pierre's right..." I wailed, the words rolling out from lips made wet with bitter tears. "Everything he said. If I had told what I knew..."

"Politics is a terrible business," Deane said, lowering himself wearily upon the settee. "You cannot be expected to have grasped its complexity. Indeed, I have little doubt but that Chaumont and this priest depended upon your innocence and inexperience as a means of controlling you. Do not be so hard on yourself, Henri."

Slowly, my shuddering sobs subsided. Gently, but firmly, I detached myself from Madame Devereux's gentle embrace and climbed unsteadily to my feet. "No more of this," I muttered, speaking to no one in particular. "I must see Dr. Franklin's bedchamber."

"To what end?" the lady asked.

"I've no idea," I replied honestly. "But the feeling is strong. Does it remain as it was when you found Monsieur Deane?"

"It does," she conceded. "I ordered one of my valets to close the door. Since then, we have all busied ourselves seeing after Monsieur Deane's injury."

"Quite so," Deane confirmed.

Nodding, I left the hearth and crossed to Franklin's closed door. Slowly, almost reverently, I turned the knob and swung the portal wide, revealing a bedchamber lit by the afternoon sun. The bed, desk and other furnishings appeared in perfect order, save for the presence of a valise upon the bed, containing much of the American's modest wardrobe. I advanced and examined this bag, as well as the other articles of clothes that had been removed from the dresser and positioned upon the bed to await packing.

I heard footsteps and turned to find Madame Devereux and Monsieur Deane at the threshold. They both regarded me with curious interest. "Whoever came for him wished to make it appear that he had left of his own volition," I observed. "Notice the valise? Their intent was to leave the impression that Dr. Franklin had fled hurriedly, but with his full consent."

"For what purpose?" asked Deane.

"To further discredit him," I proposed. "How should we expect the Comte de Vergennes to interpret Ben's disappearance?"

"He will be mortified, of course," the commissioner replied. "Benjamin's enemies will see it as an effort to flee the scandal in which he has become implicated...a means to avoid prosecution." He smiled grimly and nodded his understanding. "Vergennes will have no choice but to withdraw all support from the American Commission. Yes, Benjamin's disappearance will undermine...perhaps even eradicate...the American cause in France."

"So...Madame Truneux's murder and this abduction," I said. "They have both been orchestrated to ruin Ben as a tool of diplomacy."

"Ruthless." Madame Devereux said.

"And brilliant," Deane conceded. "Well done, Henri."

"For all the good it does us," I remarked unhappily. "Your timely arrival must have upset the villain's plan, Monsieur. After he struck you down, he could no longer risk waiting for Ben to finish his packing. So he fled with Dr. Franklin, leaving the half-completed trappings of his illusion behind them."

"Indeed," said Madame Devereux. "Look there, even his cane was abandoned."

I turned toward the window. There, resting upon the floor between the bed and the desk, lay the Crabtree walking stick. Yet, as I gazed upon it, I saw that something was amiss, though I required several moments to identify the discrepancy.

It was no longer pointing west.

The end of the cane instead directed one's attention away from the window, specifically, toward the bedside table, upon which sat a candle, a book, and something else.

I crossed the room at a run and looked down upon the last article. It was, of course, the quizzing glass, which I had, myself, placed there early this morning, when I had planned my bitter and cowardly escape. Yet, its position had changed. Instead of lying flush to the table top, the wide round lens leaned instead atop its own bob. This was an unwise position for it, as the edge of the bob was sharp, and might scratch the glass. Certainly, *I* had not lain it down thusly.

"What is it, Henri?" Deane asked from the doorway.

"I know not," I said, regarding the quizzing glass. "It..."

Then, magnified through the lens, I read once again the name and location of the firm that had imported this magnificent accessory.

Chaumont Shipping and Import. Number 124. Quay de Louvre, Paris.

Suddenly, it became clear in my mind: Dr. Franklin, faced with his kidnapper, forced to pack his belongings to help secure the illusion that he had fled. Enter poor Mr. Deane, who is struck down for his curiosity and ill-timing. In the subsequent confusion, Franklin recognizes his opportunity. There is no time to write a note, no handy quill or paper or well of ink. So he hastily repositions the quizzing glass atop its own bob, and then turns his walking stick with a toe of his shoe to serve as a marker. The clues are subtle, but he is relying upon my familiarity with his habits and upon the observation skills with which he so generously credits me.

I shall not disappoint him.

"Are you well, Master Henri?" Madame Devereux asked, her voice laced with concern.

"I am, indeed," I said, trying to contain my exhilaration. "What's more, I know where Dr. Franklin has been taken. The magnificent old gentleman has left us his forwarding address!"

Chapter Twenty-Five

"Well done is better than well said." - Benjamin Franklin

"Henri, you cannot do this!"

I moved across the sitting room in a most dire rush, collecting up my coat and cap. Deane pursued me, staggering along in obvious distress, his head wound seeping fresh blood upon Madame Devereux' bandage. The lady, herself, regarded us from the threshold to Dr. Franklin's bedchamber, wringing her delicate hands, her expression one of fearful dismay.

"Wait for Pierre!" Deane begged. Then, as if only now recalling his seniority over me, added: "Young man, I forbid this! You shall not go!"

I paused and faced him, reading his uncertainty and faux authority. This was a kindly fellow—a gentleman with a good heart. "Monsieur," I said. "What other choice can there be? If I wait for Pierre, it may be too late to affect a rescue. Hilliard, or Chaumont, or The Fox...whomever abducted Ben...may choose to move him, or kill him outright. Besides, even if I should decide to suffer such a cowardly delay, who can predict Pierre's reaction to me or my words? Given his current attitude toward me, I think it quite likely that he may murder me in his rage. You know the man as well as I do, sir."

"Edward, then!" Silas insisted. "Wait for him!"

"And if Dr. Bancroft *is* The Fox, as Pierre believes?"

"He cannot be! I don't believe it!"

"Should I take the risk?" I pressed. "With all that's at stake?"

Deane's face darkened in consternation. With less certainty, he suggested: "We should let Madame Devereux summon the soldiers."

"Another dire cost of time," I replied. "One that can be ill afforded. How could we make them believe our claim? Leray de Chaumont is a man of wealth and influence, a friend to the king. Who would move against such a man simply upon our say-so?"

Deane considered this most unhappily. "Very well, then, Henri," he relented. "Still, you shall not attend to this matter alone. I must accompany you." The commissioner stepped forward, only to sway upon his feet. A thin trickle of blood ran from his bandaged temple. Quickly, he reached out a hand, taking hold of the fireplace mantle to steady himself.

Madame Devereux was instantly at his side. "You are in no condition to set upon such an arduous task, Monsieur," she told him, guiding him toward the settee.

"But I *must!*" the courageous fellow insisted. "The boy cannot go alone."

"He shall not," Madame Devereux said, settling the protesting man down upon the cushions. "*I* shall accompany him."

"Madame!" I exclaimed. "No!"

She turned and smiled gently. "You are a clever young man, Master Henri," she said. "You may, perhaps, even be called brilliant...one day. But this business has shadowed corners that even your observant eyes cannot penetrate. There is a secret here, long kept, of which you must both now be made aware."

"Madame?" Deane asked, regarding her most quizzically.

The lady said: "Dr. Franklin and I have enjoyed a long association, far longer than anyone realizes."

Some quality in her words inspired within me a sudden comprehension. "You," I remarked in astonishment. "*You* are Ben's 'special friend' in Paris...the one to which Chaumont alluded at the gala."

She nodded slowly. "It is a very well-kept confidence that I share with you both, one which would ruin me, both socially and financially, should it become known. Dr. Franklin and I established an acquaintance many years ago, when he first came to Paris. Since then, we have exchanged letters, always using aliases. At first, we did so for fear of our mutual reputations. Later, as the political climate between England and the colonies worsened, he called upon me to serve as more than simply a friend, but as a confidant and an ally."

"But...madame," Deane asked. "What did you do for him? What *can* you do?"

"Quite a bit, sir," Madame Devereux replied. "You see, by that time, I had lost my third husband, and had taken ownership of this fine establishment. The Hôtel d'Entragues is well-respected, and patronized by the very cream of European society. I cannot begin to describe the confidences that have been broken within these chambers, many of which were subject to the careful attention of my trusted valets, who secreted themselves in small listening rooms built behind the very walls around us."

"Dear God," Deane muttered.

I glanced around at the elegant, well-appointed sitting room. "Are they here now? These listeners?" I asked.

Madame Devereux shook her head. "I do not eavesdrop upon my friends, Master Henri. This room and that of Monsieurs Deane and Bancroft are sacrosanct. But others, many others, did not enjoy this privilege, and the information so gleaned was passed on, by me, to Dr. Franklin to assist him in his long quest for French aid."

"That is a rather remarkable confession, madame," I admitted. "But it does not justify your accompanying me upon this perilous rescue."

"Quite so," agreed Deane.

The Franklin Affair

"It does for this reason, gentlemen," our hostess replied. "While I know not anyone named Hilliard, priest or otherwise, Monsieur Leray de Chaumont is not unfamiliar to me. Indeed, he has enjoyed my hotel's hospitality on numerous occasions and has, more than once, uttered confidences that I daresay he would not wish to have made public. I speak of business dealings with parties inconsistent with his status as a loyal French subject. The irrefutable details of these confidences have been carefully recorded on paper, and are safely within my possession. If Monsieur Chaumont is, indeed, involved in this horrible abduction, these confidences may be used to secure Dr. Franklin's safe return."

"Is Dr. Franklin aware of these...indiscretions?" Deane inquired.

"To a degree, but he lacks my intimate knowledge of the details. Even more, the damaging information is so prepared as to be made readily known to the interested parties within the French government should anything precipitous befall me. So, you see, Henri, you *must* allow me to accompany you. I have the means to ensure, not merely our own defense, but that of our mutual friend. You must trust me on this!"

"Very well," I said.

"This is madness," Deane exclaimed. "Utter madness!"

"Monsieur," I said, "May I suggest this course: when Pierre returns, inform him of what has happened and where we have gone. Bid him follow us as swiftly as he may, as his sword arm may be required, should Madame Devereux's memory prove an ineffective defense."

Deane looked from one to the other of us. "Madness," he said again. "But I shall comply. Henri, madame...you must show the utmost care in this business. The Fox is no one with whom to trifle. Cross him, and he will kill you."

"Sound advice," I conceded. "Come, madame. We have a great man to rescue!"

So, together, Madame Devereux and I left the

wounded and anxious Silas Deane and conducted ourselves down to the lobby, where Madame bade me go out into the street and secure a *fiacre*. She would collect her winter clothes and join me momentarily.

Upon the Rue de l'Université, the day had grown quite cold. At my request, the valet on duty obligingly addressed himself to the matter of securing our transportation. Within moments, a coach presented itself, and I availed the driver of our intended destination. He named his price, and I agreed without negotiation, which seemed to gratify him.

Then, as I stood by the carriage door, awaiting the appearance of Madame Devereux, a most unsettling sight presented itself. A second coach arrived, clattering to a halt behind our own. A moment later, a glowering Dr. Edward Bancroft emerged.

Too frightened to move, I watched as the American advanced up the carpeted steps to the hotel threshold without so much as a glance in my direction. Still, I felt not a moment's relief until Bancroft had safely vanished into the lobby. Some long minutes later, Madame Devereux appeared, wrapped in her red, hooded cloak and wearing an expression of utter distress.

"Dr. Bancroft..." she began.

"I know. I saw him. Fortunately, the reverse did not present itself."

"It did in my case," she said, rather breathlessly. "We met each other in the lobby. I did my best to appear unconcerned, but I fear that, in my anxiety, I may have poorly played my part. But, what you and Pierre said...about The Fox being an American. I kept thinking to myself: 'Surely not Monsieur Deane'! And that left Dr. Bancroft..."

"Madame. Madame, you must calm yourself," I said, as gently as my own growing anxiety would permit. "Come, we should be off."

"Yes, let us go at once. I'm sorry, Henri...perhaps I am not so courageous as I would pretend."

"You are a heroine, madame," I said, holding the

carriage door for her. "Let no one tell you otherwise."

"Gracious boy," she said as I joined her, rapping upon the underside the driver's bench to signal our preparedness.

As the coach drew away from the hotel's frontage, we both turned in time to witness Dr. Bancroft emerge upon the street, his manner most agitated.

"Oh dear!" Madame Devereux exclaimed. "I fear he's spotted us!"

And so it seemed, for within moments, Bancroft took himself to his own coach. We saw him addressing the driver, gesticulating most fervently in our direction. The man nodded and Bancroft let himself into the carriage. Within moments, the second team of horses was in pursuit of our own.

"We have trouble," I remarked dismally.

"We must find a way to forestall him," declared Madame Devereux.

Through the carriage's rear window, we could readily chart Bancroft's advance. His driver was pushing his horses quite hard, so that the poor beasts whinnied their protests and increased their pace from a canter to a near gallop.

"We must cross the Seine to reach this particular quay, mustn't we?" Madame Devereux inquired urgently.

"Indeed," I said, perplexed.

"Excellent. Henri, please instruct our driver to hesitate when he reaches the toll concession. I will need a word with the collector."

"Madame, I don't..."

"Quickly now! We shall reach the bridge within moments!"

Confused, but obedient, I rapped upon the underside of the driver's bench, shouted our instructions and received the man's muffled reply. When I turned back, my companion sat upon the bench wearing a most satisfied smile. So complete did she seem in her confidence that I felt my own flagging resolve rally itself. "Am I to assume, madame," I said, feigning consternation, "that I shall remain blissfully ignorant of your intentions?"

"Patience, Master Henri," she said, as our carriage reached the Pont Royal. Beneath us, carriage wheels clattered to a halt. Our driver addressed the toll collector, his words muted. Through the rear window, I could see Bancroft's coach turn the corner, still in fevered pursuit. Within moments, he would overtake us. What would occur then did not lend itself to hearty speculation.

Madame Devereux went immediately to the side of carriage and opened the shutter. "My good sir," she said, her tone one of fearful distress. "I regret that I find myself in a most dire position and am in need of your kindness!"

"Madame," the tollman said, most genially. "Whatever is the matter?"

"You see this coach, which comes upon us with such urgency? Within is an...acquaintance...of mine, one from whom I was forced to part under unhappy circumstances. He is angry, and seeks harm against my son and myself."

"Madame, I shall whistle for a soldier!"

"No, sir!" she said quickly. "I could not bear the scandal. Please, I beg you. We are en route to my mother's home outside the city. He knows not the address, but means to follow us there, if he may. I beg you, when he stops to pay his toll, delay him for as long as possible, so that my son and I might lose ourselves in the streets."

The toll collector seemed to consider this, looking from one to the other of us. "Very well," he said at last. "I will hold him here until your carriage is well out of sight. Have no fear, madame."

Madame Devereux sighed with profound relief. "What a gentleman! What a rescuer you are! I am indebted, sir. Deeply indebted!"

"Think nothing of it, madame. But, please, here comes the villain now. Best be off with you."

"Yes! Yes! We shall. Thank you, again!"

Then she closed the shutter and sat back once again upon her bench, as I called up for the driver to move us along with all speed.

"Well done!" I exclaimed as the carriage proceeded rapidly across the bridge.

"For every villain in the world, Master Henri," she lectured patiently, "there are five gentlemen. It may sometimes seem otherwise, but I hold that this is true. Look! Our champion is faithful to his word."

Indeed, through the rear window, it was clear that Dr. Bancroft's carriage had been detained. The toll collector was moving slowly around the coach, as though inspecting for something, while the driver and passenger uttered fierce protests. This marvelous display continued until our own carriage had turned the corner and gone from sight.

"We are safe," I said.

"We are, indeed," Madame Devereux confirmed. "And our destination is not far ahead."

Number 124 Quay de Louvre consisted of a low, timber-planked wharf, placed directly upon the frigid, gray water of the Seine, and accessible via a sturdy stairway fastened directly into the stone barrier wall with iron spikes and rigging. Above it, a long, low building offered temporary storage of incoming and outgoing goods. A weathered name board above a large oaken freight door announced the structure's owner and purpose: *Chaumont Shipping and Import*.

There was, around the building, a patch of open earth—a place for carts and wagons to be loaded and unloaded. Into this, our driver directed his team, finally bringing the carriage to a halt beside another coach, this one unmarked and well appointed.

"Do you wish me to stay, young master?" the man asked as I assisted Madame Devereux from the carriage.

"I do," I told him. "But keep a keen ear. If you hear sounds of violence from within, you are to go and fetch a constable."

"No!" Madame Devereux said quickly. "No, do not do that. Remain here, no matter what transpires. Henri, should trouble ensue, we may have need of a quick escape. We cannot be stranded here."

"Truly, Monsieur and madame," the driver said, appearing disconcerted. "This fare worries me. I don't wish trouble."

"There is within this building a parcel belonging to my son and myself," Madame Devereux most ably lied. "We hope to retrieve it without incident, but the man who has taken it from us may prove...difficult."

"Madame," the driver said. "I cannot become involved in any..."

"Sir, would you abandon a mother and her child in such dire straits?" Madame Devereux demanded, her tone in equal measures reproachful and importunate.

Looking most discomforted, the man shook his head. "Steady yourself," I told him. "Most likely, we are alarming you without cause. My mother and I shall return momentarily, hopefully with this...parcel...and with my grandfather as well. Be ready to depart at the very moment that we should appear."

"As you say, sir," the driver agreed unhappily.

Madame Devereux and I conducted ourselves toward the building. The large freight door was locked, but a small, service portal presented itself near the building's far corner.

"The presence of that fancy coach suggests that this building is far from abandoned," the lady observed. "Be most cautious, Master Henri. I beg you."

"Trust me for that, madame," I replied. Then I tested the door and, finding it unlocked, led the way within.

The corridor was poorly lit, though immediately I could discern voices from a room at the far end. As stealthily as we could manage, the two of us traversed the short hallway and soon stood at the threshold of a large storeroom. Our doorway occupied a small platform overlooking the chamber's main floor, with a staircase to provide access to the building's wares. All the windows

The Franklin Affair

were shuttered, though lamps had been stationed atop various shipping crates, lending a strange, yellow glow upon a central scene.

Dr. Franklin occupied a heavy wooden chair, his ankle shackled to its thick leg. He was wrapped, as usual, in his simple gray unembroidered greatcoat. He seemed calm. Before him stood two men, both of whom I recognized at once.

Father Hilliard, wearing riverman's garb, strode back and forth, resembling a caged beast. His companion, Monsieur Leray de Chaumont, stood close to Franklin's chair, his arms folded across his thick chest. He was scowling unhappily down upon the silent and unruffled American.

"Really, Dr. Franklin," he said, his tone patient. "There is little to be gained by such circumspection. Give us the name of your secret ally in Paris, and I assure you that your end shall be swift and quite comfortable. I will give you something to let you sleep, and then Hilliard will do what must be done, and you need feel nothing at all."

"Very generous of you," said Franklin. "But I must regretfully decline."

Hilliard paused in his pacing, his hand reaching for his sword. "Enough of this! *I* will get from him what we wish to know! Give me ten minutes, Chaumont! Now!"

"You will act when I give you leave," Chaumont replied firmly. "Remember to whom Lord Stormont awarded sway in this matter."

"Your spine is too soft for this kind of work," Hilliard said, his tone akin to an animal's snarl. "I know how to handle traitors!"

"How shall we proceed?" I whispered to Madame Devereux, keeping well in the shadows of the doorway. "Do we announce ourselves, and trust to your...persuasiveness...to earn Ben's release? Or shall we try to divert Chaumont and the priest in some way?"

"Neither," Madame Devereux replied, and I detected a degree of regret in her voice. "I'm most sorry, Henri."

Then, from within the folds of her cloak, she produced a pistol. She pressed this weapon against my abdomen and motioned for me to cross the threshold. Horrified, and too confused to form words, I obeyed her, emerging into plain view upon the platform overlooking the storeroom floor.

Dr. Franklin's eyes found mine, and the concern and dismay that I read there were belied by the pleasant tone of his voice. "Well now!" he declared grandly, as if he were a royal butler, announcing visitors to court. "The Fox, I presume!"

"None other," Madame Devereux replied.

Chapter Twenty-Six

"You and I were long friends: you are now my enemy, and I am yours."- Benjamin Franklin.

"Claudette! What the devil are you doing here?" Father Hilliard demanded. Then, at the sight of me, anger flashed in his dark eyes.

"There was little choice, Thomas," the lady replied, as her pistol continued to press menacingly against my ribcage. "Apparently, after you struck down the intrusive Deane, your charge there managed to leave behind a craftily manufactured clue as to his whereabouts, which Henri cleverly deciphered."

Hilliard fixed Franklin with a withering look, as if his elderly prisoner had, in some fashion, betrayed his trust.

"This is a singular honor, madame," Chaumont remarked, his surprise evident. "For sometime I have eagerly anticipated meeting The Fox, the masterful spy who has done so much to advance our cause. Though I have known of you for some years, your true character has always eluded me."

"As it has eluded everyone, Monsieur," Madame Devereux replied. "My sex is my most valuable asset. It shields me from the shadow of most men's suspicion. You have just joined the ranks of a very small circle."

"Henri," Franklin said to me in a carefully controlled tone. "Are you at all injured?"

"No, Ben," I said miserably.

"Are you...alone, my boy?"

I glanced at Madame Devereux, who met me with eyes like stone. "I did not believe so, Ben," I replied. "But that would seem to be the case."

"I see," Franklin said and, although his manner remained calm, I could read his agitation. "So...The Fox is actually a vixen. Madame, I beseech you. The boy has no business in this. Spare him. Do that, and I will tell you what you wish to know."

"For what little it may be worth, doctor," Madame Devereux replied, "I wish I could accommodate you. I have no desire to kill this splendid young man, but the situation regrettably demands it. I have a hotel and a life to return to, both of which are undone should either of you gentlemen ever reappear in the world."

"Ben," I said, vainly endeavoring to express my self-recrimination. "I...I'm sorry."

"No, my boy," Franklin replied. "The apologies are mine to make."

"Enough of this!" Hilliard exclaimed. "Franklin! I want the name of your secret ally...and I shall have it! Claudette, bring down your prisoner. Dr. Franklin is reticent to aid us...even to ease his own predicament. Perhaps the suffering of another will prove enough to sway his resolve."

"Monsieur!" Franklin cried, aghast. "You cannot..."

"Oh, but I can," Hilliard replied coldly, as Madame Devereux carefully directed me down the steps and into the center of the storeroom.

"We have little time," she told her two co-conspirators. "Before we left, Henri instructed Deane to inform that popinjay, Beaumarchais, of our whereabouts. He had gone out previously, believing our ruse regarding Dr. Bancroft."

"So," I said dismally. "The business of The Fox being an American was an intended deception. Your man in the Latin Quarter put up quite a performance, despite his injuries."

"It was no performance," Hilliard replied with a sneer. "I, myself, *told* him that The Fox was from the colonies. I did this against the eventuality that he should later be questioned."

"And Mademoiselle Truneux?" I asked. "Which among you is her real murderer?"

"Why, Thomas here, of course," said Madame Devereux, nodding to Hilliard. "At my instruction. We saw that it would be necessary to remove Dr. Franklin, but to do so by recognizable foul play would be to make him a martyr...something I was loathe to permit."

"Why use that poor girl?" Franklin asked.

"I can answer that," I said. I then described our foray into the Latin Quarter, and the discovery that The Fox maintained a stable of women of ill morals, conducting herself as their manager.

"You are a versatile villainess, madame," Dr. Franklin said grimly. "How did Mademoiselle Truneux learn of your espionage activities?"

"I truly was not aware that she had," Madame Devereux replied. "Not until I happened to see her at your coach that afternoon. I did not know the purpose of her contact with you, but the risk was unacceptable. I struck upon the idea of killing two birds with but a single stone. I would remove Marie as a threat, and use her death to orchestrate your downfall as well."

"Diabolical," Franklin remarked.

"But thorough," the lady replied, her manner confident. "Your reputation lies in tatters, doctor. Soon, with your disappearance, word will spread of the heinous murder you committed in the Latin Quarter."

"No," I said. "Deane knows the truth of things. He was there when I found the quizzing glass!"

Madame Devereux laughed. "Who will lend credence to Franklin's friend and fellow American? Both Deane and Bancroft will be dismissed as politically-minded dreamers, trying to form conspiracies where none exist. Parisians favor scandals, Master Henri...the more horrendous the better. Do you not agree, doctor?"

"A reasonable assumption," said Franklin. "I assume that British Ambassador Stormont enjoyed full foreknowledge of these dire events?"

"You assume correctly, doctor," Chaumont replied. "Although I, myself, was left woefully unaware of the plans for your abduction." He fixed Hilliard and Madame Devereux with accusatory looks.

"You had already offered us the use of your quayside storehouse, sir," Madame Devereux replied. "It was not necessary to involve you further. I'm rather surprised to find you here at all."

"I am Lord Stormont's direct liaison in this matter," Chaumont said coldly. "Hilliard was ordered to keep me fully informed. I was to have absolute authority over all actions perpetrated against Dr. Franklin."

"I do business my *own* way, Monsieur," the lady replied. "Ambassador Stormont is my client...not my master."

"None of this matters," Hilliard said sharply. "Stop it, both of you. Claudette, I sent word to Chaumont as soon as Franklin was secured. Those were Lord Stormont's instructions."

I fixed my eyes upon Chaumont. "And you dare to call yourself a Frenchman," I cursed.

"I am no traitor to France, Master Henri," he replied defensively. "I would never do anything to bring harm to King Louis." He motioned to Franklin. "It is these upstart colonialists who concern me. They are English, and yet dare to call themselves otherwise. Have you any notion of what toll the war across the Atlantic has wrought upon our own social structure? Already there are factions within the lower classes who clamor for change...a weakening of royal authority...perhaps an end to the monarchy, itself! How can I be expected to permit this? And...make no mistake...I would gladly deal with the devil, himself, to prevent it!"

Anger filled me like fire. Uttering a vile oath, I spit hard into Chaumont's face. He cursed and turned away, pressing a linen handkerchief to his despoiled cheek. A

The Franklin Affair

moment later, Hilliard was before me, his eyes hard. He struck me a backhanded blow that nearly drove me to my knees. I tasted blood in my mouth. "Mind your insolent tongue, Mouse!" he snapped.

"Leave him be!" Franklin cried in alarm.

"Hilliard!" Chaumont said sharply. "There's no need for that."

The villain ignored them both. He caught my chin in a vice grip and lifted my reddening face to his. "Not so clever nor so brave now, eh Mouse? What a pity. If you had honored your bargain, we could have forestalled this business in favor of the information that you might have delivered."

"Who are you, Hilliard?" I asked. "Your accent seems not what it was. I'm guessing you're not even French!"

"He's an agent of Britain," Franklin replied. "In the employ of Stormont, as is the Fox."

Hilliard grinned wickedly, so close to me that I could smell his breath. "You were *so* easy to deceive, Mouse. Tell me, does it sicken you, to know now how ill-used you were? And are you frightened...now that your fate is sealed?"

"Frightened?" I asked, mustering the nerve to meet his eyes. "Of you? Why I put you down just hours ago with nothing more than bucket of piss!"

He raised his hand again. I staunchly refused to flinch.

"Thomas," Madame Devereux said, her voice soft but her tone commanding. "Enough of that. We don't have the time for it. Bancroft suspects something, for he pursued us here. I managed to forestall him at the bridge, but I cannot say whether or not Deane divulged this location to him. We would do well to conduct ourselves elsewhere before continuing Dr. Franklin's interrogation."

"What do you propose, madame?" Chaumont asked.

"Take charge of Master Henri. I will dismiss our *fiacre*. We can all travel in your carriage."

"Where shall we go?" asked Hilliard.

"Surely Monsieur Chaumont has other holdings in the city," Madame Devereux suggested.

"I do, but none that offer such privacy as this," Chaumont replied. "Truly, madame, I am at a loss in this matter."

"Surely, Monsieur," the lady said impatiently. "You can offer some recourse!"

"I'm sure the Comte de Vergennes would happily provide a comfortable cell," Franklin remarked sardonically.

"Quiet, traitor!" Hilliard snapped, fixing him with a withering look.

Franklin offered him a mischievous smile. "I know! We could all return to madame's hotel. Enjoy some fine Madeira...perhaps?"

"Ben, don't..." I said.

Hilliard advanced on the American. "I have had enough of your damnable arrogance, you old peasant," he said menacingly. "I think it high time you were taught how to address your betters."

"Brave words!" declared a voice from above. "Uttered by a coward to a shackled old man!"

"Ah, Pierre!" Franklin said brightly. "There you are! Come join us, would you? We're having a most enlightening conversation."

Chapter Twenty-Seven

"God helps them that help themselves." - *Benjamin Franklin*

Madame Devereux seized my shoulder and, applying pressure with her weapon, induced me to turn with her. Beaumarchais stood at the top of the stairs, filling the open threshold. His saber was drawn and a fierce, warrior's grin had spread across his features. Behind me, I heard Hilliard utter an English curse.

"My apologies, Henri!" my friend called down. "It seems I had it all wrong yet again, eh? I trust I haven't missed too much!" He began to advance down the steps.

Madame Devereux withdrew her pistol from my ribcage and leveled it at Beaumarchais' descending figure. "You are in time to die, Monsieur," she muttered.

Frantically, I cast myself backward, forcing the lady off balance and sending us both sprawling to the floor. Her weapon discharged on impact, its deadly ball burying itself harmlessly in the floor planks. I heard Franklin call out a warning to me as the duplicitous woman produced a small dagger from within the folds of her dress. Twisting her body to gain the advantage over me, she lunged with her blade, her only sound a bestial hiss.

I caught her slender wrists, amazed at her strength. Beyond, I glimpsed Hilliard and Beaumarchais coming together, steel clashing against steel. Then I felt a shock of pain as the tip of Madame Devereux's blade cut into my shoulder. Her face filled my vision: eyes as wide as dinner plates, full of cold malice and murderous intent. There played upon her full, sweet lips, the very barest of smiles.

Suddenly, she was born aloft, lifted from me as if by the hands of angels. She cried out in shock and lashed forth with her weapon, but strong fingers seized the dagger and wrested it from her grasp. Then the muzzle of a small pistol was pressed against her temple. I looked into the face of my rescuer, and was quite astonished to find Monsieur Leray de Chaumont smiling down upon me.

"There now, Master Henri," he said. His one hand clutched the assassin's delicate forearm, while the other kept the pistol firmly in place against her pale skin. "This vixen shall do you no more harm, I think. Do calm yourself, madame. I have no desire to kill you. I shall save that for His Majesty's executioner!"

I scrambled to my feet, trembling and confused. Then, alarmed by the clash of swords, I turned to bear witness to a terrible duel.

Beaumarchais drove Hilliard back with smooth, precise thrusts of his saber. Hilliard retreated, his own weapon slashing furiously at the air. "You fight like a fop!" I heard the false priest exclaim, his voice laced with fury and—to my satisfaction—more than a little fear.

"Perhaps," Beaumarchais replied, parrying first one stroke and then the next, matching his opponent's rhythm, forcing him ever backward, toward a cul-de-sac formed by three large shipping crates. "However, *you* possess all the finesse of a drunken, back-alley brigand." At this, Hilliard uttered a murderous oath and slashed at the playwright's face. Beaumarchais deftly avoided the thrust, bringing his own blade in low, cutting a red path across the width of the Englishman's abdomen. Hilliard's battle cry became a howl of pain.

"Jacques!" Franklin beseeched. "For God's sake, show your pistol! Put a stop to this!"

"You're thinking like an American, Benjamin," Chaumont replied gravely. "This is a duel between swordsmen. Neither would thank me for interfering."

For myself, I could only watch the battle and marvel at the skill with which my friend conducted himself. This Beaumarchais was quite removed from the blustering, quick-tempered man I had come to know. Truly, he was now in his element: freed from the complexities of politics, left only with the purity and art of single combat.

Hilliard's back struck the side of a shipping crate. He uttered a half-maddened gasp. Then, as a cornered animal often will, he lashed out with renewed vigor, forcing Beaumarchais to take the defensive, parrying thrust after thrust, until the clash of steel upon steel resounded, filling the storeroom like the ringing of bells.

Then, with stunning abruptness, it ended. Beaumarchais avoided a final, clumsy slash, recognized his opportunity, and struck his blade home. The point of his saber slipped deeply into the British agent's chest. Thomas Hilliard's breath exploded in a great rush. His eyes turned upward. With a final shudder, he collapsed to the floor, lifeless.

Lord forgive me: I could do naught but celebrate.

Then, the playwright turned toward Chaumont, ready to do battle once more. Instantly, confusion marked his features as he recognized, as I had recognized, the earnestness by which the merchant restrained Madame Devereux.

"What is this?" Beaumarchais demanded, coming forward.

"Henri. Pierre," Franklin said. "May I present my 'special friend' in Paris: Monsieur Jacques-Donatein Leray de Chaumont."

"Chaumont!" Beaumarchais exclaimed. "Chaumont is your secret ally?"

But Franklin did not answer him. Instead, he turned and regarded me with relief, affection and—there was no mistaking it—apology.

"It was all a ruse," I muttered, feeling suddenly light in the head. "All of it. From the beginning."

"Quite so," Franklin replied. "And I am so very sorry, my boy."

"A ruse!" Madame Devereux exclaimed, vigorously shaking her head. "It cannot be..."

"I'm afraid that it is, madame," Chaumont told her gently. "As I told you when you arrived, I have eagerly awaited the opportunity to meet the elusive Fox. When I learned that you had been dispatched against Dr. Franklin, I knew that the opportunity to unmask you was at hand."

I stood aghast, sharing my attention between Franklin and Chaumont, embroiled in a great cornucopia of emotions. To Chaumont, I said: "You came to me that night at my father's country home...for Father Hilliard's benefit?"

"I did," he confessed. Madame Devereux had gone quiet. She hung limply in his arms, her head lowered in defeat. "Lord Stormont learned of Dr. Franklin's eminent arrival in France, and that he would be made welcome in your father's home in Nantes. He sent his agent, Thomas Hilliard, to that city to serve as his eyes and ears. But he did not fully trust Hilliard's discretion, and so I offered to accompany him, with the excuse that I would use my friendship with Henri's father to secure an agent within the Gruel household."

"Did you suggest to my father that I serve as host?" I asked.

Chaumont shook his head. "No, that was your father's own idea. But I *did* meet with him in Nogent-le-Rotrou and offer my dear wife's services as cook and housekeeper, which he accepted. I then traveled to Nantes, met with Hilliard, and conducted myself as you have seen."

"And you, Ben?" I asked. "From the moment you crossed my father's threshold, did you know I had been recruited against you?"

Franklin slowly shook his head. "I knew, from my

surreptitious correspondence with Jacques...Monsieur Chaumont...that *something* was planned. But I was not, upon my arrival at La Barbarie, aware that those plans involved yourself."

"Who told you?" I asked him. Then understanding struck me, as though it were a bolt cast from the hand of Jupiter. "Thérèse!" I exclaimed, throwing up my arms in consternation.

"You see, Jacques," Franklin said to Chaumont. "Clever, indeed. Yes, Henri. While you had been recruited as Jacques' agent against me, he had also recruited his wife, Thérèse, as my agent against you. Naturally, it was necessary to support your notion that Madame Chaumont spoke no English, so that you would believe her incapable of conversing with me without your knowledge and participation."

"Of course," I muttered, feeling my face flush.

"Please understand, my boy," Franklin beseeched. "I did not *know* you when this business began. We were aware that Stormont and Hilliard plotted against me...and we reasoned that they would require an agent within our circle. We simply judged it prudent to *construct* such an agent for them, someone whose true intentions would be known to us and, thusly, rendered impotent."

"Brilliant as always, Ben. And you, Monsieur Chaumont," I said sourly.

"Then why did you not inform *me* of this intrigue?" Beaumarchais demanded crossly. "You allowed me to suspect Henri, then to trust him, and then to suspect him again...when all the while he was nothing more than a subtle bit of deception!"

"My dear Pierre," Dr. Franklin said, his manner most serious. "You are an excellent friend and companion...and as fine a man as I have ever had the privilege to know. However, and do forgive me, you lack a politician's temperament. It served the deception to leave you unaware. Besides, how could I reveal Henri's true nature without revealing Monsieur Chaumont's as well...something I was absolutely resolved *not* to do?"

"You did not trust me," Beaumarchais said, clearly deeply hurt.

"Yes, Pierre," I said gently. "And you did not trust me. And I did not trust Ben, or Monsieur Chaumont, or Father Hilliard...or even poor, innocent Dr. Bancroft there at the end." I regarded Madame Devereux, the notorious Fox, who met my eyes with defiance. "In fact, the only one in whom I kept total faith was this lady here. Not so clever after all, eh, Ben?"

"Rubbish!" Franklin replied brightly. "She fooled us all. My only regret was that you were placed in such danger this day. It was not my intention. Please believe that, my boy."

"I do," I said. Then, to Chaumont: "Monsieur, when I denounced you at the Christmas Eve ball, you made it a point to communicate my refusal to Dr. Franklin, did you not?"

"Indeed," the merchant replied with a grim smile. "Your fortitude surprised and impressed me, Master Henri. Later, after you had departed, Dr. Franklin and I were able to secure a rare moment to directly converse. We realized then that, with your refusal, your usefulness to Hilliard would be ended. He might therefore choose to dispatch you, for fear of what you knew. Therefore, we resolved to remove you from harm's way."

"I see," I said. Then, to Ben: "Still, if you were so fearful for my safety, why did you leave that message for me with the quizzing glass?"

Franklin's frowned. "Yes. That. Sadly, while the true meaning behind the murder of poor Mademoiselle Truneux was clear enough, neither Jacques nor myself foresaw my own abduction. When it came about, and Hilliard revealed to me where I would be taken, I was quite beside myself. What if the mysterious Fox planned to murder me in Chaumont's quayside storehouse, with neither Jacques' knowledge nor consent? So, when poor Silas interrupted us and was stuck down for his trouble, I seized the opportunity to leave behind a subtle clue. As you had left with Pierre, I could only assume you would return with him also, and discover the message together. Then, I felt sure that Pierre would ride to my rescue alone. Imagine my horror when you arrived in his stead!"

"The fault was mine," Beaumarchais said. "I was a fool as always, thinking with my anger instead of my reason. Forgive my taking of offense, Ben. You were right to keep this business from me. I've no head for it. I only thank God that Henri was courageous enough to come for you alone, and wise enough to leave word for me with Deane."

"How did you come so quickly?" I asked him.

"By boat," he replied. "I found Deane where you left him, and he availed me of what you had both discovered. Fearing the delay required in securing a coach, I instead conducted myself to one of the *quais* near the hotel and paid its manager to ferry me here." He treated Madame Devereux to a look filled with sorrow and astonishment. "It appears that I owe Dr. Bancroft an apology."

"Time enough for that later, I think," said Franklin. "And my compliments on your resource, Pierre. As it happened, however, my situation was quite secure. My friend Chaumont arrived shortly after Hilliard and myself. With Jacques safely on hand and secretly armed, we had only to conduct ourselves in such as manner as to keep Stormont's agent at bay until the talented author of this conspiracy revealed herself, as she did." He nodded to Madame Devereux.

"I hadn't expected her to arrive with a pistol and a hostage, however," Chaumont remarked. "It was a near thing, Benjamin. Far nearer than I care to contemplate." Thérèse's husband smiled with relief. "I'm glad it all came out as well as it did."

"Agreed," said Franklin. "And now, all that remains is to see Madame Devereux safely into the custody of the Comte de Vergennes. But first...Henri, as Jacques' hands seem occupied, could I avail upon you to collect from his coat pocket the keys to my shackles?"

"Of course," I said.

What transpired then did so with alarming speed. I came to stand beside the smiling Monsieur Chaumont, who directed me to the breast pocket of his coat. I reached within, feeling for a modest ring of keys. As I did so, he turned his body, so as to provide me with simpler access. The muzzle of his pistol slipped clear of Madame Devereux's temple. The Fox saw her chance and seized it.

She twisted her body and delivered a fierce blow to Monsieur Chaumont's shin with the heel of her laced boot. He called out in pain, his hold upon her loosening. Madame Devereux then caught hold of his wrist and, turning her free hand into a claw, raked her nails viciously across the man's face. In agony, Chaumont flailed backward, his grip on the small pistol faltering. With a triumphant cry, the lady snatched away the weapon and stepped lithely aside.

"None of you move, please, gentlemen," she announced, directing the weapon at each of us in turn.

"Really, madame," Franklin said. "What is the purpose of this? There are four of us, and you have but one ball in that pistol. Should you fire, the rest will descend upon you." The others of us nodded our assent.

"I agree," Madame Devereux replied with a tight smile. "I cannot take all your lives, as is my wish. Well played, Dr. Franklin...Monsieur Chaumont...your clever machinations have ruined me."

"Surrender the weapon, madame," Beaumarchais beseeched. "There is no advantage for you here. Whatever course you choose, you cannot escape."

"Escape is not my plan, Pierre, " the lady replied. She turned her attention to the American. "Revenge is all I have now...revenge against the only man who has ever bested me. Dr. Franklin, I salute you. You are both a gentleman and a valiant adversary, and I shall welcome your company in the next world. Good-bye...dear man."

With that she aimed the pistol at Dr. Franklin's heart. He did not cry out, nor demonstrate any sign of fear. Instead, an expression of sad resignation befell the old man's face.

I have come to the conclusion that heroism is a product of instinct, rather than reason. I say this now, for surely reason played no part at all in my sudden conduct that day. I knew only that, within moments, a deadly ball of lead would strike down a great man and that I, a lesser mortal, could not—would not—allow it.

Franklin called out my name in alarm as I hurled myself forward, casting my body out into the space between the shackled doctor and the Fox's weapon.

I heard the pistol discharge, smelled the burnt powder, and then felt something strike me hard upon my chest. In mid-air, my body was cast completely over and sent crashing down upon the cold planking of the storeroom floor. My chest burned. I could not take a breath. I tried to move, but my body would not obey me.

Franklin uttered a wail of grief such as I had never imagined him capable. A frustrated cry ushered forth from Madame Devereux, who was then seized anew by Monsieur Chaumont. Pierre rushed to my side, but Franklin, despite his bonds, proved quicker. He cast himself upon the floor, toppling his chair and conducting himself toward me on hands and knees, dragging the heavy piece of furniture behind him as an anchor.

I felt him cradle my head. His face filled my vision.

"Henri! Oh dear God, no! Henri...why would you do such a thing?"

I looked up at him, at this great man whose respect and regard had become so precious to me. I spoke, the words coming forth in labored gasps. "You...are...Ben Franklin," I whispered, struggling for each new breath. "And...I...am...not..."

"But...I'm an old man! Oh dear God..."

"Ben!" Beaumarchais exclaimed. "Give him to me! Let me see the extent of his wound!"

I felt the playwright's strong hands upon me, firmly

removing me from Franklin's desperate embrace. I was laid upon my back, while Beaumarchais conducted a swift examination of my person. It was Franklin who first spoke.

"I see no blood," he said, confusion mixing with his tears.

"Nor do I," Beaumarchais remarked curiously. Then, from inside my coat, he drew forth the Gruel dagger. "What's this? A fine-looking blade!"

"And look!" Franklin said, his sobs slowly turning to laughter. "I fear it has suffered recent damage."

"Indeed it has," Beaumarchais confirmed with a grin.

"Look, a lead ball is imprisoned within the leather," said Franklin. "See the pucker it has made?"

Beaumarchais withdrew the dagger from its sheath. "Also, there is a dent upon the face of the blade," he observed. "And I see that it is not the first. This dagger has stopped a pistol shot once before, I'd wager." He looked down upon me, smiling and shaking his head. "Henri, my friend, I regret to tell you that your noble last words have been uttered for naught."

"Oh, thank the Lord," Franklin muttered, taking me up once again into his arms.

I let him embrace me, feeling a painful bruise spread across my chest, as the air, driven from me by Madame Devereux's ball, slowly refilled my aching lungs.

"Courageous boy! Don't you *ever* dare conduct yourself thusly again! Do you hear me?" Franklin demanded, laughing and kissing me upon my forehead.

"I...hear you..." I replied, closing my eyes. "...grandfather."

Chapter Twenty-Eight

"Early morning hath gold in its mouth." - Benjamin Franklin

"For the love of God, Franklin!" the unknown man at our threshold declared. "You're in Paris a week and already you have managed to close down its premier lodging establishment?"

He was a gentleman of medium height, with heavy, reddened features and a thick neck which seemed much constrained within the tight collar of his silk shirt. His nose was large and bulbous, his eyes small, and his hair thin and the color of unleavened bread. He did not so much occupy our doorway as command it, filling it as though he were monarch of the corridor beyond.

"Ah...Arthur! There you are!" Franklin replied brightly. The old man reclined upon the settee in our sitting room. I had taken the chair nearest the fire. Around us, Madame Devereux's valets—those who had not been implicated in their mistress' duplicitous machinations and arrested—moved earnestly about, conscientiously securing our belongings for travel.

Franklin addressed me: "Henri, allow me to present Monsieur Arthur Lee, my fellow commissioner...of whom I have often made mention."

The man entered the room, his manner wary. "And this is your grandson?"

"For all intents and purposes," Franklin replied. He

offered me a mischievous wink. "This is Henri Gruel, my companion and translator. So, Arthur, what news do you bring from the fair isle beyond the channel?"

"Nevermind that! As I entered the hotel, I encountered Deane and Bancroft in the lobby. They told me something of your recent disaster, Franklin."

"Disaster?" Franklin mused. "I hardly think they used *that* word."

"They may as well have. Implication in a whore's murder! Abduction by British agents! Good God, sir! Surely Congress did not deliver you to French shores for such scandalous purposes!"

"True," Franklin admitted. "However, as is readily apparent, all has come out well enough."

"I hardly think so. Such happenings only feed the fires of gossip that surround *you*, personally, and thereby detract from the somber integrity of our mission as a whole." As he said these words, Lee's small eyes regarded the valets with unhappy suspicion. "Can these ears be trusted?"

"Gentlemen?" Franklin said loudly. "Could you please give us this room?"

Madame Devereux's valets obediently departed, leaving Franklin and I alone with this unpleasant newcomer.

"Well then, doctor," Lee finally declared. "Allow me to make clear my extreme displeasure over these scandalous happenings. Frankly, sir, I fail to see how you can hope to continue to serve our cause after such a calamity. I should think it in your best interests to abandon France with your dignity intact, and to leave this mission to Deane and myself. After all, *we* are the diplomats."

"Are you, Arthur?" Slowly, leaning heavily upon his Crabtree stick, Dr. Franklin found his feet. As he advanced toward his colleague, I noted the limp that lent itself to each footstep. The old man had wrenched his ankle the day before when, in the mistaken belief that I had been mortally wounded, he had cast himself from his captors' chair, heedless of the manacle that tethered his foot. The sight of him thus distressed me and filled me with guilt. "Perhaps this will satisfy you," Franklin said. Though his tone remained genial, the cast of his eyes bespoke his anger. "These past few days I have been set upon by a ruthless and brilliant assassin. Through the fortitude of my friends...far from the least of whom is this young man here...I live to toast the successful resolution of these events. This, however, does not account for *all* of my activities while in Paris."

"Indeed?" Lee asked, offering a bitter, humorless smile. "Pray what other exploits may I expect to discover running rampant through the Paris rumor mill? An emptied wine cellar? A disgraced chambermaid, perhaps?"

Franklin's manner grew very still. "Arthur, I have met twice with the Comte de Vergennes. He is reticent, as you may have heard, to offer open support to our cause. However, in deference to my recent misfortune...and in gratitude for the final unmasking and apprehension of The Fox...he has granted me a further audience tomorrow, on the twenty-eighth." When Lee's sneer receded, the old man advanced until he had come quite close to the disagreeable fellow. "You and I have suffered our disputes over the years, Arthur," Franklin said quietly. "However, in the best interests of the fledging nation that we both hold in high regard, I propose that we set aside these differences. Whether you like it or not, I am here...and I intend to *stay* here, in Paris, until the French treaty is signed and in my hand. Now, that effort may require some considerable time, you arrogant little fool, so I suggest you grow accustomed to my presence."

Lee glowered at him, red-faced. "You shall not meet again with Vergennes without *my* being present!"

"Agreed. Henceforth, the three of us...you, Silas and myself...shall share all such duties. Edward Brancroft will, of course, continue on in his role as Secretary to the American Commission. There, does that mollify you?"

"For the moment," Lee said reluctantly. "Upon another matter, Deane has informed me that you intend to depart this establishment."

Franklin smiled thinly, though his eyes remained hard. "As we were instrumental in the ruin of its proprietor, it seemed only proper to seek other accommodations."

"What are your plans?" Lee asked.

"Edward has secured us lodgings at the Hôtel d'Hambourg on the Rue Jacob. These, however, are temporary, as Monsieur Leray de Chaumont has graciously offered us accommodations at a garden pavilion upon his estate, the Hôtel d'Valentinois, in the village of Passy, near Versailles."

"How grand," Lee remarked sourly. "Yes, Chaumont. Your hidden conspirator."

"No longer hidden," said Franklin. "Now that Ambassador Stormont and the French government are aware of his true leanings, he shall assist us more openly. As he is a man of wealth, intelligence and resource, I welcome whatever friendship he may offer."

"Of course you do," Lee replied. "Naturally, I shall be accompanying you to these new lodgings, as an equal."

"You may follow as far as the Rue Jacob. The pavilion in Passy is for myself and Henri alone. What arrangements you make on your own behalf are your own affair. Now, if you will excuse me, sir, we would like to be gone from here."

Affronted, Lee made as though to depart. At the last moment, Franklin recalled him and spoke again, his tone most serious: "One last thing, Arthur. While I may have emptied a wine cellar or two in my day...I have, thus far, refrained from disgracing any chambermaids. I'll thank you to keep you manner toward me civil, henceforth."

The new commissioner uttered a single, monosyllabic sound. Then he left us, closing the door behind him with such force that it rang loudly against its frame.

"Ben," I said in the silence that followed. "I do believe I fancy Stormont over that noxious toad."

Franklin sighed. "He will be a problem, I suppose."

I grinned. "A problem, Ben? I hardly think so. Merely a bit more rum in your cup of mortal tea!"

Franklin regarded me in surprise for a moment, and then he laughed until he had to clutch his sides. Finally, when the fit had passed, he went to me and placed a hand upon my shoulder. "Are you ready, my boy? How is your chest?"

"Merely sore," I replied. "And your foot?"

"The same. It's a blessing in a way. The pain in my ankle distracts me from the gout in my toe."

"Tell me, Ben: Will Ambassador Stormont be implicated in the attempt on your life?"

Franklin uttered a long sigh. "Highly unlikely. While it is true that Madame Devereux issued a full confession, in an effort to save her own life, Vergennes feels that the unsubstantiated word of an assassin, spy and whoremistress is insufficient cause to indict a foreign dignitary of Stormont's reputation and influence. Frankly, I agree."

"Ben! The man tried to murder you!"

"Indirectly, yes. But, Henri, this is politics...and in such a game it is always best to know well the nature of your enemy. Even if we *were* able to affect Lord Stormont's recall to England, King George would only send another sly nobleman to replace him. Stormont has suffered humiliation, both by the unofficial exposure of his villainy and by his realization of how our friend, Chaumont, has deceived him. He will behave himself, I think, at least for the time being."

"If you say so," I muttered unhappily. Then, in a more circumspect manner: "Ben, I should like to thank you...for allowing me to remain in your company."

Franklin regarded me as though I had just now grown horns and a tail. "What's this? Henri, surely you know that it was only fear for your safety that bade me desire your absence. Now that...for the moment, at least...such peril has passed, and I can think of no one in whose company I should rather find myself. No, my boy, I'm afraid you are quite stuck with me!"

"Then let us make a pact," I suggested. "Henceforth, we two shall conduct ourselves with absolute honesty toward one another. No more secrets. Agreed?"

Franklin chuckled. "No more secrets? However shall I entertain myself? But yes, Henri, I gratefully accept your pact. Well, Pierre is anticipating us at our new lodgings, and you know how cross he can become when he is left waiting. Shall we be off?"

I rose from my chair, wincing a bit as the great, purple bruise upon my chest asserted itself. Slowly, I drew on my coat. Franklin watched me with shining blue eyes. "I see that you still wear your family's dagger," he remarked.

"I do," I admitted. "And I think that I shall forever do so. I've little doubt but that there may come further cause to rely upon its magic."

With a smile, Franklin departed through the apartment door and I followed, permitting myself one final look back upon the suite that had been the site of so much adventure and intrigue. An odd, admittedly boyish nostalgia overcame me. Yet, I heartened myself with the certain knowledge that I should be leaving none of it behind me. The adventure and intrigue, truly, was walking along beside me as we descended the staircase, in the guise of a gentle, good-humored old man with mischievous blue eyes.

"Magic, you say!" Dr. Benjamin Franklin declared as he conducted me from the Hôtel d'Entragues, and out into a world fraught with danger and filled with possibilities. "Well, I should not presume to gainsay you upon that score, my boy. After all, *you* are Henri Gruel...and I am not!"

The End

Author's Note

This work falls into that ethereal genre: the historical novel. Neither true history, nor entirely fictional, the story herein revolves around a mix of imaginary characters and actual historical figures. A number of important documented relationships and events have been altered, and certain tertiary persons (such as Franklin's two grandsons who, in reality, *did* accompany him to France) have been changed or omitted entirely. For this reason, the events depicted should in no way be construed as historic fact.

As old Ben Franklin might say: he who looks to a novel for education, rather than entertainment, makes of himself a foolish pupil. Writers of fiction are, by needs, notorious liars.

Ty Drago is a writer, editor, web-designer and computer consultant, in reverse order of earned lifetime income. THE FRANKLIN AFFAIR is Ty's first attempt to change that order.

A long-time Revolutionary War buff and fan of Benjamin Franklin, Ty jumped at the chance to center a mystery novel around his favorite founding father.

Ty is the editor/publisher of Peridot Books (*www.peridotbooks.com*), a well-respected online fiction magazine. He is also the owner of a successful computer consulting and web design firm, Peridot Consulting, Inc., which created and maintains the sites for Regency Press (www.regency-press.*com*), The Reticule (*www. regencyreticule.com*), and others.

Ty lives in Stratford, NJ, with his wife Helene, and children Kim and Andy. While most of his writing is in the science fiction and fantasy genres, he hopes to soon bring his creative energies to bear on a sequel to THE FRANKLIN AFFAIR.

THE FRANKLIN AFFAIR is also available in these electronic formats:

1-929085-70-2 - Download Edition
1-929085-71-0 - Reader Edition
1-929085-72-9 - Diskette Edition
1-929085-73-7 - Cd-rom Edition

For more information about these formats, or about any of the other publications of Regency Press (full-length novels and anthologies) in a variety of formats, please call (216) 932-5319 or toll-free in the United States: 1-877-343-6299. The mailing address is: Post Office Box 18908, Cleveland Hts, OH 44118-0908. E-mail inquiries may be sent to: editor@regency-press.com